"A wild and wacky romp. . . . wood schlockmeisters such as Roger Corman, William Castle, and especially Ed Wood. . . . Sure to appeal to devotees of midnight movies and drive-in double bills. Kihn has a knack for establishing characters, no matter how zany, in a few sure strokes. . . . A fun-filled homage to monster movies in the days before huge budgets, this novel recalls the refrain of Kihn's hit 'The Breakup Song': They don't write 'em like that anymore."
—*Daily Variety* on *Horror Show*

"Well, once I picked up this take of strange folks making creature features in 1950s Hollywood, I couldn't put it down. This down-to-earth kind of quiet guy has a dark side that would make Stephen King squirm."
—*The San Jose Mercury News* on *Horror Show*

"Gets better and better as it gets stranger and stranger. . . . The action is interwoven with bits of outrageous humor. . . . The pace is fast, the interest never lags, and this novel is original enough to enchant readers of Stephen King and Clive Barker. A terrific first novel for horror fans, and I hope there are many more to come."
—*VOYA* on *Horror Show*

"Rock star Kihn's talented debut novel [is] very entertaining. . . . Not to be missed."
—*Kirkus Reviews*

"Irresistible."
—*Fangoria* on *Horror Show*

BY GREG KIHN

by TOM DOHERTY ASSOCIATES

Horror Show

Shade of Pale

Big Rock Beat

SHADE
OF ▬▬▬▬
PALE

GREG KIHN

TOR®

A TOM DOHERTY ASSOCIATES BOOK
NEW YORK

This is a work of fiction. All the characters and events portrayed in this book are either products of the author's imagination or are used fictitiously.

SHADE OF PALE

Copyright © 1997 by Greg Kihn

A Tor Book
Published by Tom Doherty Associates, Inc.
175 Fifth Avenue
New York, NY 10010

Tor Books on the World Wide Web:
http://www.tor.com

Tor® is a registered trademark of Tom Doherty Associates, Inc.

ISBN: 0-812-55109-5
Library of Congress Card Catalog Number: 97-14693

First edition: November 1997
First mass market edition: October 1998

Printed in the United States of America

0 9 8 7 6 5 4 3 2

ACKNOWLEDGMENTS

As usual, there are numerous individuals who aided me, comforted me, guided me, inspired me, taught me, and suckled me in the writing of this novel: Lori Perkins, Natalia Aponte, Peter Rubie, Joel Turtle, Kirk Iventosch, Jay Arafiles, Tananarive Due, Mike Marano, Tina Jens, Barbara Shelley, Ry Kihn, Steve Wright, Alexis Kihn, and the guys at KFOX. God bless 'em all.

CHAPTER
ONE

Jukes Wahler stood next to the glass delicatessen counter and glanced through the window when he saw her. She walked alone, gliding down Forty-second Street like an apparition.

He'd never seen a more striking woman—flaming red hair cascading behind a pale, luminous face turned, incredibly, toward him. One slender ivory hand combed through her locks, casually curling a dozen or so strands around a finger.

Jukes jolted at the first impression. Even though it lasted only a few fleeting seconds, he came away with the most poignant heartache he'd ever felt.

Something reached out and pulled at him, and it wasn't just her painfully beautiful face. There was something else. At the last fraction of a second, her head turned and she looked through the window at him. Jukes thought he saw something, a tear perhaps, glisten in the corner of her eye.

Jukes Wahler felt a sudden chill. Even through the dirty glass her gaze penetrated him. Jukes opened his mouth to speak, but there was nothing to say.

She was gone before he could react, disappearing into the sea of pedestrians, washed away.

Jukes stepped up to the window and looked where she had gone but saw only the oceanic parade of lunchtime New Yorkers.

For a moment he considered running out into the street after her, but that would have been ridiculous. He, a fifty-year-old professional man, a psychiatrist, and she . . . what? A twenty-year-old girl? What would he do? Run out and chase her through the streets of Manhattan like a schoolboy? Absolutely not. Jukes Wahler would never do anything like that, and the fact that he had even considered the notion, however briefly, concerned the hell out of him. All this in the space of two seconds.

He stood there, paralyzed, with his American Express card in his hand and a dazed expression on his face. He didn't know what he felt.

"Will that be all, Dr. Wahler?"

"Huh?"

"Will that be all?"

"Ah, yeah. Thanks."

"Are you OK? You look like you've seen a ghost."

Jukes nodded and mumbled something. Maybe he had seen a ghost; the girl certainly had a spectral quality. He signed the bill without focusing on it and looked back out the window.

Her image burned in his mind—so strange and so completely unlike everybody else. Her skin looked as pale and translucent as paper. She had an impossible complexion, like milk. He thought it must be some bizarre new makeup trend, the mutant Morticia Addams look.

The combination of her hair and skin took his breath away. *She must be a model*, he thought. With a face like that, in sensuous disproportion, with slightly oversize lips and eyes, she had to be something.

Jukes Wahler was not what anyone would call a "ladies' man," but he couldn't help but fantasize about her. Maybe he could catch up to her, ask her . . . anything.

No. Wouldn't be right. Forget about it.

He took off his glasses and wiped them with a tissue, glancing around the room. Nobody had given him a second look, and amazingly, it appeared that no one else had noticed *her*.

Jukes's long, plain features were not unattractive, but he seldom drew an admiring glance from the women he met. He replaced his glasses and looked into the mirror behind the counter. Looking back at him was a bookish middle-aged man, not altogether homely, but certainly not the type to be checking out redheads at lunch.

Yet this particular woman affected him. Something about her seemed disturbing; haunting, he would have said. Yes, *haunting*, that was the precise word to describe her.

Her beauty had something tragic about it, something brooding and melancholy. It was an inaccessible beauty, like a distant mountaintop viewed from below.

She must be flawed, he thought. *All extremely beautiful women are flawed.*

She also looked vaguely familiar. Maybe he'd seen her in a photo or on TV, but no, he would have remembered. He had the oddest sensation, and he scrambled now to define it.

When she made eye contact with him, something passed between them, some dark sentiment. It was far from a casual glance. Jukes's gut instinct told him it was purposeful, that she had pulled his face out of the crowd for a reason. Chosen him, as it were.

Jukes recalled the involuntary shiver. Now that she was gone, he wanted to close his eyes and visualize her again, to examine the mental photograph he'd taken.

"Here, Doc, a little something for the office."

Hyman Pressman, a longtime waiter at Dilman's Deli, handed him a white bag.

"What's this?"

"It's some nice fresh cheesecake, the best in town," the waiter answered. "Harry just made it."

Jukes looked inside the bag and smiled.

"It's for you, Doc, no charge."

"Hyman, you shouldn't. I can't accept this."

Hyman raised his hand. "How long have I been here?"

Jukes scratched his graying temple. "I don't know; a long time, I guess."

"Twenty years I've been here, OK? So, if I want to give away a piece of cheesecake, it's my prerogative. I see you walk in here every day, alone, eat your lunch, and pay. Never a complaint, never a problem. I wish all my customers were like that. You're a pleasure to wait on, Doc; I mean that. Besides, you've been overtipping me for years and I'm starting to feel guilty about it. Take the cheesecake."

Jukes looked at his watch. He realized he had to hurry now or be late for his one o'clock appointment.

Hyman chuckled. "You're running behind?"

Jukes nodded.

"Then go," Hyman said, patting the bag, "and enjoy."

He thanked Hyman and slid out the door, walking in the same direction the girl had gone.

The urge to look for her was irresistible, and he vainly scanned the block ahead for her hair. It would have been hard to miss. He felt light-headed as he stepped along the avenue, searching for her face in the shifting crowd. He stumbled.

Again her image in his mind's eye.

As a psychiatrist, Jukes couldn't help but see people in an analytical light, and today it seemed like everyone he saw on the streets of New York City needed therapy.

He passed some street people who were sitting on the pavement babbling incoherently. Jukes tried not to make eye contact as he hurried on his way.

A block later he passed a bag lady rooting through a garbage can. She looked up at him as he walked by. The look of recognition in her discolored eyes shocked him and made him instantly defensive. Her filthy hand shot out and clutched at his arm. He tried to pull away, but she wouldn't let go. She shouted gibberish into his face, her breath unearthly.

"You've seen her," the old woman hissed. "I know you've seen her."

Jukes recoiled with the look of inconvenience that many veteran New Yorkers get when confronted by something unpleasant. The old lady made no move to follow him as he quickly stepped away and moved past her, down the street.

He walked into his office and picked up a stack of messages. "Any calls, Ms. Temple?" He shuffled the deck of papers.

"Yes, there were several. Dr. Howard called and he's sending someone over."

Jukes looked up. "Will's sending me patients?"

She nodded. "Apparently so. Correct me if I'm wrong, but isn't Dr. Howard a GP?"

"He is. It must be a referral."

Ms. Temple smiled, professionally pleasant. "Did I mention that Mr. Avila's here?" She nodded in the direction of a man dressed as a clown.

He sat with his legs crossed on the black leather couch in the waiting area, reading an old copy of the *New Yorker*. It was Jukes's one o'clock appointment—a man who made his living as Carbinkle the Clown. Carbinkle the manic-depressive, coke-snorting clown.

"He's been waiting about ten minutes. He just came from an engagement . . . I guess."

"Let's hope so."

Jukes put the bag with the cheesecake in it on her desk and patted it. "This is for you, Ms. Temple," he said. "The waiter at Dilman's gave it to me."

"But you're on a diet," she said quickly, "and you want me to have all those lovely fat calories. How thoughtful of you. Thanks a lot." The thank-you was pure sarcasm.

Jukes shrugged.

"Before you go, sign these," she said.

"What would I do without you?" he murmured, signing the documents.

"Probably get somebody else," she replied, deadpan.

Ms. Temple handed him a file and looked across the room. He followed her eyes and found his patient sitting in an exaggerated position, legs crossed, giant clown shoes flapping, glaring at him.

"Mr. Avila! Sorry to keep you waiting. Please come in."

Late that afternoon, with the sun shining nearly horizontally through the blades of the wooden venetian blinds, Ms. Temple stood in Jukes's office.

"There's a Mr. Declan Loomis waiting to see you; it's the man Dr. Howard sent over. He seems very uncomfortable in the waiting room. Here's the file." She handed him a thin folder.

Jukes scanned the pages. "Send him in, Ms. Temple."

He read that Declan Loomis was suffering from what Dr. Howard called "delusions and hallucinations," and, he noted, the conservative Will Howard found Loomis "dangerously paranoid."

Jukes looked up as a nervous-looking, rather disheveled businessman in his early fifties entered the room.

"Please come in, Mr. Loomis. I'm Dr. Wahler."

Jukes got up and shook Loomis's sweaty hand, then carefully closed the heavy soundproof door. It latched with a satisfying click.

As soon as the door closed, Loomis started talking. "Thank you for seeing me on such short notice, Doc. I really appreciate it. I don't know where else to go."

Jukes smiled his sympathetic smile. "Well, that's what I'm here for. How can I help you, Mr. Loomis?"

Loomis looked around the room, his eyes darting from corner to corner, lingering at the window, then returning to Jukes's face. A thin patina of sweat glistened on his brow. "I don't have much time. I mean, I don't know if she's waiting for me outside—"

"She?"

"Right. You see, I know this sounds insane, but . . . To tell you the truth, I'm having trouble believing it myself, but I'm being stalked."

There was an uncomfortable silence. "I see. Why don't you have a seat and tell me about it."

Loomis sat down on the brown leather couch; Jukes took a seat opposite.

"Can you identify the person who's stalking you? Maybe that's something for the police."

Loomis blinked. "No. It's not like that." He heaved a sigh and hung his head. "She's . . . she's the angel of death and she's been following me."

"Who are you talking about?"

Loomis ran his fingers through his thinning hair. "I'm being stalked by something . . . inhuman. Something that takes the form of a beautiful young woman. But she's not a woman; she's a monster!"

"You think this woman is a monster?"

"Absolutely."

"What makes you think that?"

"I see her everywhere. She's put the evil eye on me; it's driving me crazy."

Jukes chewed his pencil pensively. "Mr. Loomis, you're a banker, right?"

Loomis nodded.

"Fifty-two years old, single—"

"Divorced."

"Divorced," Jukes repeated, "no obvious health problems, and apart from this delusion—"

"It's no delusion."

"Mr. Loomis, in time we will both come to understand and deal with this, but I want you to know, it *is* a delusion. There is no bogeyman, or bogeywoman, as the case may be."

"She's real, damn you! I've seen her with my own eyes!"

"OK, why don't we begin by you telling me when you first became aware of this . . . this problem."

Loomis wiped his mouth with a stained and wrinkled sleeve. His eyes danced wildly in his head. He lit a cigarette with shaking hands, sucked on it desperately, then blew the smoke across the room. Jukes winced; he disliked cigarette smoke.

"She came into the bank, a complete stranger. I'm in New Accounts, and my desk is near the door. She just came in and looked at me. Never said a word, just stared at me with those devil eyes."

"I see; please go on."

"I asked if I could help her, you know, like I ask all the customers. But she just stared at me. I began to get the oddest feeling—dread, I think. She scared me, Doc; she really did. I was struck dumb. For a minute I thought I was having a heart attack, but Dr. Howard says that wasn't it. It was the weirdest damn feeling; I can't describe it physically. I felt like I was paralyzed for a second."

Jukes immediately thought of the girl he had seen through the window at Dilman's. He brushed the thought away.

"I swear it, Doc; I couldn't move.

"Then I started seein' her everywhere. At the train station, on the street, everywhere. I realized she was stalking me."

"Always the same girl?"

"Always."

"Are you sure?"

Loomis nodded. "Well, for one thing, she's hard to miss. Hair as red as hellfire and unusually pale skin . . . I mean really white, like the dead. I've never seen anyone like her. She's beautiful at first; then, when you look further, she's monstrously ugly. Also, she looks like she's been crying."

A shiver oscillated down Jukes's back. Loomis was describing the girl he'd seen earlier through the window. Not only that, but the man was describing precisely the anxious feeling Jukes had experienced when his and the girl's eyes met.

It's a series of remarkable coincidences, that's all.

Jukes cleared his throat. "Why do you think she's stalking you? It could be just a series of coincidences. I see many of the same people every day; there's nothing abnormal or unearthly about it. This is New York City."

Loomis shook his head. "No, I thought of that. She only makes eye contact with me, no one else. She seems oblivious to the other people, and here's the weird part: *it's like they don't even see her.* I mean to tell you, Doc, the way she looks at me, I can feel her searching my soul. It's like she's probing for something. Gives me the creeps. It's hypnotic. Then I get that feeling again. I don't know if this word describes it, but I think it was something like a *swoon.* I think I was *swooning.* Helpless, like. There's nothing concrete I can show you, but I'm scared, Doc, more scared than I've ever been.

"I can't eat; I can't sleep; everything's going to hell at work; I can't seem to concentrate anymore. I just keep thinking about her."

These are classic symptoms of cocaine psychosis, Jukes thought. "Mr. Loomis, have you ever experimented with drugs?" he asked.

"No. Never."

"No cocaine? Amphetamines? Opiates? LSD? Marijuana?"

"Absolutely not."

Jukes treated businessmen for substance abuse problems regularly, and he could spot the signs. But something about Loomis suggested that drugs weren't the problem.

"And you have no idea who this woman is?"

"No, but I've got a pretty good idea *what* she is."

"What do you mean?"

Declan Loomis sat up, stubbed out his cigarette in the ashtray that Jukes reluctantly kept handy for his smoking patients, and sighed. "Maybe I came to the wrong place. Dr. Howard said you might be able to help me—"

"I can help you, Mr. Loomis. I can help you more than you might care to admit right now." Loomis shifted in his seat uneasily. "I want you to listen to me very carefully. I know that you sincerely believe you're being stalked by a monster. But have you ever considered that you might be wrong? Have you considered that your input, your senses, might be compromised?"

"Compromised? By what?"

"The subconscious mind. What you believe to be the truth may not be the truth at all."

"If you mean I'm crazy—"

"You're not crazy, Mr. Loomis, but you appear to be in a state of stress right now, and it's quite possible you're disoriented and maybe a little confused. You have all the classic symptoms of paranoid schizophrenia: feelings of being followed, pursued, by a nameless person, feelings of dread, loss of sleep—it all adds up.

"The mind can channel stress in unexpected directions. It can create situations that appear to be real."

"All right, fuck it." Loomis stood up suddenly and was about to go for the door when Jukes put a firm hand on his shoulder.

"Please. Mr. Loomis. I can help you."

Loomis scowled. "You think I'm hallucinating? You think I'm on drugs? Is that your only explanation for what's happening to me?"

"No. Not at all. There are hundreds of explanations. But I had to ask; it's standard procedure in a case like this."

Jukes got a good look into Loomis's eyes for the first time and felt another chill. For a moment they settled, stopped dancing, and gazed hopefully into his. The look, the absolute mark, of fear was there like a caged animal.

Loomis drew a breath and held it. "It's the Banshee, Doc. The angel of death. I'm a dead man."

"Sit down."

Loomis collapsed back onto the couch. "God help me. God help us all."

Jukes poured him a paper cup of water.

Loomis drank it down in one gulp, then crumpled the cup in his hand. "Do you know what the Banshee is, Dr. Wahler?"

"The Banshee? It's an Irish myth, isn't it? Some sort of supernatural being?"

Loomis nodded. "It's a female entity, something like the grim reaper."

"What makes you think this woman is the Banshee?"

Loomis paused, choosing his next words carefully. "I know it in my heart. Don't ask me to explain. I don't know why, but I just know."

"Have you always known about the Banshee?"

"Yeah. My grandfather told me when I was a little boy in Ireland."

"Tell me more about your grandfather."

"In my family, the Banshee had come before. My grandfather knew it; that's why he told me. You see, only certain people are marked."

"Do you believe you are marked, Mr. Loomis?"

"Yeah."

"Because of something you did?"

"Yes."

"What would that be?"

"I am born of the Loomis clan, and the Banshee knows us. The damned thing is out there waiting for me, and when the time comes, she will kill me the same way she killed my grandfather and countless others along my family line. But, most importantly, I know who she is, and the Banshee *only kills those who know her face.*"

Jukes let those words hang in the air.

"Only those who know . . . ," Loomis repeated in a whisper.

"Do you have any guilt feelings about your grandfather or anyone else in your family?"

"No, God damn it! Skip the fifty-cent psychoanalysis! You don't understand. This is real. Only the people who know her die. *I know her.* She's been following me! Don't you see? I am going to die and there's nothing you or anybody else can do about it!"

The phone rang. Jukes snatched it up expectantly, almost glad for the momentary diversion. He was strict about not being disturbed when with a patient, so he knew the call had to be important.

Ms. Temple's voice came through the receiver. "I'm sorry, Dr. Wahler, but it's your sister; she says it's an emergency."

Jukes sighed. "Cathy? All right, put her on."

Jukes looked up at Loomis and said, "Excuse me; I have a call I have to take. It'll only be a second."

"Hello?"

The voice came over the line uneasy and quivering. "Oh, Jukey, I'm so glad I found you! It's Bobby; he . . . he beat me up again! He broke the television and—"

Jukes cut her off. "Ah, Cathy, I'd love to talk to you—I really would—but I'm with a patient right now. Would it be possible for me to call you back in thirty minutes?" Jukes was careful to avoid an annoyed modulation of voice. He kept his conversational tone professionally even.

Cathy's breathless voice crackled in the earpiece. "Oh . . . OK, uhm, I'm sorry. I'm at the Doral Hotel, room 651."

"Stay where you are. I'll get right back to you; I promise. Do you have the number there?"

Cathy recited the phone number and Jukes jotted it down.

He's beating her up again, Jukes realized as he hung up. *That shithead Bobby is asking for it. Why in God's name does she stay with him? He's already sent her to the hospital once.*

Ever since their parents died, Jukes had looked after his little sister, had taken care of her. It was his father's last request.

But Cathy was wild.

Things have really been going downhill since she met Bobby. I hated that asshole photographer at first sight, with his tattoos and his leather pants.

Bobby the monster. The boyfriend from Hell. Drugs, kinky sex, God knows what else. Poor Cathy is in way over her head this time. But the more he abuses her, the more she keeps coming back.

He turned his attention back to Loomis. The good doctor, the miracle worker, was about to solve some more problems. By compartmentalizing his thinking, he was able to put the thoughts of Cathy aside and focus on Declan Loomis. He looked at the haunted, troubled face of the man across from him.

The poor bastard, I want to help him. Right after I help Cathy. Seems like I'm helping everybody.

But who's going to help me?

CHAPTER
TWO

Mrs. Willis had pains. She always had pains. Thirty years ago, when she was seventy-two years old, she had what she called "good days and bad days"; now they were all bad days.

Little aches and pains had merged into one long body ache. Her 102-year-old bones creaked when she got out of bed each morning, winter or summer.

She slowly padded her way into the kitchen and filled her teakettle with water. While she waited for it to boil, she went into the narrow living room of her row house and greeted her miniature zoo.

"Hello, little darlings," she whispered.

Her Irish accent still colored the words, though she'd been a resident of Manhattan for over sixty years. Mrs. Willis would be forever Irish. She carried it with her in every fold and wrinkle of her freckled skin, like the scent of talc and clover.

"Did you sleep well?" she asked them.

The 102 glass figurines, one for every year she'd survived, stood mute and fragile. She thrust an ancient, gnarled finger into the shelves and straightened a tiny glass elephant. Most of the figurines were smaller than her thumb and deliberately delicate. She had collected animals of every description over the decades, and when she become too old, her many loyal admirers brought animals to her from all over the world.

They resonated with her thoughts. The more fragile and tiny, the better the reception, the louder the broadcast. When she first married, her husband explained that radio waves, floating invisibly in the air, could be magically caught in a tiny crystal. Once caught, they could be listened to.

Later she discovered that miniature glass figurines could capture thoughts and ethereal "faerie messages" from beyond. Her husband told her it was because she had the second sight and that the little glass animals only triggered her psychic abilities.

They spoke to her. They told her things. They let her listen to the ocean of thoughts and emotions that roiled just outside her door. In the great city, all things were there.

"I think I'll have my tea out here in the living room, where I can think so much better."

The glass animals stood apprehensively before her. Today they were different. Today something was wrong.

Mrs. Willis sensed it.

She leaned toward the glass case that held the animals until her nose was just an inch away from a transparent matchstick giraffe.

"Are you trying to tell me something, my sweet one?"

A roar erupted suddenly in her ears. It swept into her brain like the shock wave from a nearby explosion.

She staggered back, away from the display case.

One thought filled her consciousness, one sound, unmistakable across the centuries. She'd heard it before, the night her father died, the mournful, frightening wail that always brought death.

Her song.

"Oh, my God in Heaven," the old woman rasped. "It can't be. To cross the ocean? To come here?"

She sat down wearily on an overstuffed parlor chair. The ringing in her head subsided. She clutched the arms of the chair as if the room were moving, but the figurines and everything else stood motionless.

"Sweet Jesus," she whispered. "It never ends."

The teakettle whistled sharply, like a warning siren, and she went back into the kitchen to turn it off.

She sat down at the table and poured a cup of steaming water into a dainty china cup. She lowered a tea bag into the cup and held it with her fingers.

It dangled, steeping in the scalding water at the end of a fine white string. She stared into the cup and worried.

"The time has come at last," she said. "Destiny is now."

A clock ticked; outside, an ambulance cried. Mrs. Willis sat for an hour, gazing at the string that held the tea bag. The brew was black and cold now.

She poured it down the drain and went to the closet. Behind the clothes, nestled amid the mothballs, she found the box containing her copy of the Book of Kells.

CHAPTER
THREE

Jukes Wahler thought about Loomis as he locked his office, walked across the hall, and pushed the elevator button. The windows on this floor of the Bradley Building faced the Parker Arms apartments, an older brick building. They were separated by Thirty-seventh Street. At night many of the windows were illuminated, and Jukes often wondered about the people living there.

His eyes wandered across the street.

He caught his breath.

It was she. She stared at him from one of the windows, the red hair and pale skin unmistakable. Jukes's jaw dropped.

It can't be. It's just someone else with red hair who happened to be passing by the window when I looked. Someone else with flaming red hair and impossibly pale skin, that's all. Someone else who just happens to be staring at me, across the avenue, through two panes of glass, at night. He wrestled with the idea as the elevator arrived.

Whatever this is, it's not anything supernatural, he thought. *It's either another one of those strange Morticia Addams types with red hair, or it's an incredible coincidence.*

There's that word again.

Jukes's apartment waited warm and reassuring, an emotional oasis. He lived in modest bachelor splendor, favoring bookcases and leather chairs. His prodigious jazz and classical CD collection dominated one wall. A bizarre Picasso portrait of Dora Marr stared at him from across the hall, a print he bought after attending the Picasso and Portraiture show with Cathy at MOMA. It was Cathy's idea. She loved the facial distortion and thought the colors were just what Jukes's living room needed. And of course he went along with it, not really in love with the thing, but to make her happy. And it said something about Cathy. But tonight Dora Marr made him uneasy and he avoided looking at the picture.

He phoned Cathy at the Doral Hotel, and she agreed to come right over.

For the last two years Cathy had been living with Bobby Sudden, a photographer. Jukes disliked photographers, he thought they were all voyeurs, but Bobby seemed particularly bad. When Cathy showed him some of Bobby's pictures he had to bite his tongue. Jukes thought Bobby's work violent and brutish, the worst kind of crap masquerading as art.

He leafed through a book of Bobby's photos that Cathy had given him as a gift last Christmas. He kept it out of a sense of morbid fascination, but then he kept everything Cathy gave him. And that book never failed to depress him; page after page of moody black-and-white images of girls with bored, dangerous faces, in various bondage scenarios. It was the overall attitude of Bobby's work that Jukes found offensive: the depiction of women, of *his sister*, as objects, as slaves, as unhappy victims in Bobby's perverted fantasies. Jukes found nothing erotic about it; in fact, he found it repugnant.

Wedged between two of the pages was one old photo of Cathy before Bobby. It was a color print of her first modeling card, when Cathy was an ingenue with a future as bright as her smile. Her face beamed; she looked the very essence of unspoiled beauty. In contrast, Bobby's dark images of her were of a completely different person.

Another piece of paper detached itself from the book and fluttered to the floor. As he bent over to retrieve it, he realized with a scowl what it was—a doctor bill from Bobby's last tirade. He scanned it for the hundredth time, still not wanting to believe.

That son of a bitch has beaten her up for the last time. Jukes felt his rage dilate and focus on Bobby.

Jukes looked at the doctor bill and remembered how he had insisted that she file charges with the police, which she did, and later dropped.

And then, incredibly, against Jukes's pleading and every logical argument, she went back to that monster again.

Jukes blamed himself. For all his professional training, Jukes was impotent when it came to Cathy.

He begged his sister to move out, to leave Bobby, but she stayed. For some unknown and terrible reason, she loved Bobby—and it was killing her.

Down deep, Jukes had always believed that Cathy was the reason he became a psychiatrist. Yet he never understood her, even though they'd grown up together. Everyone else, it seemed, he could help, but not Cathy, and that rankled Jukes.

She seemed to be slipping further away, and Jukes was determined to pull her back.

He shuddered to think what his parents would have said: "Instead of watching over her, you're watching her destroy herself."

But as easy as it had been for him to understand the monster Bobby, that's how hard it was for him to fathom his own sister, the victim Cathy. Knowing her background, he agonized that he could not think of one event, one unhappy period of time, one tragedy, other than the death of their parents, that would have shaped so strongly a victim's personality. Whatever events that caused Cathy's problems were part of her secret life, the part of her she never showed Jukes. The part Bobby lived in.

The doorbell rang, bringing Jukes back.

He opened the door and looked into Cathy's blackened eyes. His stomach turned.

The insanity of the situation overpowered him, and he fell into the easy grip of helpless rage. She stood there in the doorway like a monument to his failure. He stepped forward and threw his arms around her. They embraced for an unspoken minute, and Jukes felt the tears well up.

"Oh, God . . . Cath—"

"Jukey, please, don't say anything."

"You look like you've been hit by a truck," he said softly as he led her inside.

The skin around her eyes was discolored, her lower lip was swollen and split, and there were bruises the length of her arms.

"He did this to you?" Jukes asked as he examined her wounds, relieved to see nothing was broken.

"Yes."

Jukes smoldered, his face darkened. He flashed Cathy a look so uncharacteristically cold it frightened her.

"Jukey, I had no choice. We had a fight; it escalated. It was all my fault. He . . . he didn't mean it; I know he didn't. It was an accident, that's all. One thing led to another—"

"One thing led to another? Since when does a domestic argument lead to criminal assault?"

She turned away, tears streaming down her face. "This time I won't go back; I promise."

"You're damn right you won't go back!" he shouted. "You're staying here with me until I sort this out, do you understand? Jesus, it's a good thing Dad's not alive to see this or he'd kill the guy. I swear he'd get out his old shotgun and blow the asshole's brains out for this!" Jukes paused and took a breath. He gave her a look that said, *Maybe that's what I should do.*

"I don't want you going anywhere near that jerk, OK? You're lucky he hasn't killed you yet. I'll see he winds up behind bars for this; you can bet on that. Then we'll get a restraining order. I don't want him to come within a hundred yards of you."

The tears began to flow from Cathy's discolored eyes.

"Jeez, Cath. How can you let this happen?"

She fell into his arms, trembling. "I don't know."

"You've got to promise me you'll never go back to him, no matter what happens. Never, ever, ever go back."

"What about my stuff?"

"Forget about it. Just leave it there. I'll buy you all new stuff."

"But where am I gonna live?"

"You can stay here until we find you an apartment. OK? It's no biggie. The important thing is that you stay away from Bobby. We'll let the police handle the whole thing."

Cathy fell silent for a moment, but from her body language Jukes could feel the reluctance she had when the conversation turned to taking legal action against Bobby.

He took her face gently in his hands, careful not to touch the bruises, and spoke into it. "You've got to face it, Cathy. Bobby's time in your life is over. It's madness. For God's sake let it go; can't you see it's killing you? You need help."

Cathy looked down. "Can't you help me?"

"I don't think I could be objective about you on a professional level. It's just not done. I'm referring you to a colleague, Dr. James Kendall. Jim is the best in the field at this type thing."

Cathy looked hurt. "But you're so smart, Jukey. You know everything . . . you got all those awards—"

"They don't mean anything if I can't help you, Cath."

"What's wrong with me? Why do I keep going back?"

Jukes shrugged. "Why don't we let Jim Kendall figure it out. Whatever it is, we can handle it. In the meantime, let me take care of those abrasions and get some ice on your eyes."

While Cathy slept, Jukes called the police and reported the incident. He told them he'd be down first thing in the morning, with Cathy, to file charges. He next phoned his lawyer and they agreed to meet at the police station at 9:00 A.M.

This time Bobby would get what's coming.

Then Jukes made himself a drink and sat back in his leather

easy chair to think. Leaning back with a swallow of bourbon in his mouth, he let it swirl slowly down his throat and closed his eyes.

He saw the image of his father. That's how it usually began.

His father had always told him to take care of his sister; he must have said that every day of Jukes's life. He could almost hear the man's familiar voice, loud and abrasive, booming through the house: "Jukey, remember, you're the big boy. You're the older brother, and what does the older brother do?"

"Takes care of the little sister," he had replied timidly.

"Damn right."

Then his father would nod contentedly, never once considering the fact that Jukes might fail. When his father died and Cathy was only fifteen years old, Jukes swore to protect and care for her. His father had died knowing that and believing that Jukes would always be there for her.

A year later, when his mother passed away, she, too, wanted to hear those words. Little Cathy was too young, too weak, to take care of herself, she said. Jukes had to do it.

When Jukes next saw Declan Loomis, the deterioration the man had undergone in just twenty-four hours shocked him. Loomis's gaunt face looked resigned to death. His eyes were sunken orbs, frightened and dead.

He walked slowly into the office, weary and defeated. He looked at Jukes and smiled weakly. "It's almost time, Doc. She's gettin' closer."

"Mr. Loomis, have you been taking your medication?"

"Yeah. But all it does is slow me down."

"You still feel as if you're being followed?"

Loomis shook his head. "Doc, I told you. I don't *feel* anything; I *am* being followed. Except, now, she's starting to call to me, drawing me to her. And I can't resist. It's like I'm swimming against the tide."

Jukes got out his notebook and prepared to take notes again.

When Loomis spoke, his voice was dry and exasperated. "Is that all you headshrinkers do? Just write things down in your damn little notebooks?"

"All the answers are inside you, Mr. Loomis. All I try to do is help you dig them out."

"Dig them out? Christ, you'd be better off helping me dig my grave."

"Let's avoid talk like that, OK? How do you expect me to treat you successfully with an attitude like that?"

"I don't expect successful treatment. I told you; I'm going to die."

Jukes changed the subject. "Have you been able to sleep?"

Loomis rubbed his red eyes and sighed. The weight of his madness lay heavy on his shoulders. He ignored the question.

"I bought one of those disposable cameras. I figured I could take a picture of her to show you, so you wouldn't think I'm making this up.

"I started taking it with me everywhere. I saw her on the train platform, across the tracks from me. She was only fifteen yards away. I pulled the camera out of my pocket and started snappin' away. I must have got ten good pictures. She just stood there and stared. Then the train arrived and I couldn't see her anymore.

"When I got the pictures developed, there was nothing on the film. Just the train platform and the other people, but not her."

Jukes crossed his legs.

"I know that you're gonna say it's just another weird coincidence, right? Like the film lab fucked up, or I aimed the camera wrong, or she was never there to begin with. . . . But I know what I saw."

Loomis coughed and felt his pockets for a cigarette. "I've done some research, Doc. You want to hear?"

Jukes nodded.

"The Banshee, or more correctly the Bean Si or Bean Nighe, is the Irish death spirit. She wails for the members of the old families. She's a female spirit, you know, and her coming always foretells death to one of the males in the family."

An uncomfortable silence followed. Jukes raised a hand. "Let's talk about your childhood, Mr. Loomis."

Loomis acted as if he couldn't hear Jukes as he continued with his previous thought. "The wail of the Banshee is mournful beyond all other sounds on earth. . . . Believe me, I know. I've heard it. That's the final stage, hearing her song. Once she's marked you for death, there is no escape.

"When the Banshee cries, Declan dies," Loomis said poetically, a rueful grin cracked across his weathered face.

Jukes shook his head. *He's getting worse*, he thought. *Maybe the Valium was a bad idea.*

"Mr. Loomis, why do you torture yourself like this? Let's think it out together. OK? There are no ghosts; there are no Banshees. What you are feeling is a manifestation of guilt, guilt over something that must have happened years ago." He paused, hoping the words were sinking in. "It can't hurt you."

"Stop it!" Loomis cried. "You just don't get it, do you? You're looking for some kind of rational twentieth-century explanation for this. What's happening to me *defies* explanation; can't you see that? I'm talking about a curse, the bloody curse of the Banshee. It's happened countless times before. All your books and therapies don't mean shit.

"The fact of the matter is . . . the Banshee exists! And she's coming for me. When she starts singing . . . I'm going to die."

Loomis stopped talking. He sat there fidgeting nervously on the clinging leather couch.

"If you really believe that, why did you come to me?" Jukes asked. "I'm a psychiatrist, not a witch doctor."

Loomis frowned. "Where else am I gonna go? You really

want to know why I came to you? I came because I thought maybe you could help me to accept my own death."

"I'm afraid you've painted yourself into a corner, Mr. Loomis. You need help. There is a therapy that I haven't mentioned, something very effective at getting to parts of the mind which are normally closed off. It's something that I have been trained in, and it's not painful or dangerous in any way. I need to access your memories, Mr. Loomis. I need to open up the closet and look at all the skeletons. Would you be willing?"

"What are you talking about?"

"Hypnotherapy."

"Subject: Declan Loomis, September 12, 1997, 2:37 P.M., initial interrogation. Mr. Loomis, can you hear me?"

"Yes."

Jukes spoke clearly and distinctly into his cassette recorder. Loomis was in a deep hypnotic trance.

"Good. You will listen only to my voice and answer only the questions I ask. When I give you a suggestion, you will carry it out quickly and without hesitation. No harm will come to you and you will feel no pain. Do you understand?"

"Yes."

"Do you feel any guilt right now?"

"Yes."

"Do you know why?"

"No."

"Think. Go back in time. What painful memory have you suppressed that might cause you to feel guilty?"

Loomis didn't answer right away; he seemed to be searching his memory, sighing now and then and breathing in slow, even drafts. At last he said, "Francis."

"Francis? Who is Francis?"

Loomis sighed again, deeply and with great significance. He was drawing nearer to the root, the base problem, and Jukes could sense it. A tear welled up in Loomis's eye, grew fat, and escaped down the side of his face.

"Francis . . . my daughter."

"Did you do something to her, something you're ashamed of?"

"Yes."

"Tell me what you did to Francis, Mr. Loomis. Tell me and let the guilt and repression flow out as you say the words."

"I . . . I touched her . . . I—"

"Don't be afraid; nothing can hurt you. Just say it."

"I played with her!" Loomis suddenly shouted and began to cry; the dam had burst. "I couldn't help myself. I pulled her little panties down and I touched her."

There it was, lying just below the surface, something that would have caused more Banshees then the poor bastard could've counted if left to fester like this. Nothing ghostly about it, a pure case of guilt by denial. He's got a pressure cooker going inside.

Jukes immediately began to assuage Declan Loomis's fears. "Relax. No one is going to hurt you, Mr. Loomis. Where is your daughter now?"

"She's grown-up. She's a lawyer now. She lives in Manhattan, but she won't have anything to do with me."

Then Jukes's questioning took on a slightly different tack. "Do you think that's why you saw the Banshee, Mr. Loomis?"

Loomis snorted. "No, of course not. The Banshee has her own agenda. I don't know exactly why she wants me; I only know she does. Maybe it's because of Francis, maybe not. The Banshee has been haunting my family for generations."

"I want you to forget about the Banshee, Mr. Loomis. It does not exist."

There was no answer.

"The Banshee does not exist," Jukes repeated.

Loomis shook his head. "But it does!"

"If I say it doesn't exist, it doesn't exist. I want you to understand, Mr. Loomis. The Banshee is an invention of your own mind, a suggestion from the past. You created a monster from the repressed guilt of what you did to Francis."

"But I've seen it."

"Of course you have, but only in your mind's eye. That's why there was no image on the film, because it was never there. It only existed in your imagination. Now, I want you to say it, to say that the Banshee does not exist, and as you say these words, I want you to let the guilt over Francis flow away, and with it . . . the Banshee.

"Now that you've admitted the root of the problem, you've already taken the first step. You need to verbalize these thoughts, to get them out. Now take a deep breath and repeat after me. The Banshee . . ."

Loomis's voice was cracking, shaky. He seemed more afraid than ever. "The B-B-Banshee . . ."

"Does not exist. I want you to complete the sentence, Mr. Loomis. It's important that you say the words," said Jukes.

There was another moment of silence; then Loomis whispered, "Does not exist."

Jukes breathed deeply and let the words sink in. Loomis began to cry again, this time uncontrollably, and Jukes was forced to bring him out of the hypnotic state.

"When you awake you will remember nothing, except the realization of the fact that the Banshee does not exist. You will feel refreshed, rested, and invigorated. When I count to three you will open your eyes. One, two . . ."

Loomis shuddered and whimpered again.

"Three."

Loomis returned to the waking world with tears still wet on his face, unaware of what he had revealed.

Jukes smiled. "Mr. Loomis, I think we can begin our therapy as soon as tomorrow."

"I'll be dead by tomorrow."

———

Loomis left the office and went down into the street. He began to walk, aimlessly at first, then in the general direction of Saint Patrick's Cathedral.

If I'm going to die soon, he thought, *I'd better make my peace. In the holy house of God the Banshee can't possibly enter. I'll be safe there, if only for a little while.*

The church stood open and, except for a few worshipers, seemed nearly deserted. The echoes of whispered prayers reverberated around him in the close and holy shadows. He stood for a moment facing the altar, muttering his own pathetic invocation.

He entered the confessional and waited for the priest to speak. His heart pounded.

"Yes, my son?"

"Forgive me, Father, for I have sinned."

"What is the nature of your sin, my son?"

He paused, gathering what strength he could. "Ah, uhm, Father, it's hard for me to say this. . . ."

"Yes, go on."

"I . . ." Loomis swallowed a dry, forced lump. His voice dropped to a sandpaper whisper. "I sexually abused my only daughter many years ago . . . when she was young. God help me."

The priest exhaled softly. "This is a very serious matter, my son. I must ask you to seek professional help, some counseling perhaps. You can make your peace with God, but you'll have to make your own peace with your daughter, if you can."

Loomis wiped the sweat off his brow and tried to even out his ragged breathing. His voice trembled as he spoke. "I think . . . I'm going . . . to die."

"Why do you think that, my son?"

Loomis began to sob softly. "Because the Banshee stalks me, Father."

Loomis couldn't see the priest quickly making the sign of the cross and sitting up in his seat. He did hear the words, however, and the tone was unmistakable: "It is forbidden to speak blasphemy in the house of the Lord. You must pray, my son, pray for forgiveness. Pray for salvation. And may God have mercy on your soul."

He left the church sweating profusely. Intending at first to go directly home, he now felt restless and began walking again. He stopped into a bar for three quick shots of Johnnie Walker Red, then left before he could order more.

Better to keep moving.

He stumbled down the street like a madman, his bladder full and his heart galloping.

Then he saw her.

She was standing at the mouth of an alley half a block away, combing her hair. Somehow that simple act set his soul burning with dread. Loomis knew his time had come; he knew it with every tissue of his being.

Her eyes met his and she opened her mouth and began to wail. The sound rose up from the street and surrounded him, pressing in on his soul.

It began as an unearthly opera singer's glissando, then kept modulating higher and louder, until it became a deafening shriek that blotted out all else.

Loomis began to shake uncontrollably and lost control of his swollen, whiskeyed bladder. Warm fluid spread down his pants, but he was unaware of it. Declan Loomis had gone beyond caring.

He was shaking so violently that he scarcely realized he was taking step after halting step toward her, leaving urinous footprints on the dirty concrete.

CHAPTER
FOUR

Belfast, Northern Ireland

"Brendan Killian was a flake, if you ask me," said Padraic O'Connor as he tipped back a glass of whiskey. An ex–IRA Provisional Wing commando, a Provo, had no time for such nonsense as poetry. "Young Brendan spent far too much time writing poetry and not enough time on his cause, misguided as it might have been. He didn't watch his ass. And it killed him."

Sean Dolàn refilled O'Connor's glass as soon as it hit the bar. "Yeah, maybe so, but don't turn your back on our Irish literary heritage, Paddy. You'd be doin' a great injustice," he said in tired, measured tones.

"Not near the injustice that's been done us," O'Connor answered. He was a big man, over six feet tall and muscled like the forty-nine-year-old urban guerrilla he chose to be.

Dolan, the same age but a much smaller man, thin and wiry, with beard and mustache, snorted. "Agreed. But the lad was a damn good poet; let's not take that away from him." Dolan raised his own glass.

"You act as if the boy were just another customer at the bar," O'Connor hissed. "He was our bloody enemy, Sean, or have you forgotten? A damn Ulster Volunteer." He glared at Dolan, the whiskey putting a shine in his eye. "A UVF, a Protestant, what the hell more proof do you need? I can't believe we're standin' here talkin' about the little shit."

"Because he's dead. And I knew his family."

"You don't see me sheddin' no tears," Padraic snapped.

"You were at Ballymacarret. You saw what they did. Christ, Sean, how many good men have to die?"

"Killian wasn't even out of diapers yet."

"Maybe so, but that don't change anything. The boy was one of them. The enemy. I, for one, am glad he's dead. I'll piss on his grave next chance I get."

"You're a hard man, Padraic O'Connor."

"Hard, am I? Take a look outside. It's a war zone, man," O'Connor replied.

Dolan squinted through the small, grimy window, past the heavy wire mesh screen, into the dirty snow. "That's exactly what it is, Padraic. Northern Ireland is nothing but a bombed-out shell. Sweet Jesus, I can't remember when it was anything but."

"It's a sad thing," the big man said. O'Connor's eyes swept the dimly lit pub, deserted but for the two of them. At one time, in this drinking establishment, one of the oldest in Belfast, would have been filled elbow to elbow with his compatriots.

They were the proud and dangerous members of Northern Ireland's most radical terrorist group, the Black Rain, an outlaw ultra-violent splinter group of the Irish Republican Army Provisional Wing. Now there were only the two of them left, the rest killed, in jail, or in hiding. O'Connor and Dolan, the last of a dying breed.

"Curfew again tonight, better drink up," Dolan said, tapping O'Connor's shot glass on the bar. Padraic nodded.

Dolan poured an Irish double.

"Of course," O'Connor continued, "we'll have to start recruitin' again. We can't let the organization die. The trouble is these wild-eyed youths today lack discipline."

"Killian was a gifted poet, Padraic. He published some books over in the States. That's a great achievement, you know."

O'Connor considered Dolan's words for a second, then shrugged them off. "Well, the Black Rain has no time for poetry, not when our boys are being shot down in the street. I'm surprised the UVF let him publish anything, even if it was on Yankee soil. It just shows the confusion that must be runnin' ragged in their ranks.

"Make no mistake. The UVF are just as angry as a nest of hornets, and if you disturb 'em they'll come out in a swarm. Don't underestimate 'em for a minute. For Morrison to call this meeting tonight, it must be something big, bigger than the both of us. After all, he's UVF and we're Black Rain, enemies to the bloody end."

O'Connor pointed. "Don't be forgettin' that Morrison gave the orders to kill Gerry Paisley and Brian Fitt, and I've not had my revenge for that."

Like all of the members of Ireland's most radical secret society, living or dead, Padraic believed vengeance worth fighting, and dying, for.

"Surely you don't intend to kill him tonight?"

"The thought had crossed my mind," O'Connor said with cruel smile. "But no, I'll let the bastard walk away from this meeting free and clear. I'll not raise a hand to him, unless this whole thing's a trick."

"It's no trick. Morrison risks a lot."

O'Connor's eyes narrowed. "We'll face each other again, me and him, on the field of high consequence; you can be sure of that. Besides, I want to hear what he has to say. There's money involved."

Dolan lit a cigarette and inhaled deeply. "He's here about Killian."

"Ah, fuck Killian and the horse he rode in on."

Dolan forced smoke through his nostrils. "But have you even read the lad's poetry?"

"Who has time to read? For Christ sake, Sean, you sound like all those students and intellectuals we used to make fun of. This is war."

Dolan poured himself a shot while he listened, then tossed it back casually. He wiped the bar with a towel and looked across the deserted pub.

"Personal feelings aside, Paddy, this must be a matter of the gravest importance," Dolan said.

"It must be for a man like Morrison to meet with me."

O'Connor eyed his empty glass with a stare that commanded Dolan to fill it again quickly. "It's very dangerous," he murmured.

Dolan began to pour. "It is that. If any of their cronies found out that a UVF field commander was meeting with the likes of us, it'd be certain death. And the bloody Provos, I'm sure they'd do the same to a couple of old freedom fighters like you and me."

O'Connor pointed at the door. "If that's the way they want it, fine with me. We've been wronged by both sides, so what's the difference? The way I see it, there's a score to settle all around."

He let his finger drop back to his side but kept his gaze on the door, as if he expected his enemy to smash through it, guns blazing. O'Connor sighed, turned back to Dolan, and let his voice soften.

"But it's not about politics that we're meetin' this time, although never were the two sides further apart, but I've got a feelin' that this is something that cuts across party lines, cuts across all lines. . . . Except family lines, and that's it, isn't it? That's what it's all about. The families."

Dolan nodded. "They need you, Paddy. We all need you."

"When he gets here, I want you to let me do the talkin'," Padraic said. "The less they know, the better."

Dolan sighed. "I hope he's not bein' followed."

O'Connor squinted at his old friend. Dolan looked pained. They'd had this discussion a thousand times.

Dolan said, "We've made too many enemies. They all think we're a bunch of murderin' anarchists. Too free with the bombs, they say; too indiscriminate with the targets, they say; too violent, they say."

"Aw, piss on 'em all! Here's to the Cause!" O'Connor shouted, hoisting his glass high. Dolan joined him. "Here's to the day we're free from all oppression."

They drank in silence. Out on the street, some military vehicles rumbled past, shaking the old pub like a mild earthquake.

"I used to think we could change the world," O'Connor said suddenly. "The ancients always believed that, you know. They believed we would one day be the soldiers of destiny to a new world order."

"Those are pretty words, Paddy, but are they still true?"

O'Connor shrugged. "Who knows?"

Dolan looked down. "I'm tired, man. I'm old and I'm sick of fighting."

O'Connor contemplated his glass and the fraction of amber fluid it held. He'd known Dolan all his life, they'd grown up fighting together, but in Padraic's mind the skinny son of a bitch was getting soft. All this talk of wearying of the fight was nothing but cowardly horseshit. Every time he felt himself losing his passion he thought about his brothers dying in the street. It always made his blood boil.

Padraic O'Connor was a hard man.

Morrison appeared at the prearranged time, tapping the window three times, then twice again.

"That's the sign," Dolan whispered.

He hurried to let the man in, making sure no one saw them.

Morrison was thin, bald under his knit cap, with a florid face and deep-set, joyless eyes. Dolan led him to the bar and added another glass to the fray.

"You'd be Morrison," Dolan stated.

"And you'd be Dolan then, and the big feller there is O'Connor."

"That's right," Padraic spoke.

"I'll not waste your time," Morrison said with a ragged voice. "I bring word from America. As you may have heard, young Killian's dead, blown up, popped open like a can of stew. There's been some fightin' on both sides, but no one claims him." He turned to face O'Connor, leveling a gaze that could chill blood. "I think you and I know what killed him."

"Did you see the body?" O'Connor asked.

Morrison nodded. "I saw it. It's her; there's no mistakin' the mark she leaves," Morrison answered. He stopped to throw back his whiskey, and his words hung in the room.

O'Connor leaned forward. "You're sure?"

Morrison nodded. "He was bein' stalked; he told me so. It was only a matter of time."

"Why should I believe you?"

Morrison laughed. "You shouldn't. But think on this. As long as she's out there, all our families suffer, our male children. . . . Listen, O'Connor; I know that you could care less what happens to the likes of us. But it's the blood of the ancient clans that runs in all our veins, yours as well as mine."

He emptied the last trickle of whiskey from the glass into his mouth. Dolan, the observant bartender, hurried to replace it.

"This is a curse that will never end," Morrison continued. "I would go there and kill the bitch myself, but you know I'd be dead within a week. You're the only one, O'Connor, damn you. You're the only one can stop her, the only one left with the ancient knowledge."

Another pair of military vehicles rumbled past the door.

Morrison cleared his throat. "That's why I've come. God knows how she got over there, but it's our chance to stop her once and for all. The old families are fewer and far between in that part of the world. It should be easier to flush her out."

"In New York?"

"We have connections there."

O'Connor coughed. "So have I. I'll not be needin' any of your help."

"Yes, you will," Morrison snapped. "You'll need all the help you can get. I have some money."

He pulled a thick manila envelope out of his jacket and placed it on the bar.

"That's 30,000, the other half when you do the job." He paused, watching O'Connor's reaction. Padraic fingered the envelope.

"How many have you lost?" Morrison asked. "A father? A brother? Myself, I can't even remember anymore. It's gotten so that any male child in my family is damned from birth. I'm the last."

O'Connor picked up the envelope and looked inside. He sighed and slipped it in his pocket.

Morrison knew what that meant.

Dolan spoke. "And with Killian there was no bomb? You're absolutely positive about that?"

"No, no bomb, no trace of explosives. . . . The police are baffled."

Dolan shook his head. "There could have been a mistake."

Morrison sneered. "Don't you think I thought about that? I'm no fool, Dolan. Why would I spend the money if I wasn't dead sure? There's no mistake; I wouldn't be here riskin' my life if there was."

O'Connor blanched. His eyes narrowed as he leaned into Morrison's face. "How did you know to come here?"

Morrison lit a cigarette and exhaled slowly. "The old lady sent me."

"Mother Willis?"

Morrison nodded as Dolan poured another round. O'Connor should have been feeling the effects of the alcohol now, but instead of the familiar warming buzz, he felt a cold shiver down his back.

"She said you'd understand," Morrison concluded.

Padraic O'Connor, the cold-blooded terrorist, actually felt a touch of fear. "Well, I'll be damned," he whispered.

Morrison looked off, his eyes distant in the smoky little pub. "We may be enemies, Mr. O'Connor, sworn to fight to the last"—his eyes swung back into Padraic's face, flashing with passion—*"but we're still men. And we're still Irish, damn it."*

As always, O'Connor left by the back door. He moved soundlessly through the dark alley, a shadow among shadows. He hadn't gone more than a hundred yards when an explosion rocked him off his feet. He fell forward, instinctively hitting the ground and covering up. The shock wave passed over him like a sonic freight train.

Behind him, the pub burst into flames. O'Connor got up and ran. He hoped whoever planted that bomb hadn't seen him leave.

He packed his bag that night and left for New York on the first flight the next morning. He knew what he had to do and that he was the only man in the world who could do it. He felt the hands of destiny touch him. Padraic O'Connor set out to make history.

O'Connor breezed through Customs with a counterfeit passport, collected his baggage, and hailed a cab.

The gray, cheerless New York streets unfolded before him like layers of dead skin. *This is a town where a man can get anything he wants*, he thought, *anything at all*.

He bought a gun first, then set out to purchase some very unusual, bizarre items. Through the yellow pages he found an electronic surveillance retailer, a metalworks shop, and a store that sold human bones.

He thought of Morrison's last words. "We may be enemies, Mr. O'Connor, sworn to fight to the last, *but we're still men . . . and we're still Irish, damn it*."

CHAPTER
FIVE

"It's Loomis. He's dead."

Jukes stopped being careful, stopped everything. He got an odd, cold feeling when he heard the word "dead."

"What happened?"

"It's pretty bizarre."

Jukes shifted the earpiece of the phone from one hand to another. "Are you sure it's him?"

"You forget, I'm his doctor. The cops called me in around six this morning. He was carrying his billfold, full ID, everything, and, get this, no money was taken. What a mess. You won't believe it. He was difficult to identify."

"I just saw him. He was supposed to come back today."

"You saw him?"

"Yeah. I told him to go home and rest and meet me back at the office today. Jesus, I was probably one of the last people to see him alive."

Jukes could hear other voices in the background over the phone. He could hear Will saying something. In a moment he was back on the line.

"The cops want to see you. Can you come over?"

"Where are you?"

"City morgue."

"Yes. I'll see you in thirty minutes."

"Jukes?"

"Yeah?"

"You're not gonna believe this. He was murdered, ripped apart."

———

Will was right, Jukes thought. Declan Loomis's earthly remains were little more than a science project. When the coroner's assistant unzipped the bag, Jukes couldn't believe his eyes. It was not so much a corpse as a collection of loose organs. The top half of Loomis's body appeared to have been savagely mauled.

"The worst I've ever seen," said the assistant coroner.

"What could have done this?"

Will Howard was thinking. "I don't know; a large carnivorous predator?"

"Be serious. In New York City?"

The coroner grunted. "He wasn't even near the park."

Will Howard looked back and forth from Jukes to the coroner's assistant to all that was left of Declan Loomis and made his whistling sound again. "Jukes, I don't know. The preliminary look showed no mastication, no saliva, no slash marks, no powder burns, no nothing. It's as if the guy just spontaneously exploded from the inside out."

"This is weird. All week long he's raving about the Banshee, saying how he's gonna die any minute, then this—"

"I think we can rule out suicide," the assistant coroner quipped.

Will pointed to the area of Loomis's lower torso. "What do you make of this tear? Looks like, before he . . . exploded, he . . . ahh . . . seems to have split down the middle. Look how the skin separates here." He pointed. "It's torn irregularly along a central axis."

"Bizarre."

Will nodded to the coroner's assistant to rezip the body bag. The unpleasantness receded.

"There's nothing else to discern with the naked eye at this time," Will said. "The cops have requested a full autopsy, which should commence within the hour." He glanced at his watch. "There's nothing to do but wait."

It was barely eight o'clock in the morning. The two men decided to have coffee; breakfast was out of the question.

During his second cup, Jukes Wahler started to talk. "Will, Loomis was suicidal, in my opinion."

"The coroner didn't think that was possible."

"Who knows what to think? This whole thing is disconcerting. There must be an explanation, and I, for one, want to get to the bottom of it. Loomis was capable of suicide, especially if he slipped into a state of clinical depression. That shouldn't be ruled out."

"You saw his body. It would seem unlikely he could find a way to do that to himself."

"I was going to send him to Sheppard-Pratt for some treatment."

"Shocks?"

Jukes nodded. "They're doing wonderful things with electricity these days. They can be very selective."

"What about all this Banshee talk?"

Jukes poured some half-and-half into his coffee and stared at the caramel clouds. He'd been thinking about having this conversation all morning, and still he didn't know how to begin.

"I don't know, Will. You must admit, it does seem strange. Loomis was completely convinced the Banshee was stalking him; I'll say that much. He was raving. The mind can do extraordinary things under the right circumstances."

Will Howard frowned.

Jukes raised an eyebrow and said, "There must be some logical explanation."

Will cleared his throat. "I've been practicing medicine in this town for thirty years, and I've never heard of anything like this. The man was violently split open like a sausage in a microwave. The cops are automatically thinking homicide."

A stocky man with an iron gray flattop haircut, in his early fifties, approached the table, his suit unfashionably wrinkled. He walked confidently, back straight, belly forward, an unlit cigar between his fingers and his tie, one of those skinny black ties that looks as though it's been knotted with a pair of pliers, loosened at his brawny neck.

He was built the way NFL linebackers used to be in the 1950s, squat, bulldoggish.

"Detective George Jones, NYPD Homicide Department," he said. He had a five o'clock shadow even though it was only eight o'clock in the morning. "The coroner said I'd find you here; mind if I join you? I'm investigating Loomis."

Jukes stood and shook hands with George, two firm grips wrestled momentarily, then parted respectfully. Will Howard did the same.

"Please, have a seat," Jukes said.

"I missed you at the morgue, Dr. Wahler. Mind if I ask a few questions?"

"Not at all. I'd be happy to help."

George pushed back a chair and sat down casually, as if he was used to pushing his way into things. His head seemed disproportionately large for his body, padded by chipmunk cheeks and a double chin. He smelled of coffee and cheap cigars. There was also an aroma of exhaust.

A native New Yorker who knew the city well, George Jones had a reputation as a no-bullshit guy. That's why he'd become a cop: to keep the bullshit down, to keep the city safe for people—people like his parents, who hadn't been so lucky. They'd been shot during a robbery attempt when George was a still a teenager. Now he took it personally when somebody got out of line and started killing people. George was in a position to do something about it. And the city needed him.

George was the bizarre-murder expert.

"This case has some distinctive features that I'd like to discuss with you, if you don't mind," he said.

Jukes looked at his friend and back at Jones. "Sure."

"OK." The cop flipped open a tattered notebook that looked like it had been run over by a truck. The pages were greasy, dog-eared, fingerprinted, and covered with scrawl. He looked up, cleared his throat, and began. "When was the last time you saw Declan Loomis alive?"

"That would have been around five o'clock yesterday evening, when he left my office. He didn't say where he was going."

"Was Declan Loomis under your care?"

Jukes nodded.

"Well, Dr. Wahler, the department definitely suspects foul play here. As of right now, this is a criminal investigation. Dr. Howard here says that he referred Mr. Loomis to you because Mr. Loomis thought he was being followed—stalked, I believe is how he put it—by a mysterious woman."

Jukes looked directly into George's eyes and said, "I have every reason to believe that the mysterious woman was a figment of his imagination. Mr. Loomis was deeply disturbed."

"Uh-huh. Did he describe the woman to you?"

"Yes."

"Could you tell me that description?"

Jukes described the woman.

"Why did you believe she was a figment of his imagination?"

Jukes sat up straight. "That was my professional opinion, based on the limited exposure I had. Loomis was irrational; he thought the woman was some kind of monster. He insisted he saw her everywhere. He even tried to take her picture, but there was nothing on the film . . . and I think he would have realized eventually that there was nothing on the film because she only existed in his imagination. It's not uncommon for paranoid schizophrenics to have delusions like that."

"Did you know if Loomis had any enemies? Someone who would want him dead?"

Jukes shook his head. "We're walking on a thin line here, Detective. The line between cooperating in a police investigation, which I am eager to do, and violating the sanctity of the doctor-patient relationship, which I am loath to do. I hope you understand."

Jones closed his notebook. "Look, Doc. I don't mean any disrespect, but I've got a shitty job to do, OK? I'm skunked. That's the damnedest corpse I've seen in a long time. Any information that would lead to the arrest of the person or persons responsible for whatever the fuck happened to that guy"—he hooked his thumb in the vague direction of the morgue—"would be greatly appreciated. I'm not suggesting that you violate any ethics, but . . . I think we have a moral imperative here."

Before Jukes could respond, Jones spoke again. "And what's all this about a Banshee? What the hell is that? Some kind of ghost?"

Jukes looked at Will. "Did you tell him that?"

Will nodded sheepishly. "I thought it might be important."

Jones cleared his throat. "Every bit of information, no matter how trivial, or unbelievable, is important," he said.

Jukes leveled his gaze at Jones. "It was just another delusion. Loomis was convinced that the woman stalking him was the Banshee. But there are no such things as Banshees; we all know that."

Detective Jones rolled his eyes and smiled. "A homicide in New York City could be anything. I've seen copycat killers, fake vampires, satanic cults, crazed dopers, gang bangers, serial killers, secret agents, you name it. A Banshee, hell, that fits right in around here. Tell me, how does a Banshee kill its victims?"

Jukes looked away; a sour feeling blossomed in the pit of his stomach. He hated to be drawn into this conversation.

Will Howard spoke next, anxious to shed some light on the subject. "She sings, I think."

"She?"

"Yeah. The Banshee is a woman. I thought you knew that."

"The mysterious woman," Jones said.

"The Banshee sings and brings death to her victims."

"Just like some of those punk singers down in the Village," Jones replied, deadpan.

Will flickered a smile; Jukes sighed. They drank coffee.

"This is very similar to another murder we've got on the books right now."

"Like this? When?" Will asked.

Jones lit his cigar, the smell of burning garbage filled the air, and Jukes nearly gagged.

"Two weeks ago in the park," the detective said, letting a great cloud of smoke escape. "We still don't have a clue. The guy was turned inside out, ruptured outward."

Jukes made a disagreeable face. "Inside out? That's impossible!"

"Yeah, that's what we thought. But there it was, plain as day. The lab drew a blank. The victim's skin was split open in the front, and his internal organs were on the outside; portions of his skin were reversed like a coat that you pulled through the sleeves. Most disgusting thing you ever saw."

"I don't see how that could happen," Will Howard said.

"Me neither, but it did. Damnedest thing. The guy just exploded from the inside out. The punch line is, there wasn't a mark of violence on him. No knife wound, no gunshot, no incision of any kind, no trace of explosives or incendiary devices. Whoever did it must have been a magician. In many ways, it's just like our friend here, Mr. Loomis."

"How could you explode someone without explosives?"

Jones shrugged. "I don't know. You're the doctor; I thought you could tell me."

Jukes waved at the smoke coming off Jones's cigar. "Well, you can explode small animals inside a microwave oven."

Jones wrote that down. "Microwaves, that's good. Might be some kind of new terrorist weapon."

"How come I never heard about that other guy in the park?" Jukes asked.

Jones had the practiced cynicism of a career homicide detective. His voice never changed. "I don't know. The *Daily News* never returned my calls."

Jukes gaped.

"I'm kidding."

"Oh. . . ." Jukes looked at Will. Will snuffled.

"We kept it quiet," Jones said, serious now. "It's not the kind of thing the commissioner wants to see on the front page. Besides, the body was in unbelievably bad condition. What happened to him, that's something you just wanted to forget about and hope to hell it never happens again. An aberration, a fluke, completely unexplainable.

"You guys are doctors; you know that every police department has a file of stuff like this, stuff nobody wants to admit ever happened. Unsolvable cases going back generations. In this city, you can imagine what our file looks like."

Jones looked at his watch. "I gotta go. I'll be in touch, gentlemen." He got up to leave and shook both their hands.

"Who was the other guy? Was he identified?" Will asked.

"Yeah, eventually. He was an Irish writer, a poet, Brendan Killian."

Jukes said, "Loomis told me he grew up in Ireland."

Jones flipped out his notebook again and scratched a note. "That's interesting; both these guys were Irish. The Banshee's Irish, too, right?"

Will nodded. "Wasn't Brendan Killian the guy who wrote about the IRA? I think I saw him written up in the Sunday *Times*, giving a reading somewhere."

Jones laughed a short barklike laugh. "IRA, IRS, who knows? All I can tell you is he left a lot of people pissed off at him; seems he drank a lot."

Jukes felt Jones's bad breath on his face. The toadish man leaned over and whispered, "Killian was a radical; he had ties to terrorist groups."

Jones straightened and stepped away. "Dr. Wahler, Dr. Howard, it's been a pleasure. Here's my card. I'll be in touch."

Jones left as abruptly as he had arrived.

"What a character," Jukes said as soon as the cop was gone.

"They say he's a brilliant detective." Will turned to Jukes and said softly, "This is disturbing, Jukes. What do you think?"

"I don't know what to think."

They sat together in silence for a while. Then Will said, "I know this history professor over at Columbia; her name is Fiona Rice. Maybe you should go see her."

"Why?"

"She's an expert on Irish mythology. The Banshee's right up her alley. I think it might be worth looking into, Jukes, just from a research viewpoint. I'm too busy to do it, and if I know you, your curiosity is already piqued."

"And that's all?"

"Well, there is one other thing . . . now that you mention it. She's a knockout."

A big man with a ruddy face entered the restaurant and approached Jukes's table. Neither Jukes nor Will noticed Padraic O'Connor until he was standing next to them.

"Dr. Wahler? I'm Charlie O'Malley. I hope I'm not disturbing you."

Jukes looked up to see an oversize outstretched hand. He

reached for it with his own and felt a powerful, yet controlled, squeeze.

"We were just finishing up. What can I do for you?"

"I'm a relative of Declan Loomis—first cousin, to be precise."

Jukes noted O'Malley's accent. "You're Irish?"

"Yes, that's right. I happened to be here in New York on business when I heard about his tragic death."

"Well, let me offer my condolences." Jukes indicated for him to join them at the table. "This is my colleague Dr. Howard."

O'Connor sat down. "Were you treating my cousin?"

"That's right."

"And you're a psychiatrist, right?"

"That's correct."

"Was Declan crazy?"

"Oh, no. Nothing like that. He just had some conflicts and we were on the verge of working them out when . . . this happened."

O'Connor nodded. "They wouldn't let me see him. I don't understand. Do you know why that is?"

Will Howard cleared his throat. "Well, it's hard to explain, but his body . . . was in an unusual condition."

O'Connor raised an eyebrow. "Oh?"

"Yes," Will continued. "The police are looking into it."

"Was Declan the victim of foul play?"

Will and Jukes exchanged glances. "I don't think we're in a position to answer that question. Maybe you should talk to Detective Jones."

"Is he in charge of the investigation?"

Will Howard passed the business card Jones had given him to O'Connor. O'Connor read it, silently memorizing the number, then handed it back to Will.

"Thanks," O'Connor said. "Let me be frank, gentlemen.

My family is extremely upset about this unfortunate occurrence. If there was foul play, then we want it investigated." He looked at Jukes. "But I'm confused about the way he died. No one at the morgue would say anything. Can you tell me?"

"I don't think we should be discussing the case, Mr. O'Malley. While it's true Declan Loomis was under our care, the police know more about his death than we do."

O'Connor nodded. "Fair enough. But, Doctors, please . . . what in God's name happened? The last time I saw Declan, he was in fine shape. Did he have medical problems I wasn't aware of?"

"We'd be violating patient-doctor confidentiality if we told you that," Jukes said.

O'Connor sighed. "Jesus, are all you New Yorkers this evasive? I haven't gotten a straight answer since I got here. You can imagine my frustration. Look, I'm sorry to make such a stink, but I'll have to tell the folks back home something, for God's sake."

Jukes shifted in his seat, suddenly uncomfortable. "He didn't die of natural causes; I will tell you that."

O'Connor locked his eyes on Jukes's face, facial muscles setting his expression in stone. "He was murdered, wasn't he?"

Neither of the two doctors spoke.

O'Connor shook his head. "It's a sad day for my family. . . . I guess I'll have to find out what happened on my own. I just can't imagine poor old Declan gone."

O'Connor let his eyes soften. "I'm sorry to bother you. I'll be leaving now." He pushed his chair back and prepared to stand. "Oh. Just one other thing. . . ."

Sirens wailed close by. Sounds of the city teemed through the windows of the restaurant.

"Someone said there'd been talk of the Banshee." O'Connor's eyes held Jukes's, waiting for the answer, for any telltale signs that Jukes wasn't telling the truth.

"The Banshee? Who told you about that?"

"Oh, one of the fellas in the morgue."

"I guess it wouldn't hurt to tell you . . . since you're a relative. Loomis did claim to be stalked by the Banshee. He was obsessed with it, as a matter of fact."

Somewhere, many blocks away, a keening wail rose above the sound of the sirens. Jukes and O'Connor looked out the window. The sound was faint and brief but distinct amid the ambient sounds of the city. It stood out, decidedly nonmechanical, sending a shiver down Jukes's back.

When it faded a second later, Jukes and O'Connor faced each other again.

O'Connor nodded slowly. "I should have known. Yes, the Banshee, of course."

Jukes blinked. "Are you familiar with it?"

O'Connor smiled a thin, dry crack. "I come from a very old Irish family, Dr. Wahler. We have many strange beliefs, some that go back centuries. The Banshee is a recurring figure. The answer to your question is yes, I am quite familiar with it."

"Well, then maybe you can shed some light on this matter."

"There's no light to shed. Outside of a certain familial group, the Banshee is little more than a story told by old women to scare bad little boys."

"But within that group?"

O'Connor snorted. "The Banshee is a curse."

When Jukes arrived home he found Cathy asleep in front of the TV. Light from a game show flickered uselessly across her angelic face.

Watching Cathy's steady breathing as she slept triggered memories in Jukes. Memories were something he explored like tropical islands.

He let his mind drift back to Cathy's childhood.

He closed his eyes and saw her in the summer of her thirteenth year. She stood at the boat dock with a boy she'd met during vacation.

Jukes thought the boy too old for her and had told her so, but she just laughed and waved her hands, saying, "Oh, I can handle him. Don't worry about me, Jukey; worry about yourself."

Jukes didn't have any girlfriends at that point in his life. He was shy and socially backward. A late bloomer, his mother said. A nerd was more like it, he would have admitted.

Cathy was the exact opposite. She began getting interested in boys as soon as she was old enough to ride her bike. Her body developed quickly and by the age of thirteen she was already straining at her clothes and attracting the attentions of boys much older than she.

Jukes didn't like it. He thought it dangerous and foolhardy for her to act so carefree. Of course, she didn't care a thing what Jukes or anybody else thought. She just went along her way doing exactly what she pleased.

While Jukes did medical school, Cathy did the town.

Every time he tried to talk to her about it, she turned the tables on him and pointed out his lack of social grace and the fact that, at the age of twenty-three, he'd never actually been on a date.

Those memories were not pleasant, but Jukes didn't fight them. He let them come, searching for answers, looking for connections he hadn't made before. He believed somewhere deep in the fabric of his memory the explanation for Cathy's behavior lay hidden.

He visualized the small boat dock and the canoe Cathy had loved. The summer afternoon buzzed with insects. He'd just returned from fishing with Dad. While his father took the fish up to the cleaning table, Jukes doubled back to the dock to get the gear.

As he came over the hill he saw them.

The boy was older than she, maybe eighteen or nineteen, one of the tough-looking locals, with black boots and a white T-shirt. He smoked a red-tipped cigarette that glowed angrily even in the bright sunshine. Jukes had warned Cathy about the boy more than once, but Cathy just laughed.

Jukes hated the way the boy rolled the sleeves of his T-shirt up over his muscles. His jeans were way too tight. He reeked of delinquency.

And here he had Cathy by the arm.

She was shouting at him. Jukes couldn't make out what they were saying, but he could see her face, distorted by anger. The boy pulled her roughly off the dock. She jerked her arm away defiantly.

Then something happened that Jukes would not forget for the rest of his life. The boy hit Cathy. He hit her hard with a closed fist, knocking her down. She tried to get up and run away, but he grabbed her and hit her again. She fought back, kicking and scratching at the boy, but he just swatted her blows aside, laughing.

The sight of it galvanized Jukes. He clenched his fists, heart pounding, not sure what to do. His first impulse was to run down the hill and defend his sister. But the boy looked so tough, so mean. Jukes, even though older and taller, felt afraid.

He stood there for a few seconds, indecisive, burning up inside. When, at last, his rage overcame his fear, he sprang into action. He ran down the field toward them, but it was too late; his few moments of indecision had cost him valuable time.

Cathy had broken away now.

She walked back up the hill with her head down, angry tears streaming, and brushed past Jukes. When he reached out and put his hand on her shoulder she knocked it away so hard it made him yelp.

"Get away from me!" she shouted, the venom in her voice as sharp as broken glass.

He looked down the hill at the boy, who stood there glaring up at him, daring him to come down.

"What are you lookin' at?" the boy sneered. "You want some, too? Come on, tough guy."

Jukes turned and followed his sister.

"I'm waitin', you pussy!" the boy shouted.

But Jukes kept walking, flushed and frustrated.

That had been so long ago, but it still stung.

What if he had gone down and helped his sister that day? Would she have turned out differently? What if he'd stood up to the boy, win or lose? What if she could have seen that, seen him defend her against the bully? Would she have grown up the same?

Jukes often thought about that scene. It was a painful memory, one that never failed to embarrass and humiliate him. That afternoon by the lake had affected both his and his sister's lives in ways that the boy at the dock could never have known.

Jukes changed the channel on the TV to the evening news, hoping to see some sports highlights. The picture tube faintly illuminated the room, and Jukes watched a series of commercials, each one more bizarre than the last. He walked quietly into the kitchen, opened a beer, and stared off into space.

The sound of the newscast droned on in the background.

". . . the strangler is still at large. On the lighter side of the news, today in New York, man bites dog. That story after these messages. . . ."

There was a knock at the door and Cathy woke up. She sat up on the couch and rubbed her eyes. Jukes stepped back into the living room and indicated for Cathy to stay where she was. He tiptoed to the door and peered into the fish-eye security lens.

Bobby Sudden stood in the hall.

He'd shaved his head since the last time Jukes had seen him, but he looked every bit as depraved and mean. At six feet, he stood as tall as Jukes, but more muscular. He wore his usual black leather jacket and T-shirt.

Cathy came up behind Jukes; he could hear her breathing over his shoulder. Why couldn't she stay on the couch like he told her? She never followed his instructions. "Who is it?" she whispered.

He waved her back, a look of disgust on his face. He didn't want her to get anywhere near the door. "It's Bobby," he whispered angrily. "I don't want him to know you're here, OK? So, just keep quiet and stay back; let me get rid of him. I do not want you to talk to him; is that understood? Now go back into the living room."

She gave him a disconcerting petulant look and took two steps back. She didn't go into the living room, which made Jukes angry. She just hovered there, out of sight but not out of earshot. Jukes waved at her to get farther back.

He opened the door a crack, chain engaged. "What do you want?"

"Is Cathy here?"

"No."

"I know she's here, man; let me in."

"Go away."

"She needs me right now. I'm her man. I've got a right to see her."

"Forget it; she doesn't want to see you again, ever."

"Why don't you let her decide that?"

"She's recovering from the brutal beating you gave her, which was a criminal act, by the way."

"I just want to talk to her." He tried to push the door open a little more, but Jukes held on firmly, his foot planted against the jamb. The chain snapped taut.

"Don't you get it? She's through with you!" Jukes shouted.

"That's her decision, man."

"Get the hell away from my door!" Jukes slammed it shut again.

Bobby stood his ground on the other side. "I want to see her!" he shouted through the door.

"I saw what you did to her, and I've got a good mind to kick your teeth in. That's my sister, not one of your slutty models. I've already called the cops."

"You what?"

"You assaulted my sister; I called the cops. What don't you understand? I hope they put you away for a long time."

"I want to see her."

"Absolutely not." Jukes felt good saying that. He felt like he was making up for that day at the lake many years ago when he had just stood by impotently. Strength came into him as he pictured the sneer on the local boy's face. The more he thought about it, the more it fueled his indignation.

Bobby pounded on the door violently; the whole room shook.

Jukes could feel his anger rising. "Get out of here!"

The pounding continued. Finally Jukes couldn't take it anymore. In a rage, he flung the door open and confronted Bobby.

"I want to see Cathy!" Bobby shouted.

"She doesn't want to see you."

From behind him he heard his sister's voice, and his heart sank. "Bobby? Is that you?"

"Cathy? Baby?"

"Please go away, Bobby. It's over. I . . . I never want to see you again."

"Bullshit!"

"You heard her!" Jukes butted in.

Bobby pushed Jukes back into the apartment. He lost his footing, staggered backward, and crashed into the wall. Bobby was inside before Jukes could react.

As Jukes came forward to stop him, Bobby threw a punch at his face. Jukes had never been sucker punched in his life, and it caught him completely by surprise. Bobby's fist connected perfectly with Jukes's jaw and his head snapped back. Jukes went slamming back into the wall.

Bobby followed with a series of quick blows that kept Jukes covered up, but having never been in a street fight, he had no real idea how to defend himself. Bobby sensed Jukes's helplessness and took full advantage. A big right hand caught Jukes squarely on the side of the head, and he fell unconscious.

Jukes slid down the wall and slumped over. The last conscious image he had was of Bobby stepping over him.

When he regained consciousness, Cathy was gone.

CHAPTER
SIX

"How much?" asked a tall man with carrot-colored hair. Traffic streamed past; the smell of exhaust and garbage swirled.

"How much for what?" Dolly Devane answered the question with a question, a habit she had, and popped her gum.

"For a blow job and some pussy," the red-haired man asked.

Dolly looked up and down the street, another habit she had, wary of cops, competition, and psychos. Other girls were a block away, doing the same. She pulled the hem of her impossibly short miniskirt down so that it met the tops of her black stockings. "You a cop?"

He laughed. "A cop? Hell no, baby, I'm just lookin' for some *strange*." He elongated the word "strange" until it sounded like a growl. His voice hissed like a broken steam pipe.

"My name's Red." He smiled and extended his hand. She looked but didn't touch it. Most people never used their real names with her, and that was the way she liked it. "Red" would be fine.

Dolly quickly sized him up. He appeared to be a decent-looking guy in his twenties, but his hair was weird. It didn't look right. The color of it clashed with the rest of him, and he wore it shoulder-length.

She checked his shoes, a good way to spot deadbeats—they were new Doc Martins.

Red held his smile, fixed now with a peculiar glint. He said, "I got the money, if that's what you're worried about."

They stood face to face on the street.

"So?" Dolly chewed her gum vigorously. "You lookin' for a date or somethin'?"

Dolly Devane was a pro. In New York City that was a high-risk proposition. Life was never dull, or life was always dull, depending on how she looked at it. But Dolly knew what men wanted and what they would pay for it. She did OK.

Thin, with decent looks and a few shreds of her dignity still intact, when Dolly looked in the mirror she didn't see a whore; she saw a survivor. She was nineteen years old.

"Turn around," he said. "I want to see your ass."

She did. The streets had no shame; besides, Red didn't seem so bad, considering. She'd done worse. In thirty minutes she'd be out on the corner again, so what's the difference?

Way past having to justify her work, all Dolly knew how to do was take care of business. Fast. She was good at it. Wham, bam, thank you, ma'am.

There are a lot worse things than flatbackin', she told herself daily. *At least I ain't a junkie, like most of the other girls on the street.*

"Hey, I like that." Red nodded. "So give me a number, ho. I ain't got all day."

Dolly popped her gum again, which she could tell was beginning to annoy Red. It annoyed most people. "Seventy-five for a gummer, a hundred and a half to stick it in," she said with a voice as hard as uncracked pavement.

"That's a little pricey, ain't it? How do I know it's gonna be worth it?"

"Oh, you'll know, honey," she rasped, flicking her tongue for punctuation. "I'm the absolute best. Ask around."

"I did. You're Dolly, right?"

Dolly stopped chewing. "Uh, yeah. . . . Who told you about me?"

"A buddy of mine from uptown. He said you were quite a ride."

"You sure you're not a cop?"

"I'm definitely not a cop."

Dolly was looking harder now, at him, up and down the street, at the cars, at everything.

Then she said, "You got money?"

"Yeah, I got money, but I think a buck fifty's kinda high. I just want to rent your ass, not buy it."

Dolly turned away. "Then skip it, OK? I got regulars. I don't need this shit."

"Hold on a second. Let's just say I paid the tab. Where would we go?" Red asked, sounding suddenly upbeat.

Dolly turned to face him again, her face petulant. She stored the gum in her cheek and rummaged around in her purse for a cigarette. "I got a place up the street."

She fished out a Marlboro and lit it with a neon pink disposable lighter.

The man with the red hair smiled. "You gonna chew that gum and smoke at the same time?"

Dolly exhaled. "I've got a very talented mouth. What did you say your name was?"

"Red."

"OK, Red. Let's see the cash."

He pulled a wad of fifties out of his pocket and flashed it in her face.

"Good enough?"

"Good enough."

"I just got one question. My buddy says you shave your pussy. That true?"

"Yeah, nice and smooth."

"Well, then. Let's go."

Red slipped an arm around Dolly and pulled her toward him, his fingers casually kneading her buttocks, like a man checking a melon for ripeness. It was something he'd been wanting to do since he'd begun to stalk her, about a week ago. Dolly didn't know it, but Red knew a lot about her: her streets and corners, where she turned tricks, where she ate, where she lived, who her friends were, everything you could possibly glean about a whore by watching her for a period of time. Dolly, on the other hand, knew absolutely nothing about him.

When Red spoke, his voice hissed like a broken steam pipe an octave below the words. "I'm lookin' for some strange," he said again.

Dolly twisted away and took a step back. "What do you mean, strange?"

"Strange pussy."

Dolly laughed. "Is that what they call it now? Well, if you like it strange, I got some high-class strange."

Red nodded, his eyes shining mischievously. Dolly felt the uncomfortable heat of his gaze penetrate her flimsy blouse.

He liked hookers. You paid them, they treated you nice. As long as the meter was running they loved you; when the time was up they didn't know you anymore. Red thought that was a real good arrangement. He could look in his wallet and see how much love he could buy. There was no commitment or guilt, just accounting.

"All right. You want strange?" she said. "I'll show you strange, but . . ."

She turned to face him, stopped walking for a moment, and placed a hand on his sleeve. "Just one thing. No rough stuff. I'll get as strange as you want, but no hurting, got that?"

"Oh, there's no pain involved. . . . No pain at all, baby. I'm not into that," Red answered. There was something in the tone of his voice that made the brown roots of her bright red hair prickle.

The shadow of a second thought flickered across Dolly's face, and as if he could read her mind, Red held the wad of money up and fingered it in her direction. It looked like more than it was.

Dolly's attention flashed to the cash. "I got protection, you know." Her voice tried to muster all the street conviction it could. "Some real bad dudes."

"I don't doubt it."

Earlier in the day, watching Dolly from his unseen vantage point, he had shot a few pictures of her. Satisfied that she was suitably photogenic, he hungered.

They walked past the street people and garbage cans toward the Star Hotel, a run-down establishment that rented rooms by the hour or by the lifetime, whichever came first.

As they passed an alley, Red happened to glance down into the shadows, past a row of overflowing garbage cans, and saw an extraordinary woman.

Her flaming red hair caught his eye. When he focused on her, her beautiful, wan face seemed to glow like winter moonlight.

She stared at him, her big eyes wet and accusing. His heart fluttered, and he shivered slightly.

Who is this bitch? Why is she staring at me? Does she know who I am?

He felt a peculiar moment, as if a tendril of energy had darted out from her and stung him. She pulled his attention away from Dolly and held it, locked onto the other woman's ghostly face.

He almost stopped walking, almost took a step toward her.

Then he noticed pink tears unevenly bisecting her pale visage. *She's crying, and her makeup's running.* But the moment he thought that, his mind rejected it. *There's more to it than that. Why are her tears pink? What kind of makeup does that?*

He got the uncomfortable feeling that she could look inside him, that his dark desires were, to her, laid bare. A flicker of fear fired through him, resonating harmonically between the recesses of his troubled soul.

What the fuck?

This ain't right.

Why is she standing in that alley?

And why is she staring at me?

She was doing something with her hands. Red squinted into the shadows to see. The rest of the world seemed suddenly to melt away, the city and its noise, and Red was suspended in a dream.

He walked now in slow motion, time stretched like just before an accident. The rest of the universe slowed, too. Then he realized what she was doing with her hands.

She's combing her hair.

The mystery woman's eyes followed him as he crossed the mouth of the alley.

Red didn't like the way she made him feel.

He got the notion that she could read his mind, and it made him extremely uneasy. His heartbeat accelerated, in weird juxtaposition to the leaden slowness of the moment.

The intensity of her stare seemed to create a tunnel vision that pulled his eyes.

Red looked back at Dolly; she hadn't noticed a thing. She walked along, oblivious, a few paces in front of him, chewing a fresh stick of gum and acting like the queen of the block.

As soon as he'd passed the alley, out of sight of those haunted, accusing eyes, he felt better.

Whoever she is, she's got nothing on me.

He tried to concentrate on Dolly, but the ghostly face of the woman in the alley stayed with him, her likeness burned onto the retina of his mind's eye like a flashbulb afterimage. He thought how unnatural she looked, how disturbing . . . how white her skin and how red her hair. Pallid as a corpse, yet beautiful. Supernaturally so.

The gothic rock song by Procol Harum, "A Whiter Shade of Pale," floated through his head, its Hammond B-3 organ throbbing grandly. It was Red's all-time favorite classic rock tune, and now, triggered by the woman in the alley, it flooded his consciousness.

Gary Brooker's tortured vocals bit into Keith Reid's surrealistic lyrics.

"Her face at first just ghostly, turned a whiter shade of pale," Red mumbled.

Red shivered though the night was not cold.

Then it passed.

He shifted his gaze back to Dolly's tight little butt as she wiggled up the street. He blotted out the memory of the beautiful ashen-faced specter and concentrated on other thoughts.

They entered Dolly's hotel and went directly to her room, a squalid little cubicle on the third floor.

His hands began to shake a little as soon as he got past the deserted lobby. By the time they reached the second floor, he was sweating and breathing rapidly. He could smell her perfume, and it intoxicated him like a cheap, pungent narcotic. His hands fumbled in and out of his pockets nervously, unable to settle in one position.

Something dislodged from his pocket and fluttered to the floor. He stopped to pick it up. His hands were numb and unresponsive, and he couldn't get the tiny scrap of paper off the rug. He tried twice, grunting the second time, unable to see exactly what it was he had dropped.

"What are you doing?" Dolly asked. "Come on. Let's keep it movin', OK?"

Dolly turned but continued to watch him out of the corner of her eye.

Red stopped fumbling for the scrap of paper, gave up, and followed her. *Fuck the scrap; it's nothing.*

Dolly led him down a hall and produced a key from her handbag. She stopped in front of a metal door and busied herself with a series of locks. Working from top to bottom, she expertly unlocked each one, swung the door open, and pulled him inside.

He kept close.

As soon as she closed the door behind him, he turned on her. Dolly's muffled cry was short and terrible.

Red had large, strong, fast hands. They found her windpipe and crushed it easily. Red danced a macabre two-step with her as she twitched and spasmed in death's throes, jerking her back and forth as a shark would shake its prey.

He pulled up a chair, wiped some spittle off his forearm, and sat facing her. She hadn't been easy to kill, and his hands sweated inside the gloves—a problem he'd had before. But as his leather fingertips dug into her tender windpipe and the last frantic gasps came home, he got the killer's rush.

He held her long after she stopped struggling, savoring the passion of the moment. Then he walked her into a chair and stood back, studying the scene.

It was a nice composition—Dolly's arms splayed out and legs akimbo. He liked the attitude. The room was also very good, as if it had been created from carefully collected props just for this shot.

Red sat on the floor and studied it.

His heart beat at an animal's pace. He shuddered violently, locked his knees, hugged himself, then shuddered again. He began to shiver as if naked in the snow.

The killer's rush part two: the shakes.

And as he shook, from far away, he heard it.

A sound rose above the police sirens in the dense urban

night, held its pitch for a few seconds, then, unlike the sirens, modulated higher. It was a ghostly wail, standing out against the ambient backdrop of the Gotham night like a neon turd.

Not a machine, not human, not animal, not anything identifiable. It kept building in intensity, invading his head, making him anxious.

He sat upright, ears piqued, and listened until it faded back into the sound of traffic.

When the terrible frost passed and his breathing returned to normal, he removed a pocket-size digital camera and began to photograph Dolly. As he meticulously lined up her close-ups he began to whisper intimately, to tell her things. His voice was low and nearly inaudible, but he kept on talking to her as if she were still alive and really listening to his encouragements.

"That's it. Beautiful. Once more. Oh, yes. Keep it up. Very nice." The camera clicked discreetly.

He enjoyed the challenge of working with the existing light. The room was wonderfully seedy, in careless disarray, scattered with a whore's collection of junk.

"Oh, that's good . . . no smile please . . . a little pout perhaps." He stepped forward and pinched her lips fuller.

"Good. Now let's try it with the rope."

He took a length of smooth black rope from his coat pocket and looped it around her neck. He twisted it and pulled until it cut into her skin. When it was partially embedded, he stopped and admired his work.

"Looks downright nasty," he said. "I love it."

He posed Dolly in various positions for another ten minutes, taking dozens of exposures. She looked great in the viewfinder, with the vacant eyes and slack expression only death can achieve.

Satisfied now, he prepared to leave.

Scanning the room for anything he may have inadvertently

left behind, he remembered the tiny piece of paper that had fluttered from his pocket back in the hall.

Convinced that he'd left no trace here, he slipped from the room and tiptoed down the hallway.

He bent over and searched the carpet. There was no sign of whatever it was that had fallen. In the dim light, it was impossible to distinguish one bit of paper from the other filth on the floor.

He was about to drop to his hands and knees when he heard someone coming. He walked briskly down the stairs, away from the noise, and kept going.

It was maddening not to know what he'd dropped.

Probably just a scrap of something, a piece of candy wrapper maybe, some tissue, certainly nothing they can trace back to me.

CHAPTER
SEVEN

The cops could do little for Jukes, and calling them proved to be frustrating. When they arrived, he stammered and fumed, in an inarticulate rage.

"I'm not sure what happened. All I know is that Bobby Sudden knocked me out and when I regained consciousness they were both gone."

"Did your sister go willingly?" the uniformed officer asked.

"I . . . I think he kidnapped her."

"But you're not sure, right?"

"Look; I believe he kidnapped her. The same guy assaulted her two nights ago and she was going to press charges."

"But did she know the man? Were they lovers?"

Jukes sputtered a, "Yes."

The cop nodded. "This sounds like a domestic situation."

"No! She hated the guy. It was over."

"Maybe she changed her mind."

Jukes excused himself to go to the bathroom. He used the moment alone to gather himself. He splashed cold water on his face and tried to focus his thoughts. *Did Cathy go willingly?* It didn't seem possible.

When he returned he stated again his certainty that Cathy had been kidnapped.

"Are you willing to file assault charges?"

"Absolutely."

The police nodded and closed their notebooks.

After they were gone, Jukes called Detective George Jones, desperately hoping the talented sleuth could help him find

Cathy. He explained the situation to the homicide detective and waited for a response.

Jones's voice came over the line like moist sandpaper. "I'd love to help you, Doc, but it's not my department. Christ, I've got my hands full down here as it is."

"Why the hell not?"

"Well, I'm Homicide, you know? They only call me when there's a body."

Jukes held the receiver out and stared at it as if it were covered with shit. Then he slammed it down with a force that surprised him.

Jukes wandered the city for hours before appearing at the door of Will Howard's apartment.

"I'm worried sick about Cathy," Jukes said as Will led him into his comfortable bachelor's flat.

"You look it, old buddy," Will answered.

"I don't know what to do. I feel like personally searching every building in the city until I find her."

"Don't do that. Listen to me, Jukes: There's nothing you can do; it's in the hands of the cops now. They're the pros; just let 'em do their job. You should just try to relax."

"I've tried. I can't."

"How about we go out and get a couple cold beers?"

"No way."

Will sighed. "Why don't you consider doing something that will distract you from your problem? Get some distance from it, you might get your objectivity back."

"No. I gotta go home in case I get a call from Cathy," Jukes said, pacing the room.

"You got your beeper and your answering service. Besides, you don't really know if that son of a bitch kidnapped her or—"

Jukes shook his head vigorously. "Hey, wait a second; I know he kidnapped her!".

Will put a hand on Juke's shoulder and, lowering his voice, said, "Man, you were out cold. You can't be sure."

Jukes shook off the hand. "I just know, that's all. This time she was through with him. We talked about it. She was pressing charges."

"Jukes, Cathy's unstable. Consider all the possibilities, please. You can't be her guardian angel forever."

Jukes rubbed his eyes. "I can't shake this feeling that something terrible might happen, something I might be able to prevent."

Will Howard opened the closet and took out a coat. "Well, it won't do any good to worry. Cathy'll turn up; she always does. There's nothing you can do."

"That asshole actually hit me!" Jukes mumbled.

Will slipped into the coat and stepped toward the door. "Well, this time he'll go to jail. You have your beeper?"

"Yeah. I always carry it."

"Then let's get out of here."

As they walked the street, Will did his best to cheer Jukes. A few flat jokes and some small talk didn't seem to help, and Will soon fell silent.

Two blocks later, he said, "Hey, by the way, did you ever call Fiona Rice?"

"No."

"You should; you really should. She'd find this Banshee thing intriguing, and she's an expert in the field."

Jukes winced. "So why don't you look her up?"

"You just don't get it, do you?"

Jukes didn't answer. Will Howard laughed; it turned into a cough.

"Christ, for a shrink, you're pretty thick. Why do you think I gave you her number?"

"Just spit it out," Jukes said. "I'm in no mood to play games."

Will looked up and down the street, then back to Jukes. He had the expression of an umpire about to call a base runner out, his face set in a grimace.

"Dr. Rice is a babe, you idiot. I'm handing you the Holy Grail and you don't even know it."

Jukes slapped his forehead. "Oh, God."

"See? You're so preoccupied that you didn't even get the message."

Jukes blushed. "Jeez, Will, thanks, but . . . I can't be thinking about women right now, not with Cathy missing."

Will Howard stopped walking. Jukes took an extra step and stopped also. "What?"

Will pointed at Jukes. "Hey, are you the same guy that came to me last month desperate to meet somebody? The same guy whose life was an empty shell, with no one to share his pain? I'm quoting you, man. I believe the phrase you used was 'terrified of growing old alone.' Was that you?"

Jukes looked at his feet and thrust his hands deep into his pockets. "Yeah, I know. . . ."

"You *don't* know; that's the whole point. Let's face it, Jukes. Your love life is the shits. You've been crying to me for the past couple years about how important it is that you meet somebody, a soul mate. And now, after a lifetime of intense research, I come up with the perfect candidate, and you don't even have the decency to at least meet her?"

"Well, I . . ." Jukes was flushed. "I just can't right now, not with all this—" He waved his hand at the city. "You know."

"I made a vow, to you and your dad, that I would find you a suitable mate. You're in no position to do anything except what I tell you to do. For God sakes, Jukes, don't let this one get away. She's perfect, she's available, she's brilliant, she's got a heart of gold, and she's very healthy. I should know; I'm her doctor.".

"Oh, this is hopeless."

"Then you'll call her?"

Jukes sighed. "OK, I'll call her. Maybe I'll find out something about the Banshee."

The doorbell rang, and when Jukes answered it he saw Detective Jones standing with two Styrofoam cups of coffee in his hands. "Dr. Whaler?"

"Yes? What is it, Jones? Have they found my sister?"

"Well, no."

Jukes pursed his lips. "Oh. . . . Well, what do you want?"

Jones stepped forward, held out one of the cups, and smiled. "Would you like some coffee?"

"Is that what you came here for? Coffee? If you've got something to say, why don't you just say it, OK?"

George stopped; his face fell. Jukes felt a pang of remorse; he hadn't meant to be so blunt. Being blunt and mean-spirited was not his style, and it felt strange.

"Look; I'm sorry. I didn't mean to jump down your throat; it's just that I'm under a lot of stress right now."

"I know how you feel," Jones said. "It's a sick fuckin' world."

George looked past Jukes into the living room. Jukes waved him in. He handed Jukes one of the cups, and they sat facing each other in a pair of matching leather armchairs.

Jones sipped his coffee. "You know, I've been thinking about this Banshee thing and it's really buggin' me. I've been considering the possibility of a link between Loomis, Killian, and the mystery woman."

"Yes?"

"Well, I went over to Killian's apartment to have another

look at his stuff, and the landlord said that all of his poetry had
been taken by a friend of his, a guy named Sean Cheney. I
tracked this Cheney guy down, and what do you know? He's
got a bookshop down in Soho, the Turf-Cutter's Enchantment.
It's a radical Irish place; I checked it out."

Jukes nodded wearily.

"I need your help. I want to establish a connection between
the two deaths and the Banshee, an Irish connection."

"You think Loomis was mixed up with something political?"

"Maybe. Who knows? At any rate, I thought you might like
to go over there with me—you know, as a consultant—and take
a look at the man's writing. It might shed some light on this
whole thing. The fact that you're a shrink and Loomis was
under your care . . ."

Jukes sipped the coffee; its bitter scent invigorated him.
"You want my impressions?"

"Yeah, any insights you might have. If you do this for me,
maybe I can help you find your sister. I'm not promising anything, you understand, but I've got some influence around the
department. Some of the guys can be slow, unless you light a
fire under their asses. Besides, I feel bad for you. I figure you
must be pretty upset."

"That's an understatement," Jukes said. "All right, Jones,
you're on. When do you want to go?"

Jones put down his coffee. "How about right now?"

Detective Jones had mercifully let his cigar go out during the
drive, and Jukes thanked God that he didn't have to breathe
those noxious fumes again. Jones spoke conspiratorially
through his stained teeth. "Let me do the talkin'. If they think
we're cops they won't lift a finger to help us."

"OK."

The street was littered with discarded papers and empty bot-
tles. A graffiti-covered newsstand stood at the corner. The cheap

hand-painted sign on the side screamed: STRANGLER STILL AT LARGE!

They got out of the car and entered the Turf-Cutter's Enchantment.

It was a secondhand bookstore, musty-smelling and lined with overstocked, dusty shelves. The two men browsed for a few minutes, disappearing into the stacks. No salesman approached them.

In time, Jones stepped up to the counter where a bearded man sat smoking a pipe and reading a book, ignoring them.

"Excuse me, but I'm looking for something by Brendan Killian."

"Killian?" The man looked up.

"Yeah. I figured you might have something."

He put down his book. "Well, you came to the right place, mister. I happen to have all of his stuff in stock, probably the only store in the city that does. Do you like Killian?"

Jones smiled; the man had taken the bait. "Yeah, what I've read of it. He's hard to find, though, not your basic Barnes and Noble item, if you know what I mean. I couldn't put *The Rod and the Staff* down. I heard he died recently."

"Bloody shame. The man was a genius. Have you checked out *The Wishing?*"

"Lead me to it."

The bearded man came from behind the counter and showed them down one of the congested aisles. He pointed to the Killian shelf and stood as Jones withdrew several books.

"Great. I'll take all of these."

They walked back toward the counter. The bearded man seemed happy to be selling Killian's work. He obviously had some kind of a soft spot for the poet, Jukes thought. Maybe they had been friends.

"I'll be publishing some of his later work shortly. He had a great volume of poetry finished when he died," the bearded man said as he added up the sale on a piece of scratch paper.

"Really?"

The man behind the counter smiled. "I have a small publishing company here at the store; we do mostly unknown stuff. The *Visionary Poets Series*, it's called. Killian died penniless, you know, but he left me all his poetry. It's a shame; it was as if he knew he was going to die."

"You don't say." Jones was playing his role to the believable hilt.

"Oh, yes. Did you know he was gunned down by British agents right here in Central Park?"

George looked askance. "Gunned down? Are you kidding?"

"Hell, no. He was a wanted man over in England, and they feared him, feared his poetry. He had lots of enemies because he told the truth. All great men who tell the truth about Ireland are marked for death."

"Gunned down, you say? My God, it's hard to believe."

"In cold blood, no less. The New York City Police Department was in on the cover-up. That's why you didn't see much in the papers about it."

"Incredible. The things those damn cops get away with . . ." Jones was actually enjoying this. Jukes's eyes wandered to the revolutionary posters on the wall.

"It wouldn't be the first time the cops have helped the English," the salesman replied.

Jukes hadn't said a word up to this point. He feigned interest in the conversation. Actually, he was mildly amused with the quaint shop and its old-time leftist ambience. There were posters calling for the overthrow of various governments, flyers for countless rallies and demonstrations, and thousands of dog-eared esoteric books. The place smelled of revolution.

Jones pressed on. "What were his poems like at the end? He must have been into some incredible stuff."

"Want to see some?"

Jones's face brightened up instantly. "Yeah, I'd love it!"

The bearded man handed him a sheaf of printed papers. Jones accepted gleefully.

"I can sell you some of these as separates; the full collection will be out next month. It's called *Song of the Banshee*."

"What?" Jukes's ears perked up.

"*Song of the Banshee*. It's about the death of Ireland. The Banshee symbolizes Ireland's fighting spirit and the shameful exploitation of her people. Killian's skillful use of imagery is the backbone of his poetry. The man was a genius."

"I know; you said that."

Jukes and George looked through the sheaf of poems, many of them untitled. Most were short, less than a page, and shot through with the kinds of emotions Killian probably had felt in his final days. Jukes's heart leaped when he read them, and a cold wind began to blow through his heart.

> *She stalks me through*
> *The emerald night*
> *My fate is sealed*
>   *I dare not run*
> *Wherever I go*
> *She is*
> *And so I await as a lover*
>   *Should*

Jukes shivered so violently that it almost made a sound through his jacket. Killian was talking about the Banshee!

He had been stalked; that much was obvious. But Killian showed an understanding of the Banshee, an acceptance, like Loomis, and that disturbed Jukes.

Something strange is going on here, he thought. The memory of the redheaded mystery woman flooded back, and poor Loomis's rantings.

The Banshee, of course.
He read on.

Take me in the green
Where destiny calls
Dare not wait another night
I am yours, grievous angel
Freely, and of my own free will
  Proud to die in your arms
  An Irish death

Jones was looking up from his paper, too, giving Jukes strange, knowing glances. Jones handed the poem he was reading to Jukes. His eyes scanned the page.

For Ireland I join the Banshee
In tears
  Keening for the dead
  We clamor together

For all those who dream of freedom
  As we do
  As we must
The terrible beauty lives on
Death, the defiant salvation
The end of suffering
The final issue
  Resolved here and after
In the song of the Banshee

Jones purchased several of the loose poems, including the title poem of *Song of the Banshee*, as well as two books, and the two men left the store deep in thought.

George said, "I think it's time for a little more research on the Banshee. If there's a killer out there using it as a guise, Jesus, things could get unpleasant around here. Besides all these men being Irish, there must be another connection."

Jukes nodded. "I think the guy at the bookstore misinterpreted all of this. It could be political, but it could be something else entirely. Killian was being stalked by the mystery woman, just like Loomis."

Jones opened the car door and let Jukes in. This time he wasn't as lucky with the cigar smoke. The burly cop lit up and puffed on his stogie like a bellows.

"Well, Killian was a radical. He had connections to known terrorist organizations, according to the FBI. Killian had relatives within the movement."

Jukes was surprised. He looked at Jones sternly and asked, "Why didn't you tell me?"

"You didn't ask."

"You knew he was a terrorist and you didn't tell me?"

"I didn't say he was a terrorist; I said he had relatives within the movement."

"So? You should've leveled with me up front."

Jones shrugged. "Hey, I'm a cop. Whadaya want? I have my information; you have yours. I don't have to share it if I think it puts a spin on the case. I didn't tell you because I didn't want you to know, plain and simple. It might have influenced you, tainted your thought process. You got a problem with that?"

"I don't put a spin on anything! I deal in facts. I'm a doctor, for Christ sake!"

"Exactly," Jones replied. "Then you should know better. I work on a need-to-know basis. When you need to, you'll know. Get used to it, Doc; that's the way things are."

Jukes touched George's arm. "OK, I did this little errand for you, Jones; now maybe you'll help me find my sister?"

Jones blinked. "I'll see what I can do."

As Jones slipped his unmarked car into gear and pulled away

from the curb, a figure materialized from a doorway across the street.

As soon as the car turned the corner, Padraic O'Connor hurried across the street and into the bookstore.

Jukes was pleasantly surprised to find Fiona Rice to be an attractive forty-year-old woman specializing in Irish mythology and culture. She was a full professor, single, and in line to become the next department head. A bit too tall for most men, perhaps, but lithe and coltish, Fiona dressed for success in conservative tailored suits. She kept her brown hair simple and short and wore modest makeup.

Jukes felt an immediate attraction to her. Will Howard was right—she was a babe. Jukes fought off his natural inclination to be shy and slightly withdrawn in the presence of a beautiful woman.

"Dr. Wahler, so nice to meet you. Dr. Howard said you'd be stopping by. Please come in. I know it's not much of an office, but make yourself comfortable."

She led him into a pitifully small cubicle in an office shared with several other workstations.

"Dr. Howard is a wonderful man, don't you think?"

Jukes smiled. "Well, I wouldn't use the word *wonderful*, but we've been friends a long time."

"You're a psychiatrist?"

"That's right."

"Well, I'm intrigued. What can I do for you?"

"I had a patient, an Irishman named Loomis, who insisted that he was being stalked by . . . the Banshee."

"The Banshee? Really? That's interesting."

"What can you tell me about the Banshee, Dr. Rice?"

"Fiona," she said. "Nobody calls me Dr. Rice." She smiled and her eyes twinkled.

"OK, Fiona. And you can call me Jukes."

"Jukes, what an unusual name. Is that French?"

"No, just weird. My father was an eccentric."

"Well, Jukes, there's nothing I love more than talking Irish mythology." She glanced at her watch. "It's my lunch hour right now; I've got a class at one. Why don't we talk in the cafeteria?"

She gathered an armload of books and folders and led him through the door and out into the hall. After a few steps, the cargo threatened to spill from her embrace like a paper waterfall. She stopped to shift position and Jukes automatically reached out to help her. They brushed up against each other while Jukes relieved her of half her burden.

"Thank you," she said, and they both blushed slightly.

They walked together in the direction of the cafeteria.

"The Banshee is a very complex figure," Fiona said.

"The man who said he was being stalked was a banker, not the type to go off chasing leprechauns."

"You say 'was'. . . ."

"Well, he's dead. Murdered, actually."

Fiona's face creased; her brow furrowed. Jukes thought her expression of condolence was priceless. It seemed she had a thousand facial expressions, all of them wonderful.

"That's terrible," she said.

"Yes. It happened only a few days ago. Mr. Loomis was under my care. He complained of being stalked by the Banshee, and then he turns up murdered. You can see my interest. It's hard for me to gauge the sincerity of his convictions. I don't know how much he made up and how much is common knowledge, so I'm curious. The thing is, in my opinion, Loomis was suffering from paranoid delusions."

"Banshee delusions?"

"Yes."

"I see. Well, those who believe in the Banshee do so very passionately. It's not uncommon for Irishmen to experience that

phenomenon. You see, the Banshee is the Irish version of the
grim reaper. When an Irishman from certain families believes
he's going to die, he often calls forth the myth of the Banshee.
I say Irish *men* because women don't seem to fall victim. The
Banshee, you understand, is a woman."

They entered the cafeteria and Fiona put her stack of folders on a table. They stepped to the food line, took trays, and
slid them down the stainless-steel assembly line. Fiona selected
a turkey sandwich and Jukes a bowl of soup. When they
reached the cash register, Jukes pulled out his wallet and paid
the tab. The total was a surprisingly cheap $3.49.

"That's the only reason I eat here," Fiona said.

They went back to the table with Fiona's files and sat down.

Jukes looked around the room and smiled. "I'll have to remember this place; it's very atmospheric."

Fiona laughed. Jukes noted that she laughed easily, a wonderful trait to have, he thought. His shyness eased with the
blithe spirit of Fiona's company.

"The Banshee. Let's see; where should I begin? According to
W. B. Yeats, the Banshee is an attendant fairy that follows the
old families, and none but them, and wails before a death. The
keen, or *caoine*, the funeral cry of the peasantry, is said to be an
imitation of her cry.

"The Banshee has been around in myth and legend since the
fifth century. She's been called the Bean Si, the Bean Nighe, the
Washer Woman, even such quaint things as the Little Washer
by the Ford. There are dozens of variations. She haunts certain
Irish and Highland Scottish families.

"Legend has it that she appears sometimes as a woman wash-
ing the bloodstained clothes of those about to die, usually by
a desolate stream in the woods.

"The most widely believed mythos is that she is the ghost of
a woman who died in childbirth. I did my doctorate on Irish
myths and legends, and the Banshee has always been one of my

favorites, maybe because she's a woman and we women get so few good avengers."

"Avengers?"

"Yes. You see, in a way, the Banshee is the avenging angel of womanhood. I'll tell you why I say that, but this is pretty esoteric stuff; are you sure you want to hear it?"

Jukes nodded.

"I just did an informal scan on the university's data base, based on what Dr. Howard told me." She blushed. "He . . . he said you'd be inquiring about the Banshee, so I thought it might be fun to do some homework."

Jukes got the distinct impression that Will had exerted the same type of pressure for them to meet on her as he had on him, and with the same subtle message—matchmaking.

Fiona cleared her throat and went on. Jukes was captivated; he thought she was intelligent and pleasant, more so every minute.

"Anyway, I looked back at every Banshee reference I could find in the mainframe and correlated those references to the rise and fall of the great clans, and here's what I got. The Banshee usually puts in an appearance where there has been some wrongdoing to women. Fascinating, isn't it?

"Garret More Fitzgerald, the Earl of Kildare, was said to be a tyrannical woman beater, and the Banshee is referenced there by several accounts. His nephew Conn More O'Neill is said to have suffered the same fate, as well as many others of that particular lineage.

"The most notorious was Ulick Burke, who beheaded his wife, who was, incidentally, the daughter of Kildare. He was said to have lived in fear of the Banshee for many years until she took him. That was around 1504.

"For centuries she stalked the families of the great ruling clans. Names like Geraldine, Butler, Burke, and O'Brian and others. In fact, it is said that the Banshee has visited virtually

every clan in Ireland over the years, and also many of those in
Scotland. Once she gets your number . . . it's all over. The
blood of the great families still runs in hundreds of thousands
of their descendants all over the world."

"I had no idea. Tell me. What does she look like?"

"First of all, most of the people who see her die, so that
cuts down on eyewitness accounts, but as far as I can deduce
from what documentation exists, I'd say she has long red hair
and always appears crying. She wears a gray cloak over a green
dress, but that can change, depending on which family history
you follow. There have been conflicting accounts over the years.
She sometimes appears beautiful, other times horrible."

Jukes was listening intently. He hadn't touched his soup.
"You talk as if she really exists, as if you know her."

Professor Rice smiled. "Do you believe in ghosts?"

"No, but a lot of people do."

"Correct. Science can neither prove nor disprove their existence. So, I guess it's anybody's ball game. Since the Banshee is
a type of ghost, who's to say? All I can tell you is that history
is full of ghosts, in literature from the Romans to Shakespeare
to Washington Irving to Stephen King."

Jukes gave her a sly smile in return. "Do you?"

Fiona shrugged. "Kind of. I mean, I'm a historian. I spend a
great deal of time hunting them down in one form or another."

Jukes felt the warm rays of her smile, and for the first time
in his life he felt at ease with a woman. He said, "Funny, you
don't look like the type who believes in the spirit world."

She blushed. "Well, I don't really. . . ."

"What can you tell me about the Banshee's singing?"

"Oh, the song of the Banshee is supposed to be the most terrible sound imaginable. The Banshee's wail is the sound of im-
pending death, literally. Some of the research suggests that her
wailing may actually cause the death. Ulick Burke was said to
have been split in half by the sound."

Jukes sat upright. He could scarcely believe his ears. "Did you say split in half?"

Fiona took a bite of her turkey sandwich and nodded. "That's exactly how Declan Loomis died."

CHAPTER
EIGHT

O'Connor entered the old woman's crowded living room carefully, not wanting to bump into anything. Mrs. Willis had thousands of tiny figurines displayed on every available surface. Little statues, fragile bits of glass artwork, were everywhere. When O'Connor looked closely, he saw that they were all animals.

The centerpiece of her collection, a family of exquisite miniature giraffes, grazed in frozen splendor on the mirrored shelf of an antique display case.

"You like my little zoo?" Mrs. Willis asked, her voice as thin as a reed, her Irish accent thick. She was 102 years old, supposedly, and as tough and wrinkled as jerky.

O'Connor tried to whisper, his own booming voice far too overwhelming for this room. "They're so delicate, I'd be afraid to touch one."

"They are delicate, and quite fragile," she said slowly. "Come with me."

She led him through the cramped little house, into the kitchen. "Sit down, Padraic O'Connor."

He did. She sat across from him at the kitchen table and removed her glasses. There were a few minutes of silence that O'Connor chose not to break, while the old woman studied him.

"You resemble your father," she said at last.

"Did you know him well?"

"Of course I knew him well," she answered quickly, annoyed that he would ask such a stupid question. "Are you thick?"

Without waiting for an answer, she continued. "I know he taught you the secret ways, the ways of the ancients. That's how it's passed on, from father to son."

"Mrs. Willis, I—"

"Silence!" she barked. Her voice resembled a crow's, O'Connor thought, dry and hateful. He folded his hands and sat like an obedient child.

Mrs. Willis shook her finger. "In my family, after all my brothers were killed, my father gave me the knowledge in the hopes that I could someday pass it on. He knew I had the second sight, and I could see the destinies of people, and he knew that when the time came I would just see who to pass it to.

"Now there's none left but you, Padraic, a distant nephew, but that's the best I can do. I'm too old, and besides, I am a woman. A woman cannot do what needs to be done; only a man can perform that task."

O'Connor stared at her, feeling the gooseflesh crawl up his back. For the first time since he'd left Ireland, Padraic was having second thoughts. The enormity of what he was about to do suddenly blossomed in front of him as if the mist cleared to reveal a mountain.

He was used to being in charge of a situation, to being the decision maker. But here, sitting across from the century-old lady and hearing her talk, he got the feeling that he was involved with something beyond his control, something as vague and ethereal as smoke.

She leaned forward and touched his temples with dry, leathery fingers; their eyes met. O'Connor wanted to pull away but didn't. There was too much at stake. He stared into the yellowy, red-veined orbs in her wrinkled face and clenched his teeth. Her left eye twitched; her face seem to sag even more.

"She's here," the old woman whispered. "She's right here in New York. I can see her in your future."

O'Connor shuddered. He opened his mouth to speak but couldn't find words to express himself. The old woman tightened her grip, pushing in on the sides of his head.

"Now is the time," she hissed. "Strike while you can."

He found himself nodding at her, agreeing.

The old woman squinted. "You remember what your father told you?"

"Yes," he answered.

"All of it? Every word?"

"Yes."

Her hands fell from his temples, and O'Connor felt relief.

"Good. In the Book of Kells there's a coded page that gives instructions for the ceremony. I have a copy of that page and a translation. You'll need to learn the incantations."

"You have a translation from the Book of Kells? But . . . Who did it?"

She laughed a short, humorless cough and released his arm. "I did. Who do you think? Gaelic, in the ancient form, is very difficult to decipher—the old ones were a tricky lot—but I have it all right here."

She removed an envelope from her sweater and slid it across the table at him. He took it and held it reverently in his oversize fingers.

"The Book of Kells is mostly untranslated, you know. No one has seen these pages but me . . . and now you."

"OK," O'Connor said. "Supposing I know how to take care of the Banshee, how am I going to find her?"

Mrs. Willis smiled for the first time, showing her cracked and yellowed teeth. "Fate will lead you to her. It's all about intertwining lines of fate and destiny. That's the way it always has been and always will be. If fate has chosen you to be the one, then you will find her."

"Where do I begin?"

Mrs. Willis further wrinkled her already incredibly wrinkled face. She wagged a brown-spotted, bony finger in his direction. "Are you sure your father taught you?"

"Yes."

"Then you should know. Begin by clearing everything out of your mind. Start by doing nothing."

O'Connor smiled. "Nothing, eh?"

The old lady took a slow, deep breath, as if the gravity of her words pushed her down.

"Everything will be revealed in its own time. When the answers come, they will appear to be a series of unlikely coincidences, but beware. There are no coincidences."

"Damn confusing, if you ask me."

"All I want you to do right now is get everything ready. Can you do that?"

O'Connor nodded.

"Good. Now I just hope fate has chosen the right man for the job." The old woman crossed herself and muttered something.

O'Connor waited for her to speak again. She closed her eyes and seemed to go into a trance for a few long seconds.

"She will strike again soon; even now she stalks her next victim. Your job is to track her down by finding that person. Look for a sign. If you are truly chosen, a sign will come to you."

O'Connor's face remained impassive. "Can you tell me anything about who that victim will be?"

The old lady sighed. "I can't be sure. . . . I . . . I think it's someone close by."

"In this neighborhood?"

Her eyes clouded. She ignored the question and whispered, "It's somebody who is . . . two people, I think."

"Two people," he repeated.

"That's all I can say."

O'Connor waited for more, but none came.

"This is the way it has to be," she said at last, and stood.

Feeling clumsy and alien, he let her lead him to the door. She moved slowly, too slowly for O'Connor. Watching her fumble with the locks was maddening. At last she swung the door open and light flooded in. As he took a step, her cold, dry hand pulled at his sleeve.

"The doctor," she whispered. "Follow the doctor. And the cop. He's special; their destinies are intertwined with yours."

O'Connor stepped out into the sunlight. He heard the door close behind him and sighed. The old lady's words came back to him, as he committed them to memory.

"... they will appear to be a series of unlikely coincidences, but beware. There are no coincidences."

Scrupski's Metalworks and Die Casting was in New Jersey, and O'Connor had a devil of a time finding it in his rented Jeep Cherokee.

The place was big, noisy, and filthy. Harley Spinks was the foreman in charge of custom molds.

In Harley's office, O'Connor went over the specifications of a casting he wanted to have done.

"How many pieces do you want total?" Harley asked.

"Just the one," O'Connor replied.

Spinks laughed.

"What's so funny?"

"Well, this is a rather strange request, mister. We usually do poured metal casting in multiple pieces, for industrial use. One piece? Hell, I don't know. The cost is in making the mold, you know."

"I need the highest grade steel you've got."

O'Connor showed Harley the plans, spreading them out on his desk.

Harley studied the paper and shook his head. "I can save

you a lot of money and aggravation by making this in two parts."

"It has to be one piece, cast exactly as shown."

Harley lit a cigarette and rocked back in his chair. "We make precision machine parts here. I don't understand what the hell this thing is."

"It's art."

Harley nodded. "Oh, I see. Art? Christ, man, this is gonna cost you an arm and a leg."

"I've got the money. Can you do it?"

Harley squinted at the plans. "The specs are a bitch. These are metric, right?"

O'Connor nodded. "I need it polished, too."

"After it's been cast and cooled, we'll have to do another machining. Hell, this will be more trouble than it's worth."

"I'll pay the going rate, in cash, and a bonus if it's done in seven days."

Harley smiled. "Well, like they say, money talks; bullshit walks. That's gonna have to be in advance, of course. I'd hate to get stuck with a piece like this."

"Of course."

"I should be more suspicious, but since business has been down, I won't ask questions. There's nothing illegal about making precision machine parts. The government won't allow us to make anything dangerous or illegal, like bomb parts or weapons, you understand."

"I can assure you, Mr. Spinks, that this is a perfectly legal thing."

Harley looked back down at the plans again. "Well, I guess we can do this. Damned if I know what it's for."

"I told you, it's art."

"Yeah, right. Art."

"Remember, a bonus for seven days."

Harley filled out the custom order form, O'Connor signed

it using his alias, "Charlie O'Malley," and they shook on it. He paid cash. "A done deal?" O'Connor asked.

"A done deal. Pick it up at the end of the week."

After O'Connor left, Spinks studied the drawing and wondered what the hell he was going to make.

It looked like a large cylinder, about twenty inches across. There was a ridge for brackets around each end. The customer wanted the thing to be polished both inside and out.

O'Connor drove back into the city. He followed hand-written directions to a shop in Greenwich Village with the curious, yet descriptive, name the Bone Room. The tiny store had a rather specialized clientele; it sold only bones, from animal to human.

There was a display case full of skulls, some human, and another with various skeletal appendages—paws, claws, wings, tails, hands, and feet. Against one wall stood a collection of complete skeletons, all real. A sign over the door said as much. The Bone Room prided itself on having only the finest legal bones money could buy.

The atmosphere was bizarre. Having all those skulls grinning at you would have given some people the creeps, but not O'Connor. He wondered if he knew any of those poor souls who constituted the former owners of those human frames, now displayed like so much produce.

He browsed for a few minutes, examining a rattlesnake skull and the complete mounted skeleton of a wolf.

"May I help you?" asked a cadaverous man wearing a bow tie and too much cologne. His face was as gaunt and colorless as the skulls he sold. He wore a white lab coat that gave him the vague appearance of being some kind of medical technician.

"Yes. I'm looking for a certain type of human bone."

The salesman nodded, and O'Connor could see the top of his head. A few greasy gray strands of hair stuck to his scalp like spaghetti. "We have an extensive inventory of human bones, all perfectly legal and processed. May I ask what bone it is you're looking for?"

O'Connor smiled. He would make an effort to remember everything, so he could tell the story of this place later, to his friends at the pub. He stopped smiling when he realized that both Dolan and the pub were gone.

O'Connor didn't really know the name of the bone he wanted, not having a background in anatomy. The only exposure to bones Padraic O'Connor ever had was breaking them. At that he was an expert. "Well, I think it's a leg bone, about this long." O'Connor spoke with his deep Irish brogue. He held his hands up, indicating about twenty inches in length. The gaunt man in the lab coat nodded.

"I see. It looks like what you want is a femur, judging by the size you've indicated. Tell me, sir, what do want it for? I mean, what purpose do you have in mind?"

O'Connor was surprised by the question; usually people in New York took your money and asked nothing. He hadn't given it much thought, but O'Connor was a pro at dealing with people and answering difficult questions. He could think on his feet. "It's a gift," he said simply.

The gaunt man smiled. O'Connor could see that the answer made complete sense to him. He led O'Connor to the end of the counter and brought out a box containing an assortment of different-sized femurs. "We have some beautiful specimens here that would make lovely gifts."

O'Connor picked up a few of the larger bones, feeling the weight on his hand, testing the solidness of them. He smacked each one against the palm of his hand.

The gaunt man raised an eyebrow. "I'm sure you'll find these femurs to be of exceptional quality. We sell no chipped or cracked merchandise here."

"Yes, I see. These are just fine." He selected two and put them off to the side. The gaunt man waited patiently. Appar-

ently bone buyers were a picky lot, O'Connor decided. The
man had to have unlimited tolerance for eccentric people with
time to burn. O'Connor's choice took only a few minutes,
lightning-fast in the world of bone sales.

"An excellent selection," the salesman said. "Will that be
cash or charge?"

"Cash."

"Will that be all today? Could I show you something else?
Maybe something in a metacarpal? A nice tibia?"

O'Connor shook his head, aware that he was smiling again.
He realized that he was enjoying himself immensely and made
a mental note to come back here someday and buy more. A
grinning skull would look good on his mantel, leering at his
guests.

"I could gift wrap these if you wish."

"Just a box will suffice." He handed over the money, surprised at how pricey bones could be. Of course, only in New
York could you find such a shop, certainly not in Northern
Ireland. The only bones there were shattered by gunfire and
moldering in the ground, not like these perfect bleached-out
beauties.

The gaunt man wrapped the femurs and placed them in a
long cardboard box that looked like it might have been used for
flowers. He handed it to O'Connor and smiled. "I hope you'll
think of us for all your bone needs. Thank you and come
again."

Padraic O'Connor walked out into the streets of New York
with two twenty-inch human femurs in a box under his arm.

CHAPTER NINE

The atmosphere of the precinct building always seemed to be the same: desperate and depressing. Detective Jones walked through it like a holy man walked on hot coals, which is to say he rose above it.

"It's all in the mind," he said so often it became a cliché. "I don't let it get to me." Of course, on some days it did. As impossible as it was to completely tune out all the madness that swirled around him, George did his best to focus on the task at hand.

His office door did little to block out the noise and pandemonium. He took solace in the ubiquitous cup of coffee. Now on his fifth cup of the day, he was sitting down studying the police reports on Declan Loomis when the door opened and Police Captain Owen Smoller walked in.

George looked up, surprised.

"Jones, I want to talk to you."

"Sure, Captain. Here, sit down. Want some coffee?"

Smoller frowned. "That shit you drink? No thanks; that stuff is toxic. Don't you know it's bad for your heart?"

George nodded. "Yeah, they say it'll take ten years off my life, but you want to know something? It's the last ten years, the years when I'll probably be sittin' around in an old age home, waitin' for somebody to come and change my diapers. I say it's no contest. So, drink up."

The captain said, "Jones, you're so full of shit you don't know which end to squeeze. If you want to rise up in the department, you've got to show some class. Quit eating at hot dog stands and drinking rotgut coffee; it makes you look like some kind of loser."

Jones just stared at him, his lips pressed together, the mug of hot coffee between his bearlike paws. For a moment he daydreamed of throwing the hot coffee in Smoller's face, Dirty Harry style, then punching the asshole out. Nobody should talk to George Jones like that.

Nobody should, but some still did. George let people know when they pissed him off. None escaped his wrath. None but Smoller, that is.

"And tie your tie, for Christ sake."

George smiled sweetly. "Is that what you came down here to talk to me about?"

Smoller snorted. George noticed that he had some papers in his hand. The man sat down on one of the scarred wooden chairs and put the papers on George's desk. George looked at them but didn't make a move. He knew the unwritten department etiquette regarding files—you picked one up at the wrong time and presto, it magically became your file.

"People pass the buck around here so much it's damn near created a breeze," George said.

Smoller glared at him for a moment, then softened slightly and assumed a diplomatic tone. "Take the file, Jones," he said. "You'll see that it's marked SPECIAL INVESTIGATOR. That's you."

Jones picked up the folder and looked at the contents. "This the strangler?"

"Yeah, sorry. I'm gonna have to bring you in. The fuckin' commission hasn't done a thing, and the two boobs they put on it are just for show. There's been no progress and now they want you. I tried to talk sense to 'em, but you know City Hall."

"What about Loomis?"

"It's not going anywhere. You can take a heavier caseload, in my opinion. I'll give you an extra man. This strangler stuff is like dynamite; the investigation's a mess. I want a fresh mind on this. Start from the beginning; do whatever you have to do.

"The newspapers are already whipping everybody into a frenzy. But that's not the worst part."

"It's not?"

Smoller shook his head. "The mayor wants you to answer questions."

George waved his hands. "No way in Hell."

"That's what I told him. I said you couldn't break cover, I said you had death threats—believe me, I used every trick in the book—but it didn't fly. I don't want you doing this any more than you do. You're liable to punch out another reporter."

"That was years ago, and he was resisting arrest."

"Whatever. Point is, you're a loose cannon. But . . . Hizzoner insisted. He wants everybody to see that you're on the case. You're the serial killer man. He wants the press to know he's brought in his big gun."

George threw up his hands. "Aw, shit. I gotta go on TV?"

Smoller could've nodded, like a normal person, but he didn't. He was a conversational minimalist. "I'm afraid so. We'll keep it brief, but you gotta keep your mouth shut. Got that? Just give 'em the party line and play like Humble Harv."

Smoller leveled his gaze at George. He had the ability to look serious at all times.

"Don't fuck it up. I'm takin' you over there at noon for the press conference."

George let the papers drop back to the desk. He made a sour face. "I can't get involved in this kinda shit. I'll do the case, but I'm not gonna be the fuckin' mayor's monkey."

The captain was ready for that. "Look; there's nothing more to say. You got your assignment, Jones. That's it; I'm sorry. Don't give me a hard time. You want to screw up your retirement, that's your business. I'm just doing my job. Now you gotta do yours."

George felt the coffee turn to acid in his stomach.

The mayor seemed to enjoy himself at the news conference, unlike George, who was overheard by at least one reporter saying he thought it was a "cringe-a-thon."

The mayor's voice boomed in the marble hallway. "I'd like to announce that as of noon today, serial killer specialist George Jones, a detective of the New York City Police Department, is in charge of the case. Detective Jones brings a wealth of experience to the table, and an uncanny ability to understand the mind of the killer.

"He'll be heading up a team of New York's finest, and I've ordered every resource in this great city at his disposal."

Inevitably, the moment came when George had to talk. He stammered through a few generic phrases, then braced himself for questions from the media.

"Detective Jones, is it true that the killer mutilates his victims, possibly even eats them?"

George rolled his eyes. "No, that is not true."

Another voice called out a question. "Are you going to use your psychic powers to—"

"I don't have any psychic powers!" George shouted back angrily.

The same voice persisted. "But the media has reported that you seemingly make connections that other cops can't make, that you find leads that others miss."

The mayor, sensing a shift in momentum, stepped in to answer for George. "That's just good police work. Detective Jones has been on many investigations and he knows the value of detailed planning."

George looked at the mayor. *Detailed planning? What the fuck is this guy talking about?*

"So you're saying that Detective Jones is not a psychic?"

George spoke before the mayor could react. "No, I'm not a psychic. I don't believe in that crap."

The mayor bristled, clearly not pleased with George's demeanor. "I think what Detective Jones is saying is that nonscientific methods have no place in police work."

That answer seemed to placate the reporters.

George and the mayor glared at each other. Together they fielded another set of inane questions before Captain Smoller pulled the plug.

Backstage, the mayor confronted George. "You just don't know when to shut up, do you?"

George snorted. He turned to Smoller and said, "I told you this was bullshit. I hate these things."

The mayor shouted, "I give the orders around here! Jones, you made a mockery of the whole proceedings. I should have your badge for that."

"You don't like me? Get somebody else."

Smoller stepped between the two men. "OK, let's break it up. George, why don't you apologize right now and we'll get out of here."

"You can kiss my ass," George said bluntly.

"What? What did you say?" the mayor demanded.

Smoller jumped in. "He said, 'You got a lot of class.' "

Once they were outside, away from the microphones and cameras, George said, "Did you feed 'em all that psychic bullshit? Was that you?"

Smoller smiled sheepishly. "Well . . . you know how the press is; they jump on stuff like that."

George shook his head. "You're fuckin' this whole thing up, Captain. The killer was probably out there watching and having a good laugh. You want me to catch this guy or play twenty questions with these idiots?"

"You didn't have to insult the mayor."

"I didn't vote for him."

Smoller threw up his hands. "It's politics, Jones, just politics. You play ball, they write the checks."

"Exactly. He's nothin' but a damn politician. His whole job is to lie, straight-faced, to the cameras. I don't think he really cares about catching the killer, as long as he looks good."

O'Connor switched off his TV set.

He'd watched the press conference with a smile, studying George's face and listening to the answers. *These Americans are fools,* he thought. *They have no idea what they're up against.*

Later that day, the parents of Dolly Devane came into the precinct station. Smoller took them into his office and closed the door.

When they emerged a half hour later, the woman was crying. The man had the same stoic expression on his face as when he arrived, only now his brow had more lines on it and his jaw was clenched even tighter.

George watched as Smoller led them to the same desk he'd thrown the file on earlier in the day.

"This is Mr. and Mrs. Devane of Wilkes-Barre, Pennsylvania. They are the parents of—"

"Oh, yes. I know."

George had already read the report and knew who they were. He looked into Mr. Devane's eyes as he would look into the depths of the ocean from a fishing pier. He saw the bottomless sorrow of a parent with a dead child. He'd probably just found out that she'd been a whore on the streets of New York City, George thought. Nice hello.

Mrs. Devane cried the whole time. She dabbed at her eyes with a tissue and sniffed continuously.

Mr. Devane stepped forward and shook George's hand. "Captain Smoller tells me you're the best man on the force. Listen; I realize you must hear this all the time, but . . . I . . . I want this man caught. I want him punished for what he did to my daughter. My God, she was such a gentle girl, so kind and loving . . . and . . ."

Mr. Devane began to shake. George could see that he was close to breaking down. His thin veneer of composure was cracking like an eggshell.

George couldn't help but think back to when he'd heard his own bad news, that both his parents were dead and he was all alone in the world. He'd been eighteen.

Crying was something George Jones never wanted to do again. It hurt too damn much.

Watching Mr. Devane hold back his tears hurt George as much as memory allowed.

"I understand," George said. "I'll do everything in my power to bring the man in; believe me. I'm very sorry."

"If Detective Jones can't find him, he can't be found," Smoller blurted out.

Mrs. Devane looked horrified.

"What I mean to say is Detective Jones is an expert in the field. I'm sure he'll find whoever's responsible."

Cut the crap, Smoller, George thought. *These poor people just got the shock of their lives. Let's just let them go back to their hotel or wherever they came from and forget about it.*

"Don't worry; I'll do my best. Now, I'm sure you two have seen enough of the police station, so why don't you just go back and get some rest and let me see what I can turn up, OK?"

Mrs. Devane nodded. Mr. Devane led her tenderly toward the door. At the last second he turned and went back in. He came up to George and whispered, "Get this guy. Take him out of commission. Don't let him do this to someone else's daughter."

"I'll do my best."

Smoller looked back and saw them talking. As soon as he

did, he directed Mrs. Devane's attention away from the two men. He knew what they were saying.

"Detective Jones? One other thing."

"Yes?"

"Was she really like they say?"

George didn't want to answer. He could feel the probing eyes of the grieving father on his face like a lead weight. "I don't know what you mean," he replied.

"Don't play coy with me; I'm her father, for Christ sake! Was my daughter . . ." His voice trailed off.

George lifted his tired eyes from the floor. They met Mr. Devane's eyes and held. There was no getting away from it. He finished the sentence for the grieving father the only way he knew how, with the truth.

"You want to know, was she a prostitute?"

Devane nodded, blinking.

"I'm afraid so, Mr. Devane."

The grieving father sighed. "Thanks for telling me the truth."

They stood toe-to-toe for another half minute; then Devane stepped toward the door.

"Get him. Get the son of a bitch," he said softly. Then he disappeared behind the frosted glass door. George watched his figure fade away.

It took George longer than usual to get over the meeting with the girl's father. He kept drifting back to the essence, which was always the same: good versus evil. Cases changed—victims and perps—but the essence never changed.

There were other words he used, not out loud, just in his mind: *revenge, retribution, atonement.* George was a big believer in divine justice—that somehow, even if the law didn't get you, something else would.

He kept a scrapbook of cases like that; he'd even been involved in a few. Like the crack house operator who died when his pet rattlesnake bit him or the guy who beat a murder rap on a technicality and wound up having a heart attack on the golf course. It was always something. Nature had a way of evening things out.

George got the sense that this case was going to be like that. That somehow justice would be meted out. It seemed like destiny. And he was going to be there.

Front and center.

George listened to the city night, as alive as a jungle. Feeling the killer out there like a magnetic field.

He closed his eyes and let the tension pass out of him.

These evils shall not triumph.

CHAPTER
TEN

"No word from Cathy, I take it," Will Howard asked.

Jukes ran a hand through his hair, something he'd been doing too much lately. With Cathy gone and Loomis dead, Jukes was having trouble keeping up a decent front to the world. Will watched while he chugged down his beer and promptly ordered another.

Jukes stifled a burp and looked hard at Will. "Nothing. I don't mind telling you, I'm really worried."

Will Howard put his hand on Jukes's shoulder. "Listen, buddy; I don't have any answers. I don't want to upset you either; I'm your friend, OK?" He took a swig of his beer. "But you've got to consider the most likely possibilities. This guy was once her boyfriend. She may still have feelings for him, however ill-advised. I don't think you should rule that out. Can you say, for a fact, that she was kidnapped?"

Jukes thought about it; his eyes flickered downward. "I guess I can't. I don't know for sure what happened when I was lying there on the floor. Cathy's a very complex person; I suppose she could've had a change of heart. Still . . . after the beating that Bobby gave her . . . I don't know."

"It might be possible that she chose to go with him," Will said.

Jukes shrugged. "Yeah, I guess anything's possible." He ran his hand through his hair again. "At this rate, I won't have any hair left by the end of the week," he mumbled.

"Don't let it eat you."

Jukes shook his head slowly. "You go along for years, thinking everything is just fine, your life's all nice and tidy, then wham! Something like this comes along and kicks you right in the butt."

They sat in silence for a few minutes, quietly slugging away at their beers.

Suddenly Jukes spoke. His tone of voice had changed. "I talked to Jones today. He took me to this Irish bookstore in the village, the Turf-Cutter's Enchantment. I came across something interesting. Here, take a look at these." He handed Will the poems by Killian. "These are from a collection called *Song of the Banshee*, by Brendan Killian, the other guy that died like Loomis. I think you should read them. Will, I . . . I don't know what to think."

Will read the poems once, then, without saying anything, read them all a second time. Jukes drained his glass, caught the bartender's attention without speaking, and raised two fingers. The waiter brought another round.

Will looked uneasy. "Jesus Christ. This is spooky."

Jukes nodded. "*Spooky* was the word I would have used."

Will put the poems down and looked into Jukes's face. "Did you ever contact Fiona Rice over at Columbia?"

Jukes nodded.

"So? What did you think?"

Jukes suppressed a smile. "I think she's wonderful."

Will slapped his knee, delighted. "See? What did I tell you. She's perfect! I knew you'd like her. So?"

"So, what?"

"So, tell me everything. How did she like you? Did you hit it off?"

Jukes blushed. "Yeah, I think so. But mostly we talked about the Banshee."

"Did you make another date with her?"

Jukes's face froze. "It didn't occur to me."

Will Howard rolled his eyes. "You're hopeless. You still have her number?"

Jukes nodded. "But like I said, we mostly talked about the Banshee."

Will sighed. "All right. What does she say about it?"

Jukes repeated what Fiona had told him. When he was finished, he looked away.

Will picked up his beer and took a small sip, then, at second thought, took a huge swig.

Jukes drew a deep breath and spoke quietly, so no one else at the bar could hear. "You know, Will, she acts like this thing really exists."

"Doesn't sound like the same Fiona Rice I know. The one I know is as rational as the AMA."

Jukes cleared his throat. His tie, already loosened, was pulled further askew. He looked straight ahead, at their reflection in the mirror behind the bar.

"Hear me out. I know this sounds crazy. But it's possible that something extraordinary is happening here that we don't understand, something that defies logic. How do you explain the fact that Loomis and Killian were ripped in half, just like Ulick Burke in 1504?"

Will looked around, checking to see if anyone had overheard them. "Do you know what you're saying?" he asked.

Jukes answered with an imperceptible nod of his head.

Jukes's apartment stood dark and cold when he got home, late again. It had been another long and bizarre day. Nothing seemed to make sense anymore. He couldn't get Fiona Rice's last statement out of his mind. People were being split in half in New York City and there was nothing he could do about it. If it were just another serial killer, that would be one thing, but all this Banshee talk was making him uncomfortable.

When it came to the supernatural, Jukes was a clinical skeptic, but now a kernel of doubt had shattered his resolve. He wasn't so sure anymore; he wasn't so sure about anything.

This is the twentieth century, an age of enlightenment. What ancient powers and evil curses could possibly exist now?

He turned on the lights and the dark disappeared. He turned on the heater and waited for his apartment to warm up. It was as simple as that—man's own creations ruled his universe, dispelled the darkness and chased the chill. No magic there, just solid fact. It's dark; you turn on the light. It's cold; you turn on the heater. Where did the Banshee fit in? What switch did you flick to get that?

Facts were the spine of Jukes's world, even when dealing with the nebulous workings of the human brain. He was a professional, he feared nothing, and, at least before this day began, he thought that nothing was beyond his understanding.

But now, after Loomis's death, after Cathy's abduction, after Killian's poems, after Fiona Rice's revelations, what conclusions could he draw? He wasn't so sure.

He checked his messages, hoping to hear Cathy's voice. He half expected to find a message from her saying it was all a mistake, a joke, a put-on, and she'd be right home. Bobby was really just pulling a gag; he didn't mean it. He'd be right over with a six-pack and a good explanation.

The first two messages rolled by, mundane and lengthy; then the unmistakable sound of Cathy's voice jumped out at him.

"Jukey? Jukey, are you there? I'm just calling to let you know I'm all right. I can't talk right now. But . . . I'm OK, so don't worry. Look; I'll be in touch. I gotta go. Bye."

Click. The machine turned off.

He rewound and played it several times, his heart pounding. In the background, faintly, he could here some noise that might have been music. The more he listened, the more he became convinced that it was music, and he imagined that he could even tell what kind—ska. It was very hard to tell from the short piece of tape, but he thought he could hear the distinctive herky-jerky rhythm guitar. And horns. It could be horns.

Years ago, Jukes had gone with a few friends to see some ska bands in the Village. He remembered liking the crazed, speeded-up reggae dance music. The bands all had horn sections and guys with skinny ties and bad haircuts.

Jukes took the tape out of the message recorder and replaced it with a new one. He put the cassette with Cathy's voice on it in his pocket and trudged off to his bedroom.

He looked forward to getting into bed and closing his eyes.

Jukes Wahler never had a problem falling asleep. Now life was turning into one big, fat problem. He doubted sleep would come easily this night.

Even after the beers, his mind raced, twisting itself around his anxieties like a worm on a hook. He kept thinking of Cathy's voice on the tape. And the music.

She must have gone with him voluntarily. Why is Cathy like that? As a psychiatrist, Jukes felt he should have some idea.

Jukes took another mental trip back to childhood, searching, as always, for the root cause of his anxiety. He closed his eyes, leaned back, and time-traveled back to high school.

He sat at his desk and ran his fingers over the tactile surface of the wood. It was gouged and pitted with graffiti, carved deeply into it with the pointed end of a protractor, the only legal weapon in a student's arsenal in those days. He looked around at the other kids in his class and saw that they were as mean and immature as he remembered. They teased each other mercilessly and were cruel in an unthinking way that only adolescents can be. To Jukes, school life was a constant test, and everyday struggle to survive in the same world with them.

Them. Why did he care what they thought?

Why was that so damn important? he wondered *Why is it so significant for people to belong?* His life had improved immeasurably once he'd stopped trying to socialize and became the solitary man he was today.

The smells of the classroom came back to him, the singular odors of the old school building, and he realized that he'd not smelled them in thirty-five years. In his mind, it was winter, and the ancient heater warmed the room unevenly, like a campfire on a frigid night. Parts of the room were arctic, and other parts were like a sauna. As the decrepit radiator became hot, the layers of school-day life began to bake and give off a myriad of unpleasant odors. Gum, paper wads, spit, paint, puke, glue, pencil shavings, eraser crumbs, and other refuse of academe were activated and reeked like the boiler room in Hell.

For Jukes, who sat next to the wheezing metal dinosaur, it was enough to make him gag sometimes. He hated the smell of the old school building in the winter. It all came flooding back to him as he sat in his apartment decades later, looking back on those days, spying on the past, like a alien voyeur.

His gangly, ungraceful body seemed to attract accidents, constantly bumping his way through the obstacle course of life. The acne cases came and went, usually at their apex during periods of high sexual drama.

And Jukes suffered.

Shadows crept ominously in the corners of his bedroom, hiding nightmares, waiting for him to sleep. He constantly scanned the room, squinting at the darkness. His once secure and comfortable world was now filled with a hideous new uncertainty.

He tossed, searching for a comfortable position. The wind came up outside, and a light rain began to fall. A siren in the distance made him jump. It didn't sound right. . . . It sounded unreal, even vaguely human. Though he was in the center of the biggest city in the world, he felt as if he were all alone, hundreds of miles from civilization.

He read until his eyes at last grew heavy and he drifted off to sleep with the book lying open on his chest.

He had no way of knowing how long he had been asleep when nature called. It was time to pay for the luxury of those four beers. He lay there with his eyes closed, not wanting to wake up and go to the bathroom, postponing the inevitable. It felt so good, so cozy, in bed.

Jukes cleared his throat and opened his eyes a tiny bit, just enough to realize that he'd left the light on.

As soon as they were open a crack, he nearly jumped out of his skin.

The Banshee stood over him.

He had never been so shocked and afraid in his life. He jumped backward in the bed, hitting the headboard. When he tried to shout, only a dry whisper came out.

Jukes went numb and felt thousands of tiny needles prick his skin as if, suddenly, each goose bump on his body were acutely painful. Every pore on his skin flared open and secreted a dot of moisture. In a twinkling he was bathed in sweat.

The Banshee stared. Her hair undulated in a nonexistent ghostly breeze.

Fear gripped him in its icy hands; it twisted his senses until he thought he might actually hyperventilate.

The Banshee's face swam before him, liquid and changing. Her tears fell and stained the bedcovers faintly red. Jukes's eyes were riveted on hers. He whimpered like a child, afraid to move, more afraid than he had ever been, and more afraid than he could ever have imagined.

At last he found his breath and screamed. He screamed to wake the dead, again and again, sucking air and gasping loudly between shrieks.

He felt the room spinning. The Banshee never moved; she stood over him, statuelike. Her eyes, still dripping tears, drilled into him. He got the distinct impression that she was very old and very powerful. The age he could sense; the power he could feel. She was not just some hopeless spirit, aimlessly haunting the world of the living, but a thinking consciousness with a purpose—she caused change. She was causing Jukes to change.

His world was being stripped bare. Nothing would ever be the same again, now that he knew she existed.

He prayed he was dreaming.

He knew he was; he had to be. These things were impossible; they just couldn't be happening. He was having a nightmare, brought on by the stress of the last few days. That and those crazy poems of Killian's. His subconscious mind was sending him a message—*relax; you're getting too involved.*

But it seemed so real. He had never had a dream so real, so vivid. He could taste it, feel it, smell it, and, if he wanted to, touch it.

He blinked and rubbed his eyes, surprised to find that he, too, was crying. The tears came off on his hands like the residue of hysteria. He blinked at them stupidly.

Looking up, he saw her face clearly. She had a face like no other: utterly beautiful, yet ghostly, the features of it howling a tragic lament. He saw the pain there.

He looked closer and his eyes blurred. Her face seemed to swim, shape-shifting, showing a cinematic vision of mental images of her age-old misery. He felt, rather than saw, her eternal damnation and found the tears rapidly welling up in his own eyes again. The rush of emotion from looking at her made him dizzy.

His heart threatened to explode from his chest.

One by one, every conflicting passion rose up within him. It quickly became too much to take, and he couldn't bear to look at her. He tried, unsuccessfully, to turn away.

He imagined his own travails, using her as a springboard to face his own demons.

Then, as the swirling whirlpool of feelings closed over his head, he felt the last emotion, the last passionate embrace of life. He felt profound sadness for her.

Jukes got a sense of great spiritual power from the Banshee; the air itself seemed to crackle with it like static electricity. Images flashed in his mind, strobelike, as if his whole life was an open book to her, a series of pictures. Then he saw himself through her eyes for a split second.

He saw himself screaming. He saw the tears streaming down his fear-distorted face. He saw his eyes devoid of all understanding, an idiot's eyes.

He saw himself as he imagined she did—a pathetic, logic-bound huckster, turning neurosis into a livelihood.

Then she raised her hand and all his mental motion ceased. He was suddenly at peace, all his own thoughts washed away.

And he gazed at her.

"Who are you?" he asked.

You know who I am. Her voice echoed in his head telepathically; inside him a chord resonated.

"What are you?"

I am justice. Destiny.

Jukes saw his own breath making misty vapor and realized that the room had suddenly become graveyard cold. He was nearly hyperventilating. Great clouds of air, warm from his lungs, swirled in the space between them.

Jukes had merely to think his question. "Why are you here?"

I seek to intervene, before death.

He was about to ask her if that meant he was going to die when her face rippled. He looked at her now as if through heat waves; she shimmered in and out of focus.

Jukes reached out. She began to fade.

Just before she disappeared her face changed and he saw, for a split second, the face of a monstrous hag.

When Jukes awoke, the sun streamed through the windows with dazzling brightness. It blinded the pinprick f-stop settings of his sleep-shot eyes. The day was well under way, after eleven o'clock, and he was still in bed, sweating.

Was it all a dream? Jukes blinked and tried to recall the way he had felt in the Banshee's presence.

Then he saw the bedsheets, punctuated with droplets of faint pink fluid, dried now. *The tears of the Banshee.*

Those tiny dots of color shattered him.

He rejected his conclusion as quickly as he arrived at it. The tearstains had to have a logical explanation; they must. Perhaps they had come from him.

He lay back down in the bed, his head throbbing mechanically. He wanted to call the office and cancel the day's appointments but realized that he was already so late that his secretary would think something dreadfully wrong had happened to him. Why hadn't she called?

The message machine was blinking. There were several messages, but he hadn't heard the phone ring once. She had probably been frantically trying to get in touch and he had somehow slept through it all.

His head ached with the slightest movement. Things were quickly going from bad to worse and, at this rate, would soon be beyond his damage control.

Jukes faced the thought with trepidation—either he was suffering some sort of delusional neurosis because of Cathy . . . or the Banshee was real.

He stumbled to the shower. As he turned on the water, he tried to separate the nightmare from reality; then he thought, *That's exactly how Loomis felt.*

He wanted to shake off the feeling of profound sadness that he had received from the Banshee, but it clung to him tenaciously. He stepped into the hot water stream and soaped his body.

Why had she come to him? Was he being stalked now, just as poor Loomis had been? Would he suffer the same fate? Fear crept back under his skin, scratching at the outer edges of his sanity like a dog scratching at a locked door.

He let the water pound down on him, willing it to wash away the tangle of feelings. He hoped it was his own sanity that was in question and not the laws of nature.

He turned off the shower and stepped out. As he dried himself, he made up his mind to go into the office after all. He needed to soldier on and walk again in the world of the familiar. People counted on him and he could not let them down.

He forced himself to get dressed even though his hands were still shaking.

Jukes Wahler walked into a wasps' nest of missed appointments.

He did his best to pick up the threads of the day and tie them together, but his heart wasn't in it.

Later that afternoon the phone rang and Jukes picked it up absently. "Hello?"

"Dr. Rice from Columbia is calling on line one."

"Thank you," he said as he punched the button.

"Dr. Wahler? This is Fiona Rice at Columbia."

Jukes felt the bittersweet pang of irony; why did it always have to be like this? He wished he were in a better mood.

"Dr. Rice. You can call me Jukes, you know. I thought we agreed."

"Of course. I forgot."

There was an awkward silence, as if she expected him to fill in the conversation the way most men did. Fiona Rice was an attractive woman and it was her experience that men used these gaps in the conversation to ask her out on dates, make compliments, get fresh, or whatever.

So far, Jukes hadn't been at all like any other man she knew. He seemed a gentleman. He was also shy, and she found that utterly charming in a world full of bullish, egotistic bores.

For a second, she'd forgotten why she called.

"I've been thinking about the Banshee—"

Jukes sat up. "Really?"

"Yes, and I thought maybe we could get together and talk about it some more."

"That sounds good to me. I'm having myself a bad day of biblical proportions."

"Oh, I'm sorry, Jukes. Is there anything I can do?"

"Ah, no, Fiona, that's OK. I appreciate your concern."

"Sometimes it helps to have somebody to talk to, and you seem like such a nice guy."

Suddenly he had an overwhelming urge to be with her, to talk to her, to look in her eyes, to hear her voice. His throat was dry, but he managed to speak evenly. "Let's meet somewhere for dinner."

"Are you up for an adventure?"

"Sure. Why not?" he said. Normally he avoided adventures, sticking close to the familiar, to the things he knew. With Fiona he felt somewhat embarrassed by his predictability.

He thought, *Why am I doing this? I'm already lying to her. Adventure? I hate adventure. This woman, this fine woman, why would she be interested in me?*

As soon as he thought it, Jukes knew that kind of negative self-assessment was poison. He realized with sudden certainty the terrible damage he was doing to himself. But why was it happening? It was not like him. He was a trained professional, yet he was thinking more like one of his patients.

The loss of emotional equilibrium almost made him dizzy.

What was doing this to him? The Banshee? Cathy? Who had destroyed his structured, logical world and left him unable to find even the most basic answers?

He took a deep breath. *Physician, heal thyself.*

Jukes Wahler did a very unprofessional thing and canceled some of his afternoon appointments. He had never done that before, for any reason. But knowing his patients as well as he did, he knew that none of those scheduled for the rest of the day were in critical condition.

He needed time to think.

The Sir Arthur Conan Doyle Room was not crowded. Fiona had suggested it. It was a dark wood-paneled room with filtered light and lots of plants. A big Arthur Conan Doyle fan, Fiona loved the place and came here whenever the opportunity presented itself.

There was an air of respectability and refinement to the place. It was never loud or raucous. Fiona thought that was wonderful, especially here, in the heart of the most intense city in the world.

On the walls were framed reproductions of many of Sir Arthur Conan Doyle's book covers. Their table happened to be under a poster of the cover of a fifties paperback version of *The Lost World.* Across the room from them was a picture of the author with a photograph in his hand. The photograph showed several fairies dancing in an English garden.

Fiona followed Jukes's gaze. Her voice was bright. "Sir Arthur assumed that photograph, an obvious fake, to be absolute proof of .the existence of fairies," she said as they sat down together. "Photographing fairies became all the rage. Few people actually believed in them, but it was quite sensational in its day. People are always interested in things that can't possibly exist."

Jukes was too distracted to really look at the pictures. His mind was far away.

"Not unlike the Banshee." She smiled.

Jukes seemed distracted and Fiona wondered what was wrong. She felt his shyness and the great weight that seemed to be on his shoulders.

"Isn't this place great?"

Jukes nodded.

"I come here every once in a while when I want to get away. I love the decor; don't you?"

Jukes nodded again.

"Sir Arthur Conan Doyle was a fascinating man."

"Something bad has happened," Jukes said suddenly, changing the subject.

Then Jukes told her about Cathy's abduction. Fiona was shocked. She listened sympathetically, watching the hurt in his eyes grow as he filled in the details. He even gave her some background on Cathy's life, pointing out the failures he'd made as her guardian. After an hour he abruptly stopped talking and ordered another drink.

Jukes became quiet again. She found she could read him like few other men in her life—odd, because she had only known him a day or two. Something about him was so fragile, so vulnerable, and it drew her in. Jukes had never been one to hide his inner feelings from the people around him. He'd always been a guy who wore his heart on his sleeve.

Fiona let some quiet time pass.

She really liked this sensitive, caring man. His eyes were misty now, something she found extremely alluring even though it was the height of his tragedy. Her voice, soft and expressive, slid gently into the quiet minutes like a velvet glove.

"Have you thought of hiring a private detective?"

Jukes looked up. "What?"

"A private eye. They find missing people all the time."

Jukes nodded. "Well, it has crossed my mind, but isn't that just a lot of Hollywood crap?"

Fiona smiled; she had gotten through. "Not necessarily. I happen to know of a reputable agency right here in this neighborhood." She fished a card out of her purse and handed it to Jukes. "These guys are excellent. They helped a friend of mine out recently. She was trying to track down her ex-husband. They found him tending bar in the Bahamas."

Jukes looked at the card.

MERKEN DETECTIVE AGENCY
PRIVATE INVESTIGATION AND SECURITY
SINCE 1962

"You keep their card in your purse? What are you expecting to happen?"

Fiona flashed a genuine smile; her whole face seemed to light up. She had a sparkle in her eye that he hadn't seen until this moment and he suddenly became aware again of how extraordinary she was and, more important, how much she seemed to enjoy his company. She smiled at him in a way that he hadn't seen before.

Jukes found himself wondering what Cathy would think of her. Instantly that thought pulled him back into melancholia. Cathy would like her very much, he thought. She was certainly pretty enough, and intelligent.

"I don't normally carry business cards for private eyes in my purse, but this friend of mine—"

"The one with the ex-husband in the Bahamas?"

"Right. She was very impressed with them and she insisted that I put their card in my pocketbook. I mean they tracked this guy all the way down there; they must be good."

Jukes was trying not to stare at her. She seemed to get lovelier with every passing minute. He cleared his throat continuously, became aware of it, stopped, then started again, unconsciously.

"That guy probably left a paper trail and lived a normal life. Bobby is underground. I'm sure he's not running around New York using a MasterCharge and a Visa card. The man is a reptile, a bottom feeder. He's probably under a rock somewhere."

"All the more reason to call. What can it hurt? Like I said before, they're professionals."

Jukes put the card into his breast pocket. He turned his attention back to Fiona.

"I hope you don't think that I'm like this all the time. It's just that I'm rather upset right now. I really like you and . . ."

Jesus, he thought. *My sister's out there with that madman and I'm getting horny? What kind of brother am I?* He became aware that Fiona was staring at him.

"Yes?" she said.

"Ahh, I . . . well, maybe we could . . . uhm, maybe we could go out."

He waited for what seemed like a year for her to answer. It had really only been a few seconds.

"I'd love to," she said. "I thought you'd never ask."

Jukes blushed.

Jukes called the Merken Detective Agency and gave them complete descriptions of his sister and Bobby Sudden. He included everything he knew about Bobby, including the music he thought he heard in Cathy's phone call.

They seemed confident and Jukes felt a little better. At least now he could tell himself that he was doing all that could be done. Between the cops and the private detectives, something was bound to happen. The only thing that Jukes was worried about was that Bobby may have split town, taking Cathy out of the city.

But he would not fail her this time. The past would not haunt him again. This time, he would be decisive.

The image of the boy by the boat dock glaring up at him and daring him to fight lingered in his mind. The expression of arrogant stupidity on the boy's face hadn't changed in all these years. He still leered like a bully up the hill at Jukes, freezing time around that terrible moment and accentuating every detail of his own inadequate life.

He'd replayed that scene at the boat dock over and over in his mind for years. The boy, his sister, his failure to react in time, his fear.

He wondered if Cathy remembered it. He wondered if it had the same meaning for her as it did for him.

He wondered what the boy's life had been like. What had become of him? Had he become another Bobby? Was he out there now, somewhere in the world, doing the kinds of inhuman things to women that Bobby did?

Had he confronted the boy, what would have turned out differently?

Questions that had no answers swirled in his befuddled mind.

CHAPTER
ELEVEN

Heroin. Cathy and Bobby had been doing heroin.

She'd done it before a couple of times, and it didn't seem like anything that could kill you. Everybody did it, at least everybody Bobby knew. Cathy's friends had fallen by the wayside. She never saw them anymore.

But Bobby had the junk. And now Cathy wanted some more.

She woke up from a nightmare, about a weeping woman with red hair, to face the mother of all hangovers, except it wasn't really a hangover at all; it was the first stage of withdrawal. It was the surreptitious discomfort that somebody who has only done heroin a few irregular times, and thinks it can't possibly be *that*, experiences.

Cathy sat up slowly, nauseous. The room yawed and tilted. She felt her face as if the dimensions of it had shifted and swollen during the night. But numb fingers touched numb flesh and felt nothing.

She and Bobby had gotten really fucked up last night. He had started to do things.

Bobby was funny like that. He did strange things. Cathy convinced herself it was art because he photographed it. But sometimes he went beyond the normal bondage games and provoked real pain.

"Real pain for real art," he told her without a hint of irony. "If it hurts, it hurts good, because it hurts for art; it hurts for beauty."

Now, with Bobby gone and Cathy alone in his secret studio, she felt the gnaw of opiate addiction and the remorse of the night before.

She meant to call Jukes. She meant to help herself, but she only succeeded in making her way to the toilet and throwing up.

Outside, somewhere far away, a chorus of sirens wailed. The sound seemed strange to her. She became claustrophobically aware that there were no windows in Bobby's studio and only one heavily locked metal door.

A loud sound made her jump, startling her heart into an adrenaline palpitation. She fell to her knees as the room shook and the walls vibrated.

"Oh, shit!" she cried. "Oh, God!"

The floor beneath her knees pulsed with the sound. It assaulted her for a few seconds, smashing her eardrums with an-archistic noise, then throbbed into a regular pattern.

Then she realized it was music.

Music! Jesus Christ, that's what it is. Really loud, frantic, distorted music.

A rock band was playing next door.

Cathy acclimated herself to the sound and stood up, brushed off her knees, and lit a cigarette.

Jukes would kill me if he caught me smokin', she thought, then laughed. *Forget the cigarettes; how about some junk?* Smoking a cigarette would be the least self-destructive thing she'd done to herself the past few days.

The band plowed forward, cranking out mindless, repetitive ska instrumental riffs, all at the height of frenzy. Cathy thought they sounded bad.

Unpleasant music filled the room. The drummer pounded out fills that made her jump and the bass vibrated her internal organs. She considered banging on the wall, but that would have been fruitless. The noise coming from their side was overwhelming.

She crossed the room and went into the studio, smoking desperately.

Bobby's photography studio and living quarters were buried in the corner of a warehouse that had been converted into rehearsal spaces for bands.

At night the building throbbed with a dozen heavy metal bands, a few blues groups, and a large contingent of ganja-smoking Rastas.

But it was afternoon now, she thought. Without a visible clock there was no way of knowing for sure. It seemed like afternoon.

She thought about going outside to see, but she knew without checking that the door was locked. Bobby always kept it locked when he went out. She was a prisoner until he returned.

She closed the door between the two partitions and it muffled the sound of the rock band somewhat, but it still would have been impossible to carry on a conversation.

The studio was large and high-ceilinged. In the far corner Bobby's computer monitor glowed.

The light caught Cathy's eye and drew her across the room. She sat down unsteadily at the terminal and stared at the big rectangular screen. Bobby's Power Mac hummed imperceptibly before her, the menu open to a list of files.

Jukes had taught Cathy to use his Mac and gave her his old one when he upgraded. Cathy knew her way around the Apple.

She read down the screen. "Cat 41, Cat 42, Cat 43 w/flash, Cat 44 w/flash, Cat 45 . . ."

Across from the list was a corresponding list of applications. They were all PhotoShop. Cathy realized that these were pictures Bobby had taken of her with his digital camera. She knew enough to understand that these were file names for different images: "Cathy 42, Cathy 43 wo/flash . . ."

"Cat 51 w/whip." She shuddered when she recalled the terrible things he made her do, the poses and the disturbing props.

The damn music blotted everything out, disorienting her, making everything seem strobe-lit.

Her eyes wandered down the list. There were hundreds of files, many of her, but other girls' names appeared as well. Using the mouse she scrolled down and scanned the names, recognizing none.

"Dolly 16, Dolly 17, Dolly 18 w/rope . . ."

She leaned back in the chair and rubbed her face. Her fingers felt like she was wearing gloves.

Then, she leaned forward and double clicked on the "Dolly 18 w/rope" icon.

The software application opened itself and a blurred image appeared on the screen.

Cathy squinted at it. PhotoShop worked on the image; the machine hummed. Then, a moment later as the photo sharpened, she gazed in horror at the dead face of Dolly Devane.

Cathy knew Dolly was dead because no one could have survived having that thick black rope wound so tightly around their neck. And there was the glazed, lifeless stare of Dolly's eyes, so chilling.

Cathy uttered a terrible, weighty sob and shrank back in the chair, shuddering violently. She sat there, with the computer presenting Dolly's image before her like an unholy altar. She couldn't stop shaking.

"Oh, my God . . . ," she said. "Oh . . . no. . . ."

A sound in the hall, a thump that didn't sound like part of the music, startled her, and she looked around frantically.

Thump.

She heard it again. Another thump, followed by a high ratcheting sound that stood out against the muffled din of the rock band next door.

"Shit!" she whispered and moved her fingers back to the mouse. She struggled to overcome the shaking and moved the pointer up the little box in the upper left hand corner of the screen. Her hands moved like clumsy slugs.

She heard the door open and the music leap out suddenly from the open door.

Bobby was back!

She frantically moved the mouse, bearing down too hard and making it unresponsive. The sensitivity was set too high and she kept missing the little box. She clicked and clicked again, and kept missing. She heard Bobby close the door and lock it behind him.

Her heart was pounding like the hooves of racehorses, the pulse in her ears nearly blocking out the ungodly din of the music. Using all the willpower she could muster, she held her breath and steadied her hand. And tried again.

This time her hand left the mouse and went to the keyboard. With incredible luck she managed to strike "COMMAND Q," quitting the program. A box appeared asking if she wanted to save changes to "Dolly w/rope" and she clicked "no." The image winked and disappeared.

She got up and moved away from the computer, shaking and weak. The music pounded on.

Bobby entered the room and his eyes went directly to the computer. The screen was as he had left it.

"Were you fucking around with the computer?" Bobby shouted above the music.

Cathy forced herself to speak, even though her voice sounded like it had been pushed through foam rubber. "No, baby . . . I didn't go near it."

Bobby fixed her with a malevolent stare. Cathy looked back, blinking and shuddering. Bobby scared her more than she knew how to react.

Can he sense it?

Cathy sniffed her runny nose and scratched her forearms.

"What's wrong with you?" Bobby asked, stepping to her and reaching out his hands.

She looked at the hands and contemplated. If she didn't go to him and act like nothing was wrong, he'd suspect that she knew his secret. But to go to him, to touch him, was now as repugnant as touching a corpse.

"C'mere, Cat," he said.

The music stopped abruptly and the room decompressed into sudden silence. Cathy's heart seemed as loud as a cannon in the new subsonic environment. She shivered, part with fear of Bobby and part with the misery of her own withdrawal.

She willed her hand to reach out and touch his. He grasped it and pulled her roughly to him. She fell against him like a broken marionette.

Bobby's arms encircled her and she began to shake violently. She imagined those arms like pythons, able to crush the life out of her in a second. Tears streamed down her face.

Bobby broke off his embrace and held her by the shoulders. He peered into her face, now wet and desperate.

"What the fuck's wrong with you?"

"I'm sick, Bobby. I'm real sick. I been throwing up all morning."

Bobby smiled as if he were a demon in human skin. So evil was his expression that for a moment Cathy was unable to take a breath. That smile was a joyless parody of the one she knew.

"The China flu, eh? Looks like you need some of Daddy's medicine."

Cathy came alive at the sound of that word. "Medicine? You got more?"

Bobby pulled a plastic bag of white powder from his pocket and dangled it in front of her face.

"Just scored big-time."

Cathy changed. "Oh, Bobby, yeah. . . . Yeah, I need some—"

"You're strung out, bitch. You went and got yourself strung out on this shit and now you expect me to just give it to you for free? Like a fuckin' prescription?"

"No, Bobby, I . . . I . . . I'll pay for it."

"With what? You ain't got a pot to piss in, let alone the kind of dough you need for this." He shook the bag.

Cathy sweated. "My brother's got money; he'll give it to me. I know he will."

Bobby clucked and turned away. "You look like shit; you know that? You've really let yourself go. Look in the mirror."

Cathy stood. Bobby spun around and grabbed her.

"Look in the fuckin' mirror!" he shouted and pushed her to the wall where a full-length mirror hung.

She looked. The person looking back was a stranger. Cathy's once-rosy face now appeared ashen and hollow. The discoloration around her eyes from Bobby's last beating still showed, and her swollen lip refused to heal. Her hair hung limp and dirty in her face. She slumped like a hunchback.

Cathy said nothing.

"You're no good to me like that. What should I do? Kick your sorry ass out right now?"

"No, Bobby, don't," she heard herself say. Her voice now belonged to that stranger in the mirror. "I'm just a little sick, that's all. Give me the medicine and I'll fix myself up real nice for you."

"I told you to be careful with this shit. You didn't listen."

"I'll listen now, Bobby."

Cathy's tears had salted her lips, and she spoke now with the bitter irony of someone who didn't know good from evil. She hated herself for groveling to Bobby, but her craving for the drug overcame her fear. She rationalized it.

Maybe the picture was a fake. Isn't that what PhotoShop is for? Maybe it was just a well-done fake. She cleaved to that idea desperately. *And if it's not a fake, then maybe Bobby didn't kill her, maybe somebody else did, and he just took the pictures.*

Bobby stood behind her tortured face, looking into the mirror at her. Now he was the heroin messiah; the photography monster was gone.

"Please?" she sobbed.

"I hate it when you beg."

Bobby slapped the back of her head and sent her crashing into the mirror. Miraculously, it didn't break. She bounced back into his python arms, and he carried her to the couch and threw her down.

She cried piteously.

"All right, I'll cook some up. But this is the last time; got that? After this you're drying out."

"Yes, yes. . . ."

The music started again, loud, muffled, and relentless.

Bobby got up and walked over to the wall and beat on it with his fist. "Hey! Give it a break, huh?" he shouted.

After Bobby had injected the heroin into both of them, he decided he wanted to hear some real music. The crap that the band next door had been pumping out unrelentingly for the past hour was getting on his nerves.

A concert sound system stood against one wall of Bobby's studio. He stored it for a friend who rented the equipment out for rock concerts. The friend owed Bobby money, so Bobby had suggested the sound system be stored at his place, just in case.

A mammoth thing, it consisted of six huge speaker cabinets, high-frequency horns, several banks of amplifiers, and a stack of four monitor speakers.

Bobby had it rigged to his CD player.

He smiled, stoned and mischievous, and proceeded to turn on the power amps. They hummed to life.

The band next door needed to be taught a lesson.

"Cat! Bring me the sacred CD!" he shouted over the muffled din.

Cathy went over to the rack and hunted down *Procol Harum's Greatest Hits*. Walking unsteadily, she delivered it to Bobby's hand.

Bobby squatted in front of the glowing stack of power amps, adjusting levels, and laughed with fiendish delight. "You know what's so great about this song?" he asked.

Cathy humored Bobby. Stoned now, and afraid to think about the pictures on the computer, she acted contrite. The terrible memory faded as if it had happened years ago.

"I don't know."

"Everything. Keith Reid's lyrics, Gary Brooker's vocal, the Bach organ piece 'Sleeper Awake' that Matthew Fisher plays on the Hammond B-3, the gothic production, all of it, it's magic!

"And listen to the drums. Man, I love the way he rides the cymbals. I think that's B. J. Wilson. I saw these guys once in concert and it was the best show I ever saw. You can't imagine."

He slipped the CD into the changer and pushed a button.

He stood and shook his fist at the wall separating them from the horrendous band next door. Their muffled onslaught continued.

"Get ready for some real music, you assholes!"

Without warning the massive speakers quaked with the sound of the organ playing the opening strains of "Whiter Shade of Pale," by Procol Harum. The room shook. The sound flared out of the huge speakers like a jet engine, rattling their teeth at concert hall volume. It completely dwarfed the noise coming from next door.

The sound slammed into their ears as if they were standing in front of the band onstage.

The organ swirled, ponderous and grand, the magnificent

cymbals splashed along, and the incandescent production
swept them away.

Bobby's eyes swelled with moisture as the big, beautiful chorus boomed forth across the room.

This is the best part, thought Bobby. *To be high like this, listening to this song on this sound system, man, this is what it's all about!*

Bobby held onto the chair, letting the music wash over him.
His fingers dug into the armrest. The wonderful gothic production throbbed inside his head.

A whiter shade of pale.

CHAPTER
TWELVE

Detectives Jones and Panelli made their way through the street scene in front of the Star Hotel. The hookers and drug dealers hooted at them as they passed. Even though both officers were in street clothes, these people could smell a cop.

A tall man wearing a filthy Mexican blanket spit at them. "Hey, man, you ain't got nothin' on me! Get off my street! I'll give you my disease! I'll give you AIDS!"

In an alley across the street O'Connor pretended to drink wine from a paper bag. The shouting had captured his attention, and he watched as the tough old cop reacted to the situation.

O'Connor had been tailing Jones for several days.

The man in the Mexican blanket spit again and nearly hit George on the arm. George spun around and confronted the deranged street person. The tall man stopped dead in his tracks when he saw the malevolent gleam in George's eyes. The man had obviously mistaken George for one of the city's civilized, rule-abiding cops. The person who glared back at him now was as dangerous and violent as anyone else on the street at that moment.

George stuck out a big hand and put the index finger squarely in the spitter's face. The man who had initiated the sequence now felt that he had made a major mistake. The sneer melted from his lips and he didn't move; he did not make any gestures or quick movements that could have been construed as even remotely threatening. In George's mind, that would have given him due cause to kick some ass. The man in the Mexican blanket must have sensed it. The old cop with the crew-cut had an attitude he could smell.

"Did you spit at me, chump?"

The spitter in the Mexican blanket was now mute.

"I asked you a question!"

Still no response.

"All right, tough guy, let's see some ID. Now!" George stepped toward him, whipping out a set of handcuffs like magic.

Panelli knew this game; it was the old "good cop/bad cop" routine. He'd played it with George before. Panelli said, "Aw, come on, man. Let him go; he's just a bum."

Jones bristled. "He spit at me. This piece of shit spit at me! Nobody spits at me. I oughta kick his ass."

"Take it easy; this guy ain't worth it."

"Fuck you, Panelli! I'm gonna bust him."

The tall man in the Mexican blanket reacted predictably, starting his pleading right on cue. "Hey, man, come on. I wasn't doin' nothin'."

"Shut up, scumbag!" Jones yelled in his face, loud enough for everyone else on the street to notice and start to drift away.

Panelli, working from the classic script, said, "Let him go; he's not worth taking downtown. Look; he's sorry, aren't you, fella?"

The Mexican nodded vigorously.

George shook his head. "Let's just beat the shit out of him, OK? Nobody will care; when he gets out of the hospital maybe he'll show some respect for the law."

"Nah, let's just let him go."

Jones looked the Mexican blanket man up and down. "You spit on me again, you son of a bitch, and I'll break your ugly face."

The tall man stopped talking, abruptly breaking off his pleas. He turned and shuffled away gratefully under George's glare.

O'Connor slid back into the shadows. The old cop was good, he thought, tough, direct. O'Connor took note.

Mrs. Willis said he was special.

George looked at Panelli and smiled. "Nothing like a little street theater," he said.

The lobby of the Star Hotel was worn and shabby and smelled of stale cigar smoke. The clerk still read his paper and did the same thing to them that he did to everybody: ignored them completely. He was nearly sixty, George guessed, and about as sociable as a leper. George took out his wallet and put his badge in the man's face.

The man put down his paper. "OK, you got my attention. So, what do you want? I already talked to your boy here."

George smiled. Panelli rankled at being called "your boy" but kept silent.

"So now you can talk to me."

The clerk was older than George, more grizzled, unflinching, and obviously a veteran of many police interrogations. He kept his cool, used as few words as possible, and met George's gaze with a blank one of his own. "The girl came in like she always does; some guy was with her . . . I guess. I never saw 'em. I was out takin' a piss."

"That's all?"

"That's all."

"What did he look like?"

"I just told you, I wasn't here when they came in."

"What about when the guy came back out?"

"I don't remember."

"Did you see anyone leave the building?"

"Yeah, I saw lots of people leave, but I didn't really take notice of any of 'em. It's like I told your partner."

Panelli looked up, aware that he'd been promoted from "your boy" to "your partner."

The clerk said, "I don't know anything. Guys come in here all the time; they're all scum. I try not to look at 'em. They make me sick."

George nodded, acting as if everything the old clerk said made total sense. "Did you see anyone different that night?"

"I don't remember."

George put his badge away. He looked around the lobby and whistled. "Just as nice as the Helmsley," he said sarcastically. Then, turning back to the clerk, he said sternly, "OK, let's take a look at the room."

The clerk wearily picked up the key and led them up the stairs. They were the same stairs that the strangler had followed Dolly Devane up a few nights before.

Her room proved to be as drab and run-down as the lobby. The police lab team had been over it, and there were still traces of gray fingerprint powder here and there. They'd found nothing.

"The lab report said she was strangled again after she died. The first time he used his hands; the second time he used a rope. You find that curious?"

Panelli grunted. "Yeah. We're dealing with a real sicko."

As George looked around the room, he reviewed some things in the trace evidence report that had caught his eye. Speaking aloud to Panelli, George took stock.

"Christ, this rug is filthy. According to the lab, there were enough particles of foreign matter on this carpet to fill a shopping bag. They must hardly ever clean this place. With the lack of vacuuming and the frequency of visitors, it's no wonder the lab boys turned up this weird list of shit."

Looking at the rug now, its tired, threadbare pattern nearly invisible, he wondered what else they would find. A brown stain marked the spot where Dolly fell off the chair.

George squatted and examined it.

He pulled out a small notebook in which he had copied the particles from the trace evidence report.

"Listen to this. Cigarette butts, five, with and without lipstick traces, French fries, eighteen different kinds of hair, automobile oil, empty condom packets, traces of marijuana, coffee, traces of talc, bread crumbs, paper fibers, gum, beach sand, and popcorn."

"Popcorn?"

"Yeah. Why does that one leap out? There was enough trace evidence on this rug to qualify it as a city street," George said. The popcorn, however, had caught his eye.

"Did she go to the movies a lot?" George asked.

The clerk, not realizing he was being asked a question, started to leave.

"Hey!" George shouted. "I asked you a question. Did she go to the movies a lot?"

The clerk turned and shrugged. "What am I? Her mother? You think I know these people? Shit. You think I care what goes on in their miserable lives? I don't know and I don't wanna know."

The clerk asked Jones and Panelli to close the door when they were through and went back to his post.

George checked the hallway outside the door carefully. The lab boys had gone over the room, but they would have probably stopped at the door unless they had reason to continue.

George got down on all fours with a penlight and checked the floor in the hallway, from the door to the steps. His mind worked like a computer as he crawled, cataloging minute garbage.

Panelli wandered out into the hall and watched.

George cleared his throat and began to tell Panelli what was going through his mind. "The report said that this victim, like the others, had been strangled first, then placed in a sitting position in a chair."

Panelli nodded. "Yeah. Strange, isn't it? I wonder why he did that."

"The killer sat them down and then did something in front of them. He needed an audience. Why? What was he doing?"

"The guy's a psycho," Panelli snorted. "What other reason do you need?"

"Well, it's buggin' me. Try to put yourself in the scene, OK? There's the victim, freshly killed, sitting in the chair. OK, what else happened?"

"He probably whacked off," Panelli said.

"First he kills 'em; then he sits 'em up."

"Scary shit, man."

George looked up. "If he whacked off, the trace evidence would have showed semen."

"Maybe he used a towel or something."

George crept along the dirty carpet of the second-floor landing. The lab boys hadn't gone this far out the door, and George wanted to see what he could find out past the threshold.

His eyes locked on something gray and small and easy to miss on the filthy floor. He picked it up and held it to the light. It was a portion of a ticket stub. It had been ripped in half, then ripped a second time. He put the stub in an envelope and put it in his pocket.

"What's that?" Panelli asked.

"Nothin'," he replied.

They went back to the room.

George sat in the chair that Dolly had sat in after she died and looked out at the rest of the small room. It was quiet now. Outside the window the dirty wind swirled grit against the glass.

"The lab boys didn't move any furniture, so it's still the way the killer left it."

Across the room, another chair faced George. It was the only other piece of furniture in the room, except for the bed and a nightstand.

"I wonder what she faced," George muttered. "I wonder what her corpse witnessed."

"Well, the killer probably sat in front of her on this chair," Panelli replied, sitting down to face George. "Feels a little creepy, sitting in the same place the killer sat."

George nodded. "Maybe he sat there and did something in front of the dead girl. Maybe that's why he killed her. He killed her so he could sit her down and do something in front of her. But what?"

"I still say he jerked off."

"No semen. I don't think that's it."

"Maybe he used a rubber and took it with him."

"That's possible."

George sat there waiting for his mind to answer. That was the way he got most of his insights. He just sat there until a light-bulb lit up and an answer popped into his head—not exactly police procedure, but it worked for him.

But don't call me a psychic.

He looked around the room, at the yellowed curtains, the peeling wallpaper, and wondered what the Star Hotel had been like years ago when it was new.

He daydreamed about who might have stayed here when this neighborhood hadn't yet gone to the mongrels. Maybe it had been full of happy, well-heeled people. That was before the invasion, George thought, the invasion of unhappy, desperate people. Where did they come from?

The lightbulb flickered on—lonely psychotic people, the world was full of them.

Maybe he sat there and talked to her, for Christ sake. Maybe he just needed somebody to talk to. George visualized the killer sitting there in the chair and talking to the victim. It made bizarre sense. Dead people are good listeners, never interrupting or talking back.

What could you tell a dead whore?

Then another lightbulb lit in George's mind. *Maybe he took her picture.*

That made even more sense. That would explain placing the body in the chair and posing it. It even explained the second strangulation with the rope—it was a photographic prop.

George stayed there for a few more minutes, just thinking and getting impressions. Panelli seemed bored and eager to get out of the haunted room. George stared at Panelli, and Panelli stared back.

"What are you lookin' at?" Panelli said.

"I'm lookin' at you."

"How come?"

" 'Cause you're there."

"Christ, man. You're givin' me the creeps. This whole place gives me the creeps."

"Panelli, you could be a good investigator someday, but first you got to learn to put yourself inside the killer's head. Yeah, this place gives me the creeps, too, but this is where the answers are. You *want* to get the creeps. The killer might've had the creeps, too."

Panelli said nothing.

"I think he took her picture," George said.

"What for?"

George shrugged. "To sell, maybe."

"Jesus, Jones, you're a hard man to figure."

George rose and went for the door. Panelli followed. As they came down the stairs, George heard Patsy Cline singing "Walkin' After Midnight."

SHADE OF PALE   143

He walked to the desk and saw that the clerk had a small cassette tape player behind the counter. George noticed a pile of cassettes that hadn't been there earlier. He saw the titles and smiled broadly. *The Roots of Country, The Best of Ernest Tubb,* and, best of all, *Hank Williams Sr.'s Greatest Hits.* The clerk was a country music fan. Not just a country music fan, a fan of old-time, classic country music, the kind of music that George loved.

"Patsy Cline. One of my favorites," George said coolly.

The man looked up, one eyebrow raised. "Yeah?"

"Yep. I love Pasty Cline; she's my favorite singer. The world lost one of the greats when her plane went down," George continued.

"What do you know about it?"

"I told you; I love her voice. If women could sing like that nowadays, I'd get a boner every time I listened to the radio."

The old man smiled, showing his crooked teeth. It was the first sign of friendliness George had seen out of the grizzled old bastard. "You got that right."

"I take it you're a country music fan."

The old man shifted in his seat; the wall between him and George started coming down, brick by brick.

"You ever been to Nashville?"

George pulled up a chair.

They talked about country music greats and both men agreed that Hank Williams Sr. was the all-time best. Panelli got bored, wandered outside, and smoked a cigarette. George spent a pleasant fifteen minutes exchanging stories with the desk clerk and emerged from the hotel with a reasonable description of every stranger the old man had noticed coming or going the night of Dolly's murder.

"He saw a couple of guys leave around eleven, which would have been right after the murder. He didn't notice much, except one tall guy had red hair."

"How did you do it?" Panelli wanted to know. "I talked to him for hours and he didn't know a thing."

"Easy. I just went over the words to 'I'm So Lonesome I Could Cry' with him and told him it was my life story. You'd be surprised how many people fall into that category."

Something about Dolly's room stimulated George's imagination. It was just a gut feeling, but George had learned to trust his gut feelings. He went back to the office and immersed himself in thought. His mind drifted from the Loomis case to the Devane case.

Back and forth he kicked around theories, ideas, and possibilities. He looked at the descriptions of the victims and it occurred to him that they all had two physical characteristics in common: fair skin and reddish hair. Why hadn't anyone noticed that?

"I wonder if they were all Irish?" George asked out loud. "Wouldn't that be a strange coincidence?"

CHAPTER
THIRTEEN

O'Connor had extensive contacts among terrorists. Outlaws found each other. Whether it was on the international arms market or through the chemical peddlers and bomb experts, political fugitives came together.

In his time, Padraic had dealt with everybody from the Marxists to the Muslims. They all needed guns and money, regardless of their cause, and they were all out there on the edge, trying to score.

On several occasions, radical politics mixed, creating strange bedfellows. O'Connor had met Col. Mohammed Mohammed at a conference of international terrorists at the Badawi refugee camp in Lebanon.

They found they had several things in common, one of them being that they both had operations in New York City. The Libyans had tried, unsuccessfully, to mount a terrorist campaign in the United States several times. Now, with the Black Rain's help, the Libyan connection in New York had become a reality. The net result was an exchange of money, weapons, explosives, and technologies that helped both groups.

At a dimly lit Middle Eastern café on the edge of Elmhurst, Mohammed Mohammed waited for O'Connor's arrival. They hadn't seen each other in years. Both had been busy making life hell for the British and Americans.

O'Connor and Mohammed both used code names when they contacted each other, to protect the security of both sides. Mohammed was "the Viper," and O'Connor was "the Hare."

The Hare walked in and took a seat at the same table with the

Viper. The Viper poured him some tea and the two men drank
in silence for a few minutes, waiting to see if they had been followed. A man sitting nearby got up and went outside to check
the street. He returned a minute later and nodded.

When the coast appeared clear, the Viper spoke. "It is good
to see you, my friend. How goes the struggle against the evil
empire?"

O'Connor, speaking as quietly as possible, answered, "It
goes well, and you?"

"We live to fight another day," the Viper said. He took an-
other sip of tea, his eyes sweeping the room, checking the door.
"I must admit, however, I was surprised to get your message.
Tell me, what can I do for you today?"

O'Connor, as cautious as Mohammed, pulled his chair
closer, so that the two men were practically nose to nose. "I
need something," he said.

The Viper nodded knowingly. "Tell me what it is and I will
tell you if I can get it."

O'Connor looked around again. His voice dropped even
lower. "It is something unusual, and I was told that you had
some experience dealing in this type of thing."

"I have experience dealing in many things. What is your particular need?"

O'Connor swallowed; even for a Libyan terrorist, this would
be a strange request. The atmosphere in the café seemed to become darker by several shades.

"Human skin," he whispered.

The Viper's left eyebrow raised. He looked questioningly at
O'Connor. The silence washed across their faces. O'Connor
said no more.

Mohammed said, "I see, and what kind of skin does the
Hare require for his purposes?"

"The skin of our enemies, of course."

Mohammed Mohammed rocked in his chair. He took another sip of tea and contemplated his reply. "Nice, pale, English skin? Pink and soft?"

The Hare nodded.

"That is surely a strange request, my friend, very strange."

O'Connor kept still. His face was as cold and unemotional as a statue. Even though he was in the heart of New York City, O'Connor felt thousands of miles away. The café was quiet; some dishes clinked in the back room. Water ran.

The Viper stared at him, making him feel slightly uncomfortable. Mohammed studied the Irishman, trying to fathom what this request meant. *It must have some symbolic meaning,* he surmised. Terrorists often sent messages to their rivals that way.

The Viper looked away, his face dispassionate, flat and unconcerned. "How many hides?" he asked casually.

"Two."

"With what will you pay?"

"American money."

"We have American money."

"Plastic explosives, then."

The Libyan nodded. It was a strange trade, but he would do it. He liked the new plastics. In the next few minutes they agreed on a price and a delivery date.

O'Connor left as soon as it was decided. The Viper immediately began considering whose skin it would be. He left the café ten minutes later by the back door.

O'Connor placed a call to Scrupski's Metalworks. "This is Mr. O'Malley. Is my piece finished yet?"

"O'Malley? Yeah, it's ready for pickup; came out real nice, too."

O'Connor asked what its weight was.

"It weighs sixty pounds; would you like to make shipping arrangements?"

"No, I'll be over to collect it in person."

———

From Elmhurst O'Connor drove back into Manhattan and visited a store that sold electronic surveillance equipment. He bought an array of high-tech items, all designed for spying. The gear was the best available and very expensive. An expert in the field, O'Connor knew brand names and specifications.

Satisfied with his purchases, he stopped at a phone booth and used directory assistance for the telephone number of Dr. Jukes Wahler.

Padraic O'Connor made his appointment with Jukes under the name Charlie O'Malley.

Jukes recognized him as soon as he came in. "You're Loomis's cousin, aren't you?"

"That's right, Dr. Wahler. I'd like to talk with you."

Jukes smiled, even though something about O'Malley him made him uncomfortable.

O'Malley's size and firm handshake were intimidating. The singsong lilt of his Irish brogue made little melodies of the sentences, seducing Jukes's attention.

"That's what I'm here for," Jukes said. "Please, come in and sit down. I'm sorry about your cousin. Are you looking for some grief counseling?"

O'Connor shook his head. "No, it's a personal matter."

"No problem, Mr. O'Malley. My door is always open."

O'Connor sat. "Let me get right to the point. I think I can help you find your sister. But I need you to help me first."

Jukes's jaw dropped. "Cathy? How did you know about that?"

O'Connor's face was impassive. "I know a lot of things about you, Dr. Wahler."

"I don't like the sound of that."

"Well, it's all a matter of public record. That, and a bit of investigative work of my own."

Jukes stood up. "What do you know about Cathy?"

O'Connor put up his hands. "Sit down, man. I didn't say I knew anything; I just said I wanted to help. These are troubled times, Dr. Wahler. A man has got to accept help where he can find it; now don't you agree?"

"Are you a private investigator?"

O'Connor pressed his hands together, as if praying. "In a way, yes. However I'm not licensed, and I don't really want any compensation for my work. Call it an exchange of professional services."

"Then what's in it for you?"

"I'm looking for the Banshee."

Jukes stared at him. "The Banshee? The Banshee doesn't exist."

O'Connor/O'Malley laughed. "I'm afraid that's not entirely correct, you see. It's true she doesn't exist in the conventional sense, on our level of consciousness, but I can assure you, she does exist, and she's here in New York City."

Jukes tried to mask his surprise. "But . . . But that's absurd. You can't expect me to believe that."

"You shouldn't disbelieve something just because you don't understand it, Dr. Wahler; that's a very unscientific way to think. I know more about the Banshee than you might expect."

Jukes said, "But what good would I do? What makes you think I have any connection?"

O'Connor straightened, and his voice took on a magisterial tone, colored by his engaging accent. Jukes was compelled to listen.

"The Banshee travels along the lines of destiny. Your destiny has already crossed it. You now have to play out the scenario."

"You're talking gibberish."

O'Connor smiled. "Then pretend that I'm crazy and try to cure me like you did poor Declan. I don't care. Don't you see?

The lines of fate have already been cast and there's nothing any of us can do about it."

O'Connor paused, letting his words linger.

"You're acting just like I expected you would, Dr. Wahler. You're approaching this thing as if it had a logical explanation. I respect that. I'd have been disappointed if you didn't. But there is no logical explanation. You can't rely on science, because I'm talking about something science can't explain."

"Oh, for God's sake, O'Malley, get to the point!"

O'Malley nodded. "I think my cousin came to you raving about the Banshee. You probably treated him much the same as you're treating me right now. But the Banshee got poor Declan before you could figure out what was happening.

"At that point, though you were unaware of it, you crossed her path. Because of Declan Loomis, you see. And he told you about her; he spoke her name many times. She's aware of these things, Dr. Wahler. Declan passed it along to you like a virus. Chances are you saw her even before you met Declan. Sometimes she knows in advance what poor bastard to haunt."

Jukes's face went pale. His mind flashed back to the girl through the delicatessen window, hours before he met Loomis.

Yes, it was she.

O'Malley rocked forward in his seat. "Am I right?"

Jukes answered the question with a blank stare.

O'Malley said, "The tendrils of fate that link us together are slender and subtle sometimes, but their connection is as strong as iron.

"You see, the Banshee is always among us, attached to some human being or other. She keeps moving, going from haunting to haunting until she finds someone she wants to destroy.

"Then, depending on the diabolical whim of that murderin' bitch, she'll either reveal herself to you and move on to someone else in the circle, or she'll kill you."

Jukes needed a drink of water. His throat felt dry and hopeless as he tried to say something to counteract the terrible gravity of those words. All he managed to say was, "Ah, ah, ah . . ."

O'Connor walked over to the watercooler and filled a paper cup. He handed it to Jukes. "Have a nice, cool drink of water, Dr. Wahler. I have a proposition for you."

Jukes accepted the cup and drank, never taking his eyes off O'Connor.

Jukes cleared his throat. "You realize all this is just a lot of delusional rhetoric, don't you? It's the kind of story a child would dream up."

O'Connor chuckled. "Of course. That's only logical. From your perspective, what else could it be?" He looked around the room, appraising Jukes's office and nodding approvingly. "Not bad; nice place. You make good money from explaining the likes of me away, don't you? Armed with your bloody logic, you go out there and fight the good fight, until the end. That's the kind of guy you are Dr. Wahler. A real company man."

"There's no need to insult me."

O'Malley raised a hand. "Sorry. What I mean to say is I would expect you to take the logical course and be a disbeliever until you see proof with your own eyes. That reasonable enough?"

"Yes."

"Good, good. Now that we both understand each other, let's have a drink of this fine New York springwater and ruminate for a moment. I think you're going to find what I have to say interesting."

Jukes allowed himself to relax. Delusional or not, Charlie O'Malley was interesting.

They drank in silence; then O'Connor put down his cup. "I'll find Cathy for you, if you'll help me find the Banshee."

Jukes exhaled, surprised that he'd been holding his breath.

"Look, O'Malley, I'd love to get Cathy back, but I don't have the slightest idea where the Banshee is. In fact, I don't even think she exists, outside of your imagination."

"Right. But that has nothing to do with it, don't you see? She doesn't give a fuck if you believe in her or not. As I've explained, once you're on her dance card she'll hang around until she takes you, or she'll pass over you to someone else, some other poor soul in the intricate web of destinies, someone who's crossed *your* path."

Jukes shook his head. "And how will you find Cathy?"

"Let that be my concern. I've done work finding missing persons before, and I've been known to get results. I can be more effective than the police. You get Cathy back; that's the main thing. Are you willing to try?"

Jukes didn't know what to say. Part of him rebelled against carrying on any type of dialogue with this madman, to acknowledge even the possibility that the Banshee could be real. But Jukes desperately wanted Cathy back, and something about the man who called himself Charlie O'Malley suggested he just might get the job done.

"Damn," Jukes said. "I don't know how to react to you, Mr. O'Malley. You're in your own world and you're convinced of this whole bizarre scenario. If I play along with you, it might lead you to some sort of irrational behavior. You might hurt somebody."

O'Connor snorted. "You're right. I might hurt somebody. I might hurt Bobby Sudden."

Jukes's ears rang when he heard Bobby's name. Revenge presented itself to him on the tongue of a madman, and Jukes felt its narcotic tang. When Bobby punched him and took Cathy, something inside Jukes broke. The old Jukes would never had contemplated revenge, but now it seemed an attractive choice. At that moment he felt like it would have been like going against nature itself not to reach out and grab this opportunity.

"You see? It's fate, terrible fate," said O'Connor. "The worst fuckin' thing you can imagine, ain't it? Now you're forced to consider the possibility that I'm right, and that galls you.

"But if you got your precious Cathy back, why, I don't think you'd begrudge me my little request."

"But I can't find the Banshee for you."

"That's where you're wrong. You won't have to find her at all. She'll come to you, when she's ready."

"But why do you want to find her?"

O'Connor smirked. "I've got my own reasons, which don't concern you. Suffice it to say that the Banshee is evil. The damned thing's killed scores of good men, destroyed so many great families over the centuries . . . you have no idea. I myself have lost a brother.

"Any attempt to shelter that monster, or side with her in any way, is absolutely treasonous to mankind. You must understand that.

"Never underestimate the explosive nature of this creature. She kills again and again, and has kept on killing for centuries.

"But, you're probably wondering, how can I find Cathy for you?"

Jukes nodded.

O'Connor let his voice drop. "It's my destiny. I'll find Cathy, and the Banshee, and Bobby Sudden as well. I can no sooner fight destiny than I can change the world. All I have to do . . . is just be there when it happens. Events will occur. They will appear to be a series of unlikely coincidences. I don't expect you to understand that, but it's true.

"I am a warrior. This is my battlefield."

Jukes's face turned cold. "I don't really care, as long as I get Cathy back."

O'Connor smiled, his Irish eyes twinkling with intensity. "Exactly. You get Cathy back; I get the Banshee. Fair enough?"

Jukes found himself nodding, wanting to say no, but being

unable. He felt as if his body were betraying him, acting on its own. The more he wanted to stop agreeing with O'Connor, the harder it became. "Fair enough," Jukes said.

"I'll start by looking through Cathy's belongings, listening to any tapes you might have of phone calls, correspondence, things like that. Somewhere here is the clue I need to proceed to the next level."

"You really think you can do what the police can't?"

O'Connor winked. "Yes, I do."

O'Connor/O'Malley left with a hodgepodge of possible leads on Bobby's whereabouts. The message tape with the music on it seemed a good place to start. It took O'Connor an afternoon to run through all the band rehearsal spaces in Manhattan and make a second list of those places that also rented to artists and photographers.

O'Connor agreed with Jukes that the music in the background was ska, and that narrowed it down even more. There were only so many ska bands rehearsing in New York.

The old lady's words came back to him like a song remembered.

"They will appear to be a series of unlikely coincidences, but beware. There are no coincidences."

Working at her suggestion, O'Connor started in the vicinity of Mrs. Willis's house. He spent the next day looking around, visiting the most likely spaces. Bribing and threatening people to get information, he narrowed the list down considerably.

CHAPTER
FOURTEEN

The newspapers made a big deal out of the murder of Dolly Devane, especially the tabloids. Their headlines screamed things like: BOWERY STRANGLER STILL AT LARGE! almost daily. When the reporters tried to milk George for information, he gave them a shoulder so cold you could freeze ice cubes on it. He locked himself in his office and drank coffee.

George arranged all the evidence on his desk and stared at it until he got a notion. He didn't know it, but he was doing exactly what psychics did, only he called it "getting a gut feeling." George dismissed anything that smacked of the supernatural as "crack-pot."

But no one could argue with his batting average: best in the department, too good to promote.

He stared at the evidence, held it in his hands, played with it, smelled it, and lived with it until it began to tell him things.

He was particularly interested in the portion of ticket stub he'd found in the hall. He studied it meticulously and got the distinct impression that it came from the killer. Another "gut feeling."

He held the ticket stub in his hand.

Popcorn. Ticket stub.

Most theaters changed ticket colors every day so that people couldn't cheat and use the same one twice. This one was ripped in an odd way, though, he thought, in quarters. It had been torn, then torn again. George knew that tickets were torn in half when you entered a theater, but torn again?

He thought about the kind of movies to which the killer might have been attracted—porno was the first thing to pass through his mind. George closed his eyes. Yeah, that made sense, but it was too obvious. Obvious things always bugged George; only on TV could you make a connection that easy. George used his bloodhound sense to play with it, kick it around.

Hell, it could be any kind of movie.

Maybe the strangler watched movies because his own life was such a disaster. Then he went out and killed prostitutes and took pictures of them. George put down the ticket stub and picked up his coffee.

He placed his feet up on the desk and tried to visualize the killer. The desk clerk had mentioned a guy leaving later that he didn't recognize—a tall guy with red hair. George closed his eyes.

First he kills them; then he strangles them.

The more George considered it, the more sense it made—the rope was a prop. The killer twisted it in deep so you'd be able to see in the photos that the victim was really dead, not just faked.

He picked up his phone and called Panelli.

"Yeah?" a voice answered. "Panelli here."

"Let's go downtown. I want to check on something."

Panelli sighed. "Sure, George. I'll bring the car around."

They drove down to the area near the Star Hotel. George said he wanted to cruise the neighborhood. He hadn't told Panelli or anyone else about the ticket stub, another Jones idiosyncrasy.

It wasn't really evidence; it didn't even come from the room; he just had a hunch. Lying out there in the hall, it could have come from anyone, and there was no physical reason to believe that the killer had dropped it. Still, the thought intrigued him.

"What are you looking for?" Panelli asked.

"I don't know; I'll know when I see it."

There were many porno theaters in the neighborhood, one after another, but sprinkled among them were a few legitimate places. One was showing a Laurel and Hardy festival, another an Italian art film, and the next a kung-fu movie.

"I want to check all these places."

"Why?"

"I'll tell you later. Let me out on the corner. I think I want to walk around a little."

Panelli was exasperated. "What the hell for?"

"Panelli, you amaze me. How did you end up in Homicide?"

"Just lucky, I guess."

George laughed. Panelli could be funny when he wasn't trying. "OK, let me spell it out for you. The killer doesn't seem like the kind of guy who's hangin' out on the street. Chances are, in this neighborhood, he's not gonna be drivin' a car either."

"Why not?"

"Well, look around. Where would you park? No place is safe here; it'd be stripped in an hour. All the people you see on the street here use the subway or cabs. So, I figure he was probably on foot the night he killed Devane."

"So?"

"So, he had to be walkin' around; maybe somebody saw something. He picked up the girl somewhere, right? People notice shit. You'd be surprised."

Panelli nodded.

George continued, "He probably found her on the street around here. We can start by asking the other girls who work this area if they've seen anyone strange."

"But they've already gone over this."

"Yeah, but it's my investigation now, and I'm going back over everything."

O'Connor, following in a cab, passed Panelli's car and turned the corner. He paid the tab and doubled back. George Jones was easy to spot. Careful to stay half a block away, O'Connor pretended to look at the girls in the movie posters.

George said, "I'm gonna start flatfootin'. Catch up with me at the corner place, after you park the car."

Two blocks later he found a gaggle of working girls.

"Hey, Officer, you want a date?" one of the girls shouted. They all laughed.

"Is it that obvious?"

"Where'd you get those shoes? Honey, I didn't think they even made shoes like that anymore."

George smiled and flashed his badge. "I'm looking for the guy who killed Dolly Devane. I thought maybe somebody saw something."

"Dolly baby? I swear that was a damn shame. She was always real nice to me."

"Did you see the guy she went with the night she died?"

"Nope, but maybe one of the other girls did."

After talking to all the rest of the street girls, George found one who said she thought she might have seen Dolly that night walking with a man with red hair. Her name was Sugah, and she spoke with a southern accent.

"He was weird-lookin'. Plus I seen him before once or twice checkin' out the action."

"What did he look like?"

"He had goofy-lookin' hair, kinda long. It was a real dumb shade of red, carrottop. I can't really remember anything else. Plus I'm not sure what night that was."

George walked around the neighborhood some more, checking each of the movie theaters. It turned out that they all used gray tickets at least once a week. It was impossible to identify the theater that had issued the one he had found.

He met Panelli at the diner and ordered coffee.

"Well, our boy's been around the neighborhood. One of the girls saw him."

Panelli nodded. "That's great. What do we do next?"

"We check all the buildings within a ten-block radius."

"That could take days!"

"Yep."

They paid for their coffee and walked past the porno theaters. The sky darkened with storm clouds, and the smell of rain blew on the urban wind.

George liked the rain. The city needed it. It washed away some of the filth, although never quite enough. George looked up at the marquees as they went by. There was only one legitimate theater left in the block—the Temple Theater, a 1940s movie house that had seen grander times. On the marquee it said: CINDERELLA, except the last A was missing, so the sign read: CINDERELL.

George thought that was funny.

The hamburger was greasy and fries were cold. Bobby was alone in the diner except for a couple of teenagers talking loudly in a corner booth. Things were damn fine. He was nice and relaxed since his photo session with Dolly. Even Cathy was in line.

The pictures were definitive, perfect. He'd captured the elusive face of death like a butterfly pinned and mounted.

He was looking forward to a day at the movies. He liked to spend a whole afternoon at the theater, slipping out occasionally to the bar across the street for a few pops, then back to the movie.

Bobby didn't have too many days like this. It usually only

happened after he'd had a good photo shoot. He felt alive, free.

He knew that soon he'd have to split for a while, and he wanted one last blast of the old neighborhood.

He finished up his lunch and walked out into the street just as it started to rain. He slipped his hands in his pockets; Bobby was always putting his hands in his pockets or pulling them out, a nervous habit he had. He felt the reassuring weight of his Smith & Wesson .38 Special, its two-inch barrel snug against his thigh.

Bobby seldom went anywhere without the gun these days. It was a necessary fashion accessory in this part of town, one that any self-respecting tough guy should never be without. He liked the .38 'cause he could pack it easy in his jacket and it didn't show.

He turned the corner and saw the movie theater up ahead. It was time to see the wicked stepmother again; she was so much like Bobby's real mom. In fact, Bobby fancied himself to be very much like Cinderella. *Life's like that*, he thought, *a real unfair trip*. At least, in the movies it had a happy ending. He looked up and saw the sign, CINDERELL; he was so used to seeing it without the final A that he had all but forgotten it was ever there to begin with.

It was time to see his old buddies again, the same ones that he'd visited when he was a kid.

He walked up to the old woman behind the glass. "One for *Cinderell*."

She took his money and gave him a ticket. He entered the theater and the doorman took the ticket and tore it in half, dropping one piece into a cigar box and handing the other back to Bobby.

He walked down the center aisle and waited for his eyes to adjust. Kids skittered past him laughing and spilling popcorn. He cussed at them and made his way toward the front, close to the screen.

The movie began and Bobby slid back into his seat and relaxed. Life was grand, at least for a few hours until he had to go back out into the real world again. Until then, he was a citizen of the magic kingdom.

He watched in rapt attention while the evil stepsisters made Cinderella's life a living hell. They baited her and teased her, gave her all the dirty jobs to do. *Man*, he thought, *ain't that the truth.*

Bobby knew the movie by heart and he was sailing along, deep into another viewing, when he saw something that made him sit up.

He looked around, wondering if anybody else saw it. Then he realized that everybody around him was a kid.

He looked back up at the screen and became somewhat confused. Why hadn't he noticed this character before?

Bobby figured that the theater had gotten hold of a new version, a new print, with a new character in it. He stared up at the screen and wondered why the new character looked familiar to him.

The new character wasn't interacting with the others in the story; it seemed to be preoccupied with something outside the screen, something beyond the frame. Bobby couldn't pull his eyes away.

I've seen her before.

He wanted to laugh, to throw his head back and howl like a dog. Something about that new character was making him feel crazy.

He leaned forward in his seat, his shoes making sucking sounds as they shifted on the sticky, gum-splattered floor beneath him. The new character leaned out of the screen, out of the movie itself, and pointed at him.

Bobby nearly jumped out of his seat.

It was a woman, a real babe in Bobby's estimation, with wild red hair and ivory white skin. Her eyes were neon intense, an unnatural shade of green, and Bobby could see a tear running down the side of her face.

Where did she come from?

Something about her hypnotized him and he couldn't wrest his eyes away long enough to blink.

Her animated beauty seemed to shimmer on the screen.

The thing Bobby thought was cool was that the woman reached right out of the movie and pointed directly at him. 3-D at its finest, and he wasn't even wearing the special glasses. Wow!

How did they do that?

Bobby jumped back in his seat as the pale, slender finger extended from the screen and stopped a few inches from his face.

The red-haired woman stared at him and whispered something.

Bobby kept looking around, but none of the kids seemed to notice. His eyes went back to the screen. The woman whispered again. She said, "Dolly. What did you do to Dolly?"

George Jones cursed the fact that he didn't have an umbrella. Panelli cursed the fact that George was making him tromp all over the city.

They went from one seedy apartment building to the next, asking everyone they met if they had seen a man with red hair.

The trail was getting colder and Panelli was starting to sneeze.

"Let's try one more place; then we can go back to the station."

"Thank God."

George asked a guy who worked at the newsstand if he'd seen a man with red hair. The newspaper vendor was small, like a jockey, but had a tough face with a long scar across his cheek. He chain-smoked unfiltered cigarettes and coughed constantly.

George believed newsies always knew what was going on in

a neighborhood. People bought the morning paper, cigarettes, magazines, and gum, even in the worst part of town. They came and went, but newsies usually noticed the regulars. George knew from experience that they were a valuable resource.

He bought a cigar and struck up a conversation.

"Red hair?"

"Yeah."

"Tall guy?" He spit. "Dresses in black?"

"Yeah."

The man squinted at them and said, "I seen a guy like that, but only once. Red hair. He's not a local, though, or I'd know him."

"Was he checkin' out the girls?"

The newsie nodded, coughed, and spit again. "Could've been."

"Would you recognize him?"

"Maybe. You gonna bust him?"

"Yeah, if I can find him."

"You guys are cops, right? You take me for a fool? I don't rat on anybody out here; otherwise I'd be dead meat. If word got back that I told the cops anything, something real bad might happen."

George brought his new cigar to life with a wooden match and bellowslike cheek muscles. "I'm not interested in the local lowlifes. I'm looking for the strangler."

The newsie's eyes lit up. "No kiddin'? The strangler? Man, that's cool. That's one motherfucker I hope gets caught; he's makin' everybody crazy."

George turned to Panelli. "See? The food chain has been interrupted. Girls stay away, customers stay away, money stays away. This community wants to rid itself of the cancer. Pretty soon they're gonna spit him up like a hairball."

Panelli flashed a wry smile. "That's deep."

George puffed his cigar and perused the magazines on the stand.

The newsie watched. "So you're the new guy they called in? The ringer?"

"Yeah."

"I seen you on TV."

"That's me."

"Hey. Would you pay me for information?"

George nodded. "I might."

The newsie scratched his chin. "It might be worth big money."

"You won't be able to retire on it," George said, "but if it's the right information, I'll go something decent for it."

"You say you're looking for a guy with red hair?"

George looked at Panelli. "Yeah. . . ."

"So maybe I might be able to turn you onto somebody."

"Who?"

"How much money you got?"

George pulled out his wallet and counted out five twenties. "Try this," he said, and handed it to the newsie.

"There's a guy I know, a small-time street dealer. He told me he was lookin' for a red-haired guy who burned him on a dope deal."

George was listening intently. "A dope deal, huh? That's interesting. The red-haired guy was buyin'?"

The newsie looked down at George's wallet. "The answer to that question is also for sale."

George counted out another hundred.

The newsie snatched it up with the same hand that still held the first hundred. "The answer to your last question is no." He looked at George and grinned. "He wasn't buyin'; he was sellin'. That's how come my buddy got burned."

"Let me get this straight. Your buddy was gonna score from the red-haired guy, and he got burned?"

"Yeah. He took the money in front and never delivered."

"What's your friend's name?"

"That'll cost you another bill."

George frowned. "How do I know you're tellin' me the truth?"

The newsie laughed. "I ain't goin' anywhere. I'm here every fuckin' day of the year. If you find out I'm lyin', come back and break my legs. We're livin' in a fishbowl, man."

George counted out another hundred, this time borrowing half of it from Panelli, who acted like it was all he had. When the money was in the newsie's hand, he went back into his little booth and motioned for George to come closer.

"If it gets back that I talked to you guys, bad stuff might happen."

"Nobody's gonna get popped except the strangler. You have my word."

"My buddy's name is Tony B. He's usually out on Tenth Street, two blocks over. The B stands for Brooklyn, Tony Brooklyn. He's got a mustache and wears a fringe jacket, looks Hispanic, black hair with a ponytail, midthirties, short."

Jones and Panelli crossed the street and made their way through the thickening raindrops toward the haunt of Tony B.

They found him just where the newsie said he would be.

As soon as Tony got a good look at them, he sprinted down the street like a halfback.

Had it not been for Panelli's quickness and agility, Tony would have gotten away. But the athletic detective ran him down like a linebacker and pinned him to the pavement in front of a red neon sign proclaiming: LOVE ACTS.

By the time George caught up, out of breath and limping a little, Panelli had Tony up and handcuffed from behind.

Tony screamed, "You fuckin' fuckers 'r fucked!"

"Wow, did you hear that?" George said. "I didn't think that was possible, man. I'm gonna have to write that down, I think you just made a breakthrough in the English language. You managed to use the word *fuck* as a noun, a verb, and adjective, all in the same sentence. That's quite an accomplishment."

"Fuckin' fuckers," said Tony, sputtering like a dud fire-cracker.

George wheezed. "He's doing it again."

"Where were ya goin', man?" Panelli asked. "We just wanted to talk to you."

"I got nothing to say."

"Search 'im," George told Panelli.

Panelli patted him down, went through his pockets, and found a wrinkled plastic Baggie containing several packets of white powder. Panelli held the Baggie up and said, "That was too easy. No wonder he took off."

George smiled, pulled out his badge, and showed it to Tony. The big gold detective's shield glinted, a symbol of righteous indignation. "Well, looks like you got big problems now, ass-hole. What do you have to say for yourself?"

Tony struggled like a trapped insect. "I ain't sayin' nothin, man."

George affectionately wiped a piece of dirt off Tony's shoulder. Tony looked at him as if he'd just looked in the mirror and noticed that George cast no reflection.

"This is a very delicate situation," George said. "We got you here red-fucking-handed, man. And now you're telling me you don't wanna talk. That's very discouraging."

George spoke to Panelli in a stage whisper. "What do you think we should do?"

Panelli's reply was much louder. "Bust him; lock him up. What else is there?"

Tony struggled anew. "Shit, man! What you want me for? I didn't do nothin'."

George thrust his hands in his pockets and rocked back and forth on his heels. "You wanna walk, Tony? Is that what you wanna do? You wanna walk away from here and never see us again? I'll bet you'd love that, wouldn't you? Walk your candy-ass right down the street, huh?"

With his wrists bound behind him, Tony's struggles were so hopelessly futile as to be almost comical. His head was the only thing that moved now, as if it were trying to detach itself from the rest of his body. "What are you sayin', man?"

"What I'm sayin' is you might have one chance to walk. It's all up to me. I could set you free as a bird or make your life a living hell. The whole thing's at my whim. And frankly, I gotta tell ya, Tony, after that run, I'm in a pretty shitty mood right now."

Tony looked from cop to cop, his eyes crazy in the reflection of red neon. "What do you want? Just tell me, man."

"We want to know about the guy with red hair."

Tony laughed a short bark. "That asshole? You wanna know about him? Shit. What do you want him for?"

"Suspicion of murder," George said before Panelli could tell Tony it was none of his business.

Tony smiled, showing a mouth with several missing teeth. "Whoo-ee. I knew that fucker was trouble; I knew it right from the start. He's not from around here, you know, just comes down once in a while. I bought shit from him before, man, couple of times. Real good shit, uptown stuff. Then last week, he takes my money for a quarter and burns my ass. Now I got guys lookin' to cut me, you know what I mean? It's real ugly 'cause of him."

"Do you know where he is?"

"Shit, if I knew that, I'd go get my money."

"What's his name?"

"Just called him Red. But, you know, that's a big joke, too. Dig it. The hair's fake, man. The dude was always in disguise. Tell you the truth, I thought he was weird as shit."

Jones and Panelli relaxed; Panelli lit a cigarette and Jones stoked up his cigar. Rain had fallen briefly, but now it was clear. The streets shimmered with an oily iridescence.

"You sure about that? He was wearing a wig?" George asked.

"That's the word, man. Gave me the creeps, too, but I never let on that I noticed. You know? He had such sweet shit, I didn't really care. None of my business. But I swear to God, he was wearing a fuckin' wig and makeup. I got some friends who are TVs, you know, and I can tell that shit a mile off."

George said, "You sound like a real interesting guy, Tony. I tell you what—I'll make you a deal. You find this guy for us, we'll let you go."

George's face was earnest. He delivered the lines like Brando in *On the Waterfront,* only more believably.

Tony's relief was instant. "All right! Let me go, man. You won't regret it. I'll find that fuckin' fucker for ya. We'll nail that fuckin' fucker till he's fucked. He owes me money."

"You have the soul of a poet," George said.

CHAPTER
FIFTEEN

Jukes walked in a daze, something he warned his patients never to do. The big city could be a dangerous place for a space cadet. After nearly getting run over by a taxi, he snapped back to reality.

Christ, he thought. *I'm falling apart here. I've got to get ahold of myself.*

He needed a drink and a shower and sleep. He had a massive headache. He'd been thinking about Cathy, O'Connor, and the Banshee.

It was dusk in New York—the magic, sinister time of half day and night. The big city seemed somehow undecided on which side it should show.

Jukes's once-logical thought process spun its wheels. He mentally bounced back and forth between their faces, always returning to her face—the unforgettable face of the Banshee.

Dying light rays slanted through the skyscrapers, bending in the prismatic windows far above, then slanting down on him. Jukes was bathed in the unnatural colors only sunset through smog can bring.

He walked down the block, away from his building. A friendly supple hand grasped his shoulder.

He jumped.

Jukes spun around and looked into the face of Fiona Rice.

"I'm sorry, Jukes; I didn't mean to startle you."

Jukes breathed a sigh of relief, glad it was a friendly face he had turned to greet. "Oh, Fiona, I had no idea . . . Sorry I jumped. I'm so tense these days."

Fiona smiled. "After we talked, I felt so bad for you . . . Well, to tell you the truth, I was on my way over to see you. Will Howard gave me the address. I thought you might want to talk some more, or maybe just need a shoulder to lean on." She paused. "Besides, I have some more information on the Banshee that I thought might interest you."

"That's very kind of you," Jukes stammered.

Fiona looked into Jukes's eyes, surprised at how bloodshot and sunken they'd become. His hair stood uncombed, and his tie was loosened. He needed a shave. He bore little resemblance to the man she'd met earlier. Yet the kindness in his face remained. His gentle way and sensitivity were unchanged; that much she could tell at a glance. "Why don't we go someplace? We could have a drink or something. Have you had dinner yet?"

"Well . . . I don't know. I'm not really in the mood right now," Jukes replied.

Fiona showed concern. "Oh, Jukes. . . . You look like you've got the weight of the world on your shoulders. How about a cup of coffee?"

Jukes made a sour face. He said, "I'm not feeling all that sociable, and besides, I must look like hell."

"You look fine. A man like you never looks all that bad."

Jukes managed a weak smile; he wasn't used to compliments from pretty women, or any women. "All right. You win. I could use some nourishment. It's been a tough day."

He let her lead him by the arm.

Any other time and Jukes would have been flattered that a woman would pay this much attention to him. Right now he just wanted to crawl into a hole. The accumulated stress showed on his face. He knew it and could do nothing.

Their relationship, still in its infancy, was at the first crucial turning point. He didn't want to show her his weak side, but there weren't that many sides left to Jukes Wahler.

He looked at Fiona and realized how badly he didn't want to

lose her. This time he would get it right, he vowed. Suddenly he wanted a shave and a change of clothes in the worst way.

I'm blowing it.

But when he looked, she was smiling. Her face seemed encouraging and radiant. The more he basked in her warm glow, the better he felt.

I'll just be honest with her and take my chances.

"I'm afraid I'm not much of a conversationalist tonight," he said.

"That's all right," she said. "I'll do all the talking. Why don't you just relax. Where do you want to go?"

"There a place in the next block. They have great chicken noodle soup."

"Ah, a traditionalist. Sounds perfect."

They sipped their soups together and watched day dissolve into night. Fiona kept conversation to a minimum and let Jukes rest.

He spilled some soup on his tie and she immediately leaned across the table, dabbed her napkin in water, and swabbed at it. "Hold on; let me fix that for you." When she was done with the tie, she smoothed his hair and adjusted his collar.

He felt her hands touching him, fussing over his appearance, and liked it. Another new experience. He wondered what it would be like to live with a woman like Fiona—to have that kind of attention all the time, to swim in it. *It must be intoxicating*, he thought.

"Uhm, thanks. . . ." He still felt a thousand light-years away.

Jukes had never been in love, and he wondered if that was what was happening to him now. The prospect of it warmed his soul. And scared him, too.

He found himself staring at her, wondering what she'd be like as a lover.

God, he thought. *How can I be thinking about that? I must be a real cold and callous piece of crap to think about sex while Cathy is missing.*

Fiona batted her eyelashes.

Why does she like me?

Her enthusiasm for these little flirtations became infectious and Jukes found himself playing back, smiling and blushing like a schoolboy.

He found himself anxious to hear what she had to say, anxious merely to hear the sound of her voice.

And he was tempted to spill something else.

Fiona said, "If you'll recall our last conversation on the subject, I told you that the Banshee started turning up around the fifth century. Well, I was going through some recent Celtic translations, new discoveries from the Dublin Archives, and lo and behold! Banshee legends date back even earlier than that, a hundred years earlier as a matter of fact.

"Like the legend of the Vampire, the Banshee predates most of all the commonly held Christian beliefs about death and spirits. Of course, as with most ancient records, symbolism is the key."

Jukes nodded.

Fiona's voice was musical. "Saint Patrick, you'll remember, drove the snakes out of Ireland. . . . Actually, there were never any real snakes; that was a metaphor. This was during Roman times. The political situation in what was then part of the Roman Empire was very unstable. Warlords controlled small areas and fought among themselves. Life was hard.

"Anyway, Saint Patrick returned to Rome while he was still young. He'd been held captive by one of the tribes roaming the countryside. Before he left, he became involved with the chieftain's daughter, not a very saintly thing to do under the circumstances, but these were lusty people, earthy and simple.

"You must remember that the kind of intellectual, religious posturing we associate with the church was still centuries away.

Most of the world was still barbaric at that time, and people lived by their wits and muscles. Superstition was real.

"The chief's daughter got pregnant. There's no way of knowing whether it was Patrick's baby or not, but her father became extremely upset and beat her mercilessly. She died during childbirth. It was said that she had consorted with the devil.

"Later, when Patrick returned to drive the evil out of Ireland, she came back to him in the form of an avenging angel. She stood at the side of Saint Patty and battled her father's clan.

"Over the centuries, whenever a young girl was murdered or abused by a male descendant of one of the old families, she sought revenge."

Jukes had become absorbed in Fiona's story. He'd momentarily forgotten all about Cathy. Incredibly, he also found he was losing his skepticism about the Banshee.

Fiona said, "She became the avenger of womanhood."

Jukes wondered if he should tell Fiona he'd actually seen the Banshee. *There will never be a better time,* he thought. *But will she think I'm crazy?*

He decided he was tired of keeping secrets.

Full disclosure. I have to come clean about this or it's going to drive me crazy.

"Fiona?" He shifted in his seat.

"Yes?"

"I don't know how to say this . . . without just coming right to the point. But I think I've seen it."

Fiona just sat there and stared, saying nothing. Jukes wondered if she'd heard him and repeated his claim. "I think I've seen the Banshee."

Fiona sipped from a glass of water and looked around the room distractedly. Worry lines creased her forehead.

Jukes said, "Did you hear me? I said I think I saw the Banshee. I've seen her on at least two different occasions."

"I heard you." Fiona's tone of voice had changed. She sounded concerned.

"I saw her right before I met Loomis for the first time; she was walking down the street in broad daylight. Later, that same day, I saw her again, from my office window. The same woman Loomis described, the Banshee. I got the strangest feeling when I saw her, almost like an anxiety attack, but different."

Fiona let some time go by, a handful of ticks on the clock. She said nothing.

"You think I'm crazy, don't you?" Jukes asked, fearing he'd made the wrong decision telling her.

Finally, she spoke, her voice as quiet and soothing as she could muster, without being patronizing. "I believe you. I don't think you would lie."

"So, you don't think I'm crazy?"

Fiona looked into his eyes. Jukes felt a warm rush of emotion, a thrill, as their eyes locked. "No, I don't think you're crazy. If you say you saw her, then I believe you."

"Thank God. Fiona, I was afraid to tell you. Obviously I haven't told anyone else because . . ." His voice trailed off. "I can't believe I'm saying this."

"You don't have to justify yourself with me."

"Jesus, the Banshee was probably stalking me and I didn't even know it."

Fiona sighed.

Jukes continued. "That's not all. I got a visit from an Irishman named O'Malley, who claims to be Loomis's cousin. He offered to find Cathy for me . . . if I lead him to the Banshee."

Fiona said, "That's interesting. Then he knows about the Banshee, too. But why does he want to find her?"

Jukes shrugged. "If he brings Cathy back, I don't care."

Fiona studied Jukes's face. He looked forlorn. "Why does he think you could lead him to the Banshee?"

"He said I'd already crossed her path, that I was already marked."

"Can he really find Cathy?"

"He thought so. He said he would get clues, that they would appear to be a series of unlikely coincidences."

Fiona nodded. "The lines of fate."

Jukes tried to smooth the look of dread on his face. "The Banshee might've killed Loomis. What else could have done that to him? He was torn in half, right down the middle."

Fiona looked into his eyes, her face and voice working in concert to make him understand. She'd already thought this out, using the symbolic key, and now she wanted to say it to him without making it sound absurd.

"That represents the dual nature of man, good and evil. One half is good; one half is bad. She merely separates the two," she said softly. "Symbolism."

"And Killian, he spontaneously exploded."

"The true nature of man is within; the inner truth must come out. I guess you could say the Banshee brought it out."

Jukes rubbed his eyes. "They said it was like he was turned inside out, like an overcoat. His internal organs were exposed."

"Yes, the wrong side was on the outside. It symbolizes one man's inhumanity to women, his inner monster, so to speak. She reversed it, pulled the monster out."

Jukes looked back into her green eyes and asked, "Are you telling me that they all died for their sins? That they had all committed crimes against women?"

She nodded. "They must have."

Jukes leaned back in his chair. "Loomis maybe. I don't know about Killian. They said he had terrorist connections. . . . I suppose it's possible."

"Cruelty to women activates the Banshee."

They stared at each other for what seemed like minutes.

Jukes's mouth was hinged open slightly. He blinked and swallowed.

"But I've seen her, too," Jukes said with a razor voice. "Does that mean I'm next?"

Fiona shook her head. "You don't impress me as the kind of guy who does bad things to women. At least, as far as I know, and I'm a pretty good judge of character. In fact, you're the exact opposite of those guys."

Jukes immediately thought of Cathy and his inability to help her. He thought of the boy at the boat dock, and he thought of all the chances he'd had to change the course of her life. Maybe that was it; maybe he'd failed to act, and that was his crime.

"I could have helped Cathy, but I didn't," he said.

"Listen, Jukes; you can't blame yourself for that. You're not responsible for anyone else in this world but you. That's just the way things are. People are individuals, each one different. You've done all you could over the years to help her and a thousand other people, but you can't solve all the world's problems. It's ludicrous to try."

He didn't answer.

Fiona spoke more forcefully now. Jukes had yet to see this side of her, and it intrigued him. She was a much stronger, more dynamic person than he'd imagined.

She said, "There's more to the Banshee mythos that you should know. Please listen carefully, because this pertains directly to you. Down through the ages, I've noticed a curious pattern. Every few generations, certain men have seen her and not died. You see, someone had to write the accounts, the witnessings, someone who'd seen her and lived. I realized this after reading several references. I thought, *Who wrote this?* and, *What did they know?* They run through Banshee history like a thread, popping up regularly every hundred years or so. These men were sympathetic, I believe. I get the distinct feeling that they'd somehow helped her, or she helped them. It goes all the way

back to Saint Patrick. In other words, once in a great while, a
man comes along that she singles out as an empath."

"An empath? Someone to whom she reaches out? You know,
I dreamed something like that . . . that she asked me to help her,
to set her soul free."

"That makes sense, considering she is a ghost, a trapped
soul."

Jukes shook his head. "I've never heard of a ghost blowing
people up or splitting people open. Ghosts can't affect physical reality, can they?"

"This one can. She's not your common garden-variety,
haunted-house ghost. The Banshee is complex. Somehow she
must be able to channel all the anger, misery, and injustice of
her lineage through her and back out into the world in the
form of this violent energy. Suffering, or the suffering of
women, to be more precise, seems to make her stronger, more
focused."

Jukes heard her but didn't hear her. He put his hands over
his eyes and sighed. He was numb. "This is all too fantastic, too
hard to believe. It flies in the face of everything I know." He
paused and stared down at his soup bowl for a few seconds,
then up into her eyes.

They left the restaurant together, holding hands. Their path
took them past Jukes's apartment building. He hesitated.

"Would you like to come up for a minute? We could have a
drink or some coffee or something. . . ."

Fiona smiled. "You don't want to be alone tonight, do you?"

Jukes blushed. "No . . . I don't."

It was completely dark when they entered his apartment, and
the lights of Manhattan were at full illumination through the
window.

The things Fiona had told him were bizarre, far too improbably for his mind to embrace. Yet she'd believed him when he told her he'd seen the Banshee. If she trusted and accepted what he said, why couldn't he believe what she said? The mythos existed; she hadn't made that part up. People had recorded it, believed it, and feared it for centuries. All Fiona had done was make sense of it, and her insight was extraordinary. Why was it so hard for him to believe her and accept it?

He switched on the lights and they stood in the middle of the floor, awkward as two newborn foals.

"Wow, look at this view," she said, going to the window.

The streets below teemed. The city just kept going, he thought, its gears meshing and grinding like a big, impersonal machine. Lives began and ended, personal empires were destroyed and created, but the city kept on boiling.

"Sometimes I think it looks like an ant colony down there," Jukes said.

Fiona stood close; her electric proximity tingled his skin. Jukes, too shy to put his arm around her, stammered for something to say.

"Would you like something to drink?" he asked.

She opened her mouth to answer, but in that split second before her moistened tongue could form the words she changed her mind and leaned forward and embraced him.

Jukes stood with his hands at his sides, unable to react. Every one of his senses vibrated. He felt the soft orbs of her breasts against him, smelled the flowery scent of her perfume, and melted. Slowly his arms came up and surrounded her.

He looked into her face and kissed her without thinking.

She returned his kiss the way he'd always fantasized a woman would, with delicate, intelligent passion that made him swell.

"Oh, Fiona . . . I didn't know if that was the right thing to do."

She closed her eyes and brought her face to his. "Do it again."

Their second kiss lingered. Jukes forgot about everything but the reality of her mouth. He wrapped his arms around her tighter and squeezed gently, eagerly. She responded by snuggling deeper into his grasp.

There were no more words. Jukes realized anything said now would only break the magic, so he willed his heart to stop pounding and his hands to not sweat and enjoyed the moment.

They spent the next hour on the couch, quietly and deliberately wrapping their bodies together.

When the time for Fiona's leaving passed and it was obvious that she would stay the night, Jukes led her to his bed.

They undressed awkwardly and slipped between the covers like two young adventurers. Their bodies met and shared warmth, then affection, then passion.

Jukes didn't dare say it, but it was the one great lovemaking of his adult life. He entered her gently, but with all the resolve and commitment of an experienced lover.

With her, he felt no constricting inhibitions, and he grew to know her in ways that were impossible mere minutes before. They made love eagerly, and when he was about to climax, he whispered for her to tell him what to do.

"Come in me," she said. "It's OK. I want all of you."

Waves of liquid excitement coursed through him like fire, and he pumped into her the years of frustration and emptiness he'd been holding back. His sweet release spoke volumes.

She accepted it without hesitation and with equal ardor.

When it was over and they lay in each other's arms, Jukes felt like crying. He'd been transfigured. In the warm afterglow of their passion, Jukes lived years.

The sounds of traffic drifted in from below, a Manhattan lullaby, weighing on his eyes.

They slept the sleep of lovers.

They both dreamed of green fields. And a white horse with a beautiful woman rider. Her red hair flowed behind her as she neared.

Jukes recognized her. He could hear her sobbing.

Jukes looked at his hand and saw that it was glowing. His whole body glowed. He was translucent and lighter than air. He thought, *Maybe on this side of the dream, she's real and I'm the ghost.*

This time, instead of fear, Jukes felt compassion for the Banshee. He surprised himself by approaching her boldly.

She dismounted and stood by her horse, the green of her dress morphing with the rich vegetation beneath.

Being in her presence was overwhelming, and Jukes felt the field of energy she radiated. It warmed his skin and bathed his soul.

But something had happened since their last meeting. Jukes had changed. By making love to Fiona he'd opened a door and crossed the threshold into a new experience. He felt strong and confident, infused with life.

Jukes Wahler faced the Banshee now a different man, pure of heart and unafraid.

He studied the breathtaking beauty of her face—it haunted rather than seduced. The exquisite sadness of her expression against the flawless milky angles of her skin mesmerized him. She stood before him more like a goddess than a ghost.

With great effort Jukes forced himself to speak.

"Why are you crying?" he asked.

"Because I can never be free," the dream voice replied.

"I wish I could help you," Jukes said. "You seem so infinitely sad."

The Banshee's face blurred.

"Come; let's walk together," she said. Her words echoed eerily through the dreamscape. Her soft voice, with its tuneful lilt of Irish brogue, made hymns of the words. Every note resonated in his heart like a melody that made him want to weep.

"Help me, man of the modern world. Free my soul."

"But how? How can I help you?" he asked.

The pity he felt for her was like a great ocean around his feet, swirling with eddies and currents. His feet began to sink in the sand like when he stood on the beach as a child. The waves licked at his ankles. The wind blew mournfully across a robin's egg blue sky. He heard people sobbing in the distance.

Behind her accent, the Banshee's voice sounded familiar, and he thought for a moment that it was Cathy's voice, then Fiona's, then his mother's. It affected him in conflicting ways, bringing tears one second, joy the next.

It was this constant shifting of emotions, he realized, that seemed to accompany the Banshee and made it so hard to be in her presence.

"Are you suffering?" he asked.

"I suffer for womankind," she said. "As womankind suffers."

"Why did you come to me?"

"I come to warn you. Your sister, Cathy, is in great danger. You must save her from the evil man."

Jukes was galvanized. "Where is she?"

The Banshee shook her head. "I do not see the present; I only see the future and the past. I live outside of the moment. Ask me where she will be."

"Where will she be?"

"At the turning point, the place of your first failure."

"Where is that?"

"It's in your past. You will come full circle."

Jukes wanted to shower her with questions but stopped himself. Her answers were enigmatic.

He saw the Banshee as he had not seen her before, as a force of good.

Then, before his eyes, she began to grow old. Older and older still, until she became a withered old hag. Her beauty was corrupted into ugliness as foul as the grave. Jukes stepped back in horror.

He wanted to run, he wanted to scream, but his body would not obey. The mutant Banshee disappeared.

Jukes began to cry in his sleep.

Fiona awakened with a start, jolted from the same dream into the same reality. She found Jukes awake next to her and moved into his arms. Tenderly he pulled her close.

They were both sobbing.

"Oh my God!" Fiona said. "I dreamt I talked to the Banshee!"

"So did I," Jukes said, astonished they'd both had the same dream, at the same time.

"It seemed too real, not like a dream at all."

Jukes felt his face and remembered the time before when he'd dreamed of the Banshee and how it had blurred reality. He wasn't sure then and he wasn't sure now.

"I think it was a dream, but I don't think it was the same kind of dreams we know. This was like being thrust into another dimension."

Fiona used the sheet to wipe her tears. "Where is this place she said Cathy would be?"

"The place of my first failure . . . I don't know. Someplace in my past."

CHAPTER
SIXTEEN

The old house smelled of mothballs and disinfectant and something else. Mrs. Willis had failed to answer the door. Padraic O'Connor forced it open and entered, his anxiety growing as he walked further back into the stifling atmosphere of the old lady's house.

An ungodly smell came from the kitchen. O'Connor recognized the unmistakable odor of death.

He found Mrs. Willis facedown on the linoleum floor, stretched out stiff and cold. She'd been dead for several days. He looked around and saw that the ancient texts were still spread out on her kitchen table, the pen still clutched in her skeletal hand.

She'd been working on the final translation when she died. Her handwriting was nearly illegible, but O'Connor could see the columns of Gaelic phrases and their English translations.

He studied the words, trying not to breathe through his nose. He gathered all the papers on the table and stuffed them in a folder.

He couldn't escape the oppressive biosphere of the old lady's house fast enough. As he hurried through the living room to the door, he happened to glance at the old lady's menagerie and noticed something strange—all the glass figurines of animals were shattered. They hadn't fallen off their shelves or been smashed; they stood exactly where they had always been, each one shattered individually in place.

He looked closer and saw that many of the tiny glass legs still seemed to be standing at attention, but the rest of the animals were disintegrated.

O'Connor shivered when he saw those shards of glass.

Only sound waves could have destroyed them so cleanly, he thought. *Another aspect of the Banshee? Has she been here?*

O'Connor hurried back to his hotel room and placed all the materials he'd gathered on the bed. The time had come to pull together all the phases of his plan.

The time is now.

He carefully unwrapped the metal cylinder and two human skins.

On the streets, later that day, Padraic O'Connor was relentless. He heated up his karmic poker and burned a hole in the side of New York big enough to crawl through. Driven by a new level of apprehension since discovering the old lady dead, he had became obsessed with finding Bobby.

O'Connor had visited three band rehearsal facilities before he found this one, the one with the ska music coming out of the filthy glass warehouse windows. The speeded-up reggae tempo caught his ear like a razor.

He smiled. *This one could be it.*

It was a huge building, almost half the block, made of old brick, divided into a warren of studios. The entrance stood crowded with scruffy musicians, smoking and drinking beer. O'Connor decided to check the rear. He found a locked metal door and a loading dock facing a garbage-strewn alley. He was about to leave when the loading dock opened.

The corrugated garage door raised with a metallic clatter and a man as big as O'Connor stepped out. He stopped when he saw O'Connor.

"What are you doin' there?" he said menacingly.

O'Connor stepped forward. "I'm lookin' for somebody."

"You a cop?"

O'Connor shook his head and took another step. He moved like a cat, light for person of his size, up on the balls of his feet as a dancer would.

The man he was talking to had a Mohawk haircut and two muscular arms covered with tattoos. The shaven sides of his scalp rippled as he addressed O'Connor. "This is private property, man. You're trespassing. You can avoid trouble by leaving now."

"I'm lookin' for somebody," O'Connor said again.

"Hey, man! I'm not gonna tell you again! Get the fuck outta here!"

O'Connor smiled. Mohawk came forward.

"I'm lookin' for a guy named Bobby Sudden."

Mohawk came threateningly close and poked his finger sharply into O'Connor's chest. "OK, last time, asshole. Move it!"

O'Connor casually raised his hand and grasped the offensive finger. He expertly bent it back until it cracked. Mohawk shouted and brought his other arm up, fisted and ready. O'Connor pushed the elbow of the arm attached to the finger he had just broken into the man's face. As he did this he pivoted, drawing Mohawk down in a swift circular motion.

O'Connor's attacker went down hard, uttering a short profanity as the breath went out of him on impact.

In one smooth motion, O'Connor pulled Mohawk's arm back and inserted his thumb on the small fleshy pad between Mohawk's thumb and first finger on the outside of his wrist. He twisted the hand back into his body and applied pressure.

Mohawk tried to roll onto his side, but O'Connor countered. With a grunt he screwed Mohawk's arm 360 degrees counterclockwise. This time the sound was more like that of branches breaking on a dead tree.

Mohawk screamed, blocking out the satisfying crunch of breaking bones to O'Connor's ears.

The Irishman leaned over and spoke quietly, directly into the side of Mohawk's agonized face. "I just broke your arm in three places and your wrist in two, and I've only just started. Do you understand?"

Mohawk nodded, wincing back all manner of tortured sounds.

"I said I was looking for somebody. I think you know who it is. Now where is he?"

"I don't know," barked Mohawk through the pain.

O'Connor's voice rose in anger. "Don't piss me off!"

He twisted again; there were a few more sounds like rubber bands snapping; then Mohawk began to shriek.

"You broke my fuckin' arm! You broke my fuckin' arm!"

"Shut up!" O'Connor put his foot on the man's neck and pressed down. "I'll take the cracked bone and shove it up your ass."

"No! Please . . . don't! I'll talk. I'll tell you whatever you want to know."

Somewhere, a few blocks away, a car alarm went off. O'Connor looked up and down the alley.

"I'm not convinced. I'll have to do some more damage. You see, what I want from you is your undivided attention. The only way to get it is with pain. Lots and lots of pain."

"No! Please, I'll tell you anything! Just let go!"

O'Connor released Mohawk, who rolled over in pain, whimpering like a child.

"All right, let's try again. I'm looking for Bobby Sudden. I have reason to believe he rents a studio here. Which studio is it?"

Mohawk looked on the verge of passing out. "Bobby's in the secret studio in the back, last room in the corner. There's a black dog painted on the door."

O'Connor picked up Mohawk by his pants and heaved him into the dumpster, where he collapsed among the garbage. The physical exhilaration of the violence had invigorated O'Connor. He'd been fallow too long. He believed a warrior must fight to remain himself.

Padraic entered the building stealthily, threading his way down the corridors, past the doors behind which thrashing rock bands of every description played at deafening volume. As he approached the corner, he heard a ska band playing louder. O'Connor's face tightened.

The door with the black dog painted on it was at the end.

CHAPTER SEVENTEEN

George Jones found Tony Brooklyn entertaining. After George bought him a hamburger and fries, the diminutive street dealer became talkative and spoke at length on a great many topics. George shut him up periodically, directing his wandering attention back to finding the red-haired man. But the conversation was lively and George actually laughed out loud several times.

Panelli failed to see the humor in anything Tony had to say and was anxious to get back to the station. "Come on; let's get on with the hunt," Panelli said.

George had a peculiar expression when he answered, one not quite as bemused as annoyed. "This is the hunt, Panelli. Relax. I think Tony's about to come up with the big break any minute now. Right, Tony?"

"That's right, boss."

"Just remember, Tony, Rikers Island needs men, nice-lookin' boys like you, with nice tight buns. I know some old cons up there; they send me out recruitin' new prospects all the time. I do them a favor, they do me a favor. Right now, I'm doin' you a favor by not draggin' you in for that dope we found. So don't forget it."

"I won't."

George's voice became stern. "There's places this guys hangs out around here?"

"I've checked 'em all, man. I told ya, I've been lookin'."

George looked up at the ceiling, as if the answers to his questions were written there like graffiti. He closed his eyes and took a deep breath. Another moment of intuition passed and he made a connection that had been building for hours. "How about the movies?" he asked. "Did he go to the movies?"

Tony's eyes opened wide. "Hey, man! Wait a second. . . . You know, there was a place."

"Where?"

"Well, now that you mention it, I remember once, he went to the movies right after we jazzed. We just scored some excellent brown and he took a taste. After he got buzzed, he says he's goin' to the movies. I thought it was kinda strange, you know? But he said it was nice and dark in there and he could nod and nobody would hassle him. Makes sense, when you think about it. I asked him why he just didn't go someplace free and he said he dug the art when he was high."

George listened intently. "What do mean 'he dug the art'?"

"The art, you know. . . ."

"The films?"

"Yeah, he dug the films. I thought he'd be into some porno or some other heavy shit. But the dude liked cartoons, those corny old Disney cartoons, you know?"

George looked at Panelli with an expression like he'd just fitted two halves of a peach together. "I got a hunch," he said. "Popcorn, ticket stub . . . It's a long story. It just came to me."

"Are you goin' psycho on me, George?"

George's face flushed; he frowned. "It's psychic, not psycho, and I'm not. You know I don't believe in that shit."

Panelli folded his arms. "OK, you had a hunch. So spit it out."

"There's a movie theater down the block; it's gotta be the only one in this neighborhood showing *Cinderella*. I noticed it earlier."

"Right," Tony said. "The Temple. That's the place. He dug the art there."

"How come you never looked there?" George asked.

Tony shrugged. "I don't like cartoons."

"You don't think he'd be there now, do ya?"

Panelli laughed. "Come on; you're dreamin'. That would be way too easy."

"That's what you said when you pulled the dope out of my pocket," Tony said.

George found the Temple Theater box office and showed his badge to the old lady behind the scratched Plexiglas window.

"Police, ma'am. We're looking for a white male, tall, with red hair. Anybody by that description buy a ticket today?"

The old lady squinted at George. "I don't know; my eyes are no good. Ask the ticket taker."

George found a black teenager named Ray at the door, taking tickets. George held his badge out and smiled. "I'm looking for a guy who may have passed this way. He's tall, has red hair, comes in here a lot."

The teenager nodded. "Yeah, I've seen that guy. I think he's in there right now."

George couldn't believe his good luck. "Are you sure?"

"I think so."

The movie was nearly over. Panelli had handcuffed Tony in the car for safekeeping.

"Let me ask you a question, OK? Let's say a guy comes in here and you rip his ticket in half and then he leaves, like he forgot something in his car, but he wants to come back in. Would you take the half of the ticket the guy had and rip it again?"

"Yeah, that happens sometimes. Like if the guy steps out for a minute, I remember his face and the quarter-ticket."

"You ever do that for the red-haired guy?"

"All the time, man. I know because he's one of the only people who ever goes out once the show starts. I think he gets high or something."

George's heart was pounding. *It might be Dolly's killer.*

"How many people are in the theater right now?"

Ray tried to count in his head how many tickets he'd taken so far today. It wasn't that many. "I think about twenty," he answered carefully.

"How many are kids?"

Ray looked surprised. "Why, most of 'em, I guess. Except for a couple of teenagers and the big guy down in front."

Shit, George thought, *a theater full of kids. That's all I need. Why couldn't this guy have gone to the X-rated places like all the other pervos? No, he has to come here, where all the kids are.*

Panelli covered the back exit. George went inside, wondering how he was going to handle this.

First I'll have a look. If I see the guy, I'll call for backup.

Inside, on the screen, mice were singing. Kids were scattered throughout the cavernous room completely absorbed. Their little faces turned to the screen, eyes wide. A group of teenagers were eating popcorn near the door. George could hear the rattle of their bags.

George's eyes adjusted to the dark slowly. He couldn't see a thing at first, so he took an aisle seat near the door and waited. He wanted to be able to discern the silhouettes of the patrons before he continued toward the front. He had a small penlight flashlight in his pocket, but he dared not use it for fear of alerting his suspect. He had to stay in the dark.

His eyes scanned the old theater, built during Hollywood's golden age. It was an art deco palace, complete with back-lit gargoyles and ornate wooden scrollwork.

At last, his pupils dilated and he slipped out of his seat and stealthily made his way down toward the front. A couple of kids came up the aisle on their way to the refreshment counter or rest room. They looked at George and pointed as he went by. He heard them giggling as they passed, and he found himself wishing they'd stay in the rest room.

This is where I should radio for backup, but the damn radio's all the way in the car. Besides, I'm just taking a look.

George could see Red's shape clearly outlined against the screen. He was in the third row, his feet up on the chair in front of him. He stood out like a giant among pygmies. Luckily, there were no children in his immediate vicinity.

George slowed to a careful creep and crouched down. He slipped into a seat, about six rows back.

This is as close as I get.

His heart was pounding now. He was in a theater full of kids with God knows what kind of maniac. He slid his right hand inside his jacket and wrapped his fingers around the walnut grip of his gun.

Can't use that here.

His foot touched an empty soft drink cup and he kicked it accidentally. It rolled noisily in an arc toward the front.

Red turned.

George slid down in his seat.

Ray the ticket taker watched intently from the rear of the theater. He saw the figure of the guy down in front turn suddenly and face Detective Jones. There was something about the way both men moved that told him there was going to be trouble.

He slipped farther back into the darkness.

Then he saw the guy in front jump up from his seat and pull something from his pocket. Ray knew right away that it was a gun, even before the first shots rang out. He could see its outline against the bright movie screen.

He decided to call the cops on the cops.

George saw Red go for his pocket. He dived to the ground between the seats, jerking his own huge handgun from the holster.

There's too many kids in here; no way do I fire my weapon.

Panelli was on the rear exit, and to get out the front the suspect would have to get past George. Red was trapped.

Kids started screaming. They jumped up from their seats in a panic and ran for the exits. Everybody in the room had seen the two men square off against the movie screen; their silhouettes were sharply defined. The gun was clearly visible in Red's hand.

Red began to move. He hunched down behind the seats and started to make his way toward the door to the right of the screen. George hoped Panelli was ready.

"Back off, motherfucker!" Red shouted.

George stayed down, crawling through the gum and candy wrappers, working his way toward the door also.

Suddenly Red ran for the exit. George raised his head and called out.

"Police officer! Freeze!"

Lying down behind some seats near the door was ten-year-old Karen Sweeny. Red scrambled down between the seats and almost stepped on her. She was crying vigorously. He saw her and smiled like the devil. He reached down with one of his hands and yanked her to her feet, twisting her tiny arm behind her back. Karen screamed. George could hear the terror in her voice, and his mouth went dry.

"Hold it, cop! I got a kid! So just back off!"

George felt sick. Red began to slide down the aisle toward the exit at the side of the screen.

"Stay down! Don't fuck with me!"

He was almost to the door and George couldn't do a thing. He wished he had called for backup, but there'd been no time.

The movie was almost over; it was getting late. They could have lost him forever.

Red felt the utter helplessness of the kid in his arms and the frailty of her twiglike arm. He wanted to snap it off like a drumstick and howl at the ceiling. The kid was nothing in his hands, just a sobbing hunk of useless crap. In his mind, she deserved to die, but she was his ticket to ride.

George could see the kid clearly now; Red had her by the arm and was using her tiny body as a shield. He backed into the door, and liberation. With his free hand he pushed the lock bar down and put his shoulder into it. Keeping his eye on George, he pushed it out forcefully, nearly ripping it off its hinges. Light exploded into the dark theater, blinding them both momentarily.

It looked like the doorway to Heaven. George had a perfect shot at him, his body clearly defined in the light, but the kid was too close. He couldn't risk it.

Red released the kid, took two steps, and ran directly into Panelli, who was crouched just outside. Panelli was knocked back by the force of the collision, completely surprised. His gun came up too late; Red fired down on the cop at point-blank range. Panelli's body jumped.

George ran to the exit, heard the shot, and paused. On the screen music was playing and the credits were rolling. On the other side of the door his partner was dying.

Red took off down the alley like an Olympic runner.

George cautiously opened the door and peered out. He saw Panelli on his back and cursed.

Sirens were approaching.

George looked up and saw a patrol car come down the alley. He pulled his badge out and shouted, "Officer down! Call an ambulance."

He ran after Red.

Police swarmed the area. They found a red wig in an alley nearby and used dogs to track the killer through the dense urban jungle. A few blocks away, the trail ended abruptly.

When Panelli died on the way to the hospital, Red became a cop killer and the entire force mobilized against him.

George followed the trail, intent on nailing Red's ass to the wall of justice.

CHAPTER
EIGHTEEN

Jukes and Fiona held each other like lovers who'd been separated for years, instead of two people who barely knew each other. Jukes knew that the short time of intimacy had changed everything about them. They were inseparable now, as one.

Neither of them had spoken so much as a word since awaking from their parallel dreams. They stared at the ceiling deep in thought.

Finally, Jukes broke the silence. "It's early, only eleven o'clock. We must have gotten back from dinner around seven. That means we've only been asleep for an hour."

"You mean we both fell out and had the same dream right off the bat? That's unbelievable. This whole evening has been unbelievable. God, I don't know what to think."

"I don't know about you, but I think I've been working too hard. The stress must've caught up with me. I'm mentally exhausted. There's no way I can go back to the office for a while."

"I know. I can't concentrate on anything . . . except you and me . . . together . . . and the dream."

Jukes stretched and sighed. "Yeah, the dream. I can't get it out of my mind. I've been thinking about what she said. I might have an idea."

"An idea where she said Cathy was going to be?"

"The place of my first failure. I think I know where that is." Jukes told Fiona the story of the boy at the lake and how that incident had colored his life. He traced his frustration with Cathy and his own social inadequacies to that moment, the moment the bully challenged him and he backed down.

"God, if I ever had one moment in my life to live over again, that would be it," Jukes said.

Fiona propped herself up on one elbow. "Let's go there."

"Now?"

"Yes, exactly. Now. How far is it?"

"Only about an hour-and-a-half drive upstate."

"We can be there by twelve-thirty. You just told me how much you need a rest, how stressed out you are, so why not do something impulsive and go there? We can make it a three-day weekend. I'll call your answering service and tell them you'll be unavailable till Monday."

Jukes nodded. "I could get back to the roots of my anxiety. It should be therapeutic."

"Don't forget what the Banshee said. If you're right, it's where Cathy will be."

"The more I think about it, the better it sounds. We can have some downtime together."

Fiona sat up in bed, her naked body pale in the darkness of the room "All I ask is that we stop at my place so I can throw a few things in a bag."

Before leaving, Jukes called George Jones. The line clicked and he got George's voice mail.

"Detective Jones, this is Dr. Jukes Wahler. I'm driving to my family's cabin upstate at Lake Pierce. I have a hunch that Cathy may show up there, and I want to be there if she does. I'll leave directions with my answering service if you need to get in touch with me. There's no phone up there, so I won't be reachable until Monday."

Jukes hung up and felt strange, as if he'd just put another ball in play in the pinball game of life.

The words of the Irishman came back to him: *"They will appear to be a series of unlikely coincidences."*

Tom Rayburn was cooking some of the catfish he'd caught that morning when the phone rang, which surprised the hell out of him. He hardly ever got phone calls, especially in the off-season.

Tom wasn't the most popular guy in the world. In fact, he was downright cantankerous. The people in town stayed away from him in droves. They didn't like him and he didn't like them.

He spent the winter baby-sitting the cabins on Lake Pierce. He spent the summer fixing people's boats and running the only bait shop on the lake. Summer was a time to try to enjoy what few pleasures life still held for his seventy-six-year-old body. Winter was a time to do some serious drinking.

The fall was a transition period. He checked the cabins, pulled the boats out of the water, and went to the liquor store to stock up. With nobody around, he didn't have to keep up the charade of sobriety. If he wanted to get falling down drunk and piss in his pants, he did it. And fuck the world.

Tom Rayburn knew how to cook catfish, though. The smell of it filled his cabin and stuck to his skin like a lightly breaded, aromatic sweat.

Heaven's Glen, the next closest town, had a population of around two hundred people, most of whom were pissed off at him.

The phone jangled his nerves.

"Hello?"

"Hello? Mr. Rayburn?"

"Yeah, Tom Rayburn here. What can I do you for?"

"Mr. Rayburn, this is Jukes Wahler."

"Harumph. . . ." There was a pause and Jukes could hear

something sizzling. A moment later, "Little Jukey Wahler, the kid with the braces?"

"Yes, except I'm grown-up now. I'm a doctor, as a matter of fact."

"A doctor? Well, bless my soul and kiss my hairy balls! A doctor! Well, don't that beat all! Say, I've got this pain in my leg that keeps gettin' worse; maybe you could look at it sometime," the old man said.

"Actually, I'm a psychiatrist."

Tom worked the spatula expertly, flipping the fish and a glob of greasy burnt cornmeal. "What is that, a headshrinker? Well, I'll be damned! I guess I spoke out of turn, Doc. I may be old, but I ain't crazy. What's the occasion?"

"Well, Mr. Rayburn, I'm coming up to the lake tonight. Could you get the cabin ready?"

Goddamn city slicker. Don't he know anything? The weather's changing; everyone is gone now.

"Well, ahh, I don't think you understand; the season's over. There's nobody here. The place is all shut down, for Christ sake!"

Tom removed the fish from the pan and turned off the burner. He was about to hang up when Jukes Wahler spoke again.

"I'm driving up anyway, Mr. Rayburn. I'll be there in about two hours. Do you know which cabin I mean?"

Rayburn squinted at the phone. His mood was not good. He had been looking forward to a quiet evening of catfish and bourbon. He coughed directly into the receiver. Rayburn imagined a big hunk of spittle flying out and hitting Jukes on the side of the head. *Serves him right,* he thought.

"Of course I know which cabin you mean! What do you think I am, an idiot? Your sister damn near tore the place down last summer! Say, you're not plannin' any kind of wild sex orgy, are ya?"

Jukes laughed. "No. No orgy. I just have a little family business I have to tend to."

"What the hell for?"

"It's personal."

"Yeah, I'll bet it's personal. What are you, some kind of a drug dealer?"

"No, Mr. Rayburn, I told you; I'm a doctor. Can you do me a favor and get the place up and running for me? Your fee is twenty-five dollars, right?"

"It's a hundred now," the old man grumbled. "That includes turning on the 'lectric, gas, firin' up the heater, checkin' it out for critters, gettin' the water pump runnin'. You sure you want all that?"

"Yes," Jukes replied firmly. "By the way, have you seen anybody up there in the last twenty-four hours?"

"Haven't seen a soul."

"Good. Well, keep an eye out; there may be somebody else. If you see them, let me know."

Aha! So that's it. Must be some kind of secret rendezvous. Maybe Jukey Wahler is one of them homosexuals now, Tom thought.

"No problem. I'll just give you a holler on my cellular phone."

"What?"

Tom realized his sarcasm was lost. "You don't get it, do ya? It's late, and I'm not goin' up there tonight. I'll get over there when I get the chance, probably tomorrow. That's the best I can do. My truck's been actin' up lately; I don't even know if it'll start."

"Mr. Rayburn, it's really important that you do it tonight. I'll pay you 200 bucks."

"Two hundred? Christ, you're the one that needs a psychiatrist." Tom looked at the catfish and pondered the offer.

The fish'll keep; the booze ain't goin' anywhere. That's good money. Too good to turn down.

"OK, I'll do it, but I still think you're crazy."

"Thanks. I appreciate it. I'll be up in a couple of hours."

Tom Rayburn slammed the phone down and cursed. "God-damn city slicker. Crazy as a shit-house rat."

Jukes rented a car and drove north toward Lake Pierce. The weather was cold and clear. His fatigue faded from him like a streak of bad luck. With Fiona at his side, he was full of the strongest resolve he'd felt in years.

He was going back.

It was nearly one o'clock in the morning when they arrived at the lake. Shafts of silver light sliced through the tall pines, bisecting the road with the moon's waxing radiance. He'd taken a few wrong turns, which was to be expected after so many years, but for the most part he knew where he was going. The area had changed very little since he was a young man, and except for a few housing developments and convenience stores, it was still a quiet rural drive.

Tom Rayburn was right: the place was deserted. They drove past the tiny supply store and one-pump gas station and took the lake road into the resort. Built in the 1950s around what was then a thriving fishing spot, the rustic cabins were clustered on the periphery of the small lake like prehistoric wooden beasts gathered around a watering hole. Modest, even funky by today's standards, the Lake Pierce Vacation Paradise and Travelers Club Approved Campgrounds held the charm of another era. Boating was now the major attraction here, and the lazy canoe pace of his youth had been replaced by the much faster and noisier pace of the water-ski rigs that now dominated the summer scene.

The serious fishermen had gone elsewhere, but the old-style family-oriented recreational atmosphere still existed. The modern world had taken its toll here, as everywhere, but Lake Pierce fought back valiantly. Jukes liked it; it was a solid and soulful reminder of simpler times.

Jukes hadn't seen another car for miles.

Fiona had fallen silent as soon as they left the main highway. She stared out the window, deep in thought.

The road went from two-lane blacktop to one-lane blacktop to dirt to ruts. The closer he got to his destination, the faster his heart beat. He felt as if he had a rendezvous with destiny up ahead, in the moonlight, among the pines. He rounded the lake where the ghosts of his youth still dwelled.

There was his father, waving from a rowboat, his fishing tackle in his hand, wearing a plaid flannel shirt rolled at the sleeves. A hat with a collection of fishing lures jabbed into it sat jauntily off the side of his head.

Jukes watched with his mind's eye as the old man rowed slowly out into the center of the lake and disappeared.

Jukes rounded the next bend and came face to face with the bittersweet memory of his mother. There was a picnic basket at her side, and she sat on a red-and-white checkered tablecloth in a moonlit meadow. He could hear the singing of cicadas in the tall grass of his memory. His mother looked as fragile and delicate as china, a reflection of beautiful desperation.

The rising moon shone full on her face. Its icy fluorescent colors gave incredible depth to the scene, making her stand out like she was in his old stereoscopic View-Master, the one he had spent hours playing with as a child. Jukes wondered what she had in the basket, some of his childhood favorites no doubt: fried chicken, peanut butter and jelly sandwiches, homemade pickles, a slice of blueberry pie, maybe some potato chips.

The images of his early years tugged at Jukes's heart like a hooked rainbow trout on his old Zebco fishing rod.

He knew he would see his sister next, paddling a canoe past

the boathouse with all the skill and cunning of Hiawatha. God, it hurt to think of her with Bobby.

Jukes saw the boat dock where the nightmare began, where the most painful memories of all culminated and died. He could see it in the shadows, the water lapping against its pilings. It stood there like a memorial to Jukes's youth, somewhat sagging now. His failure filled the air like the odor of the lake in midsummer. He saw the local boy, all toughness and arrogance, standing in his dreams, daring him to come down the hill and defend his sister.

"That's the place," Jukes said. "That's where the bully stood, down by the dock, and I was afraid to walk down that hill. I can still feel the humiliation."

Fiona touched his knee. "What's important is that you're here, ready to confront it."

Jukes's hands tightened on the steering wheel, turning his knuckles white. He silently cursed the boat dock and drove on.

Jukes pulled up the dirt road, passed his father's cabin, and drove around to the rear, so that the car would be out of sight to anyone driving up. He killed the engine.

The water was as still and quiet as black glass. From where he sat, it looked as deep as the ocean. They got out of the car, took the overnight bags they'd packed out of the trunk, and walked up to the porch. Crickets and frogs resumed their song. The moon loomed high in the sky.

"It must be beautiful here in the summer," Fiona said.

"Look at the stars," Jukes said.

They both looked up into a celestial canopy of countless brilliant dots of light.

Fiona sighed. "God, there's millions of them. I never saw anything like it. . . ."

"The city blocks out most of it, but when you come out here, away from the lights, you really see the immense scope of the universe. Really gives you perspective. Man is so small in comparison."

He looked at Fiona, saw the moist affection in her eyes, and kissed her. Her mouth was warm and soft against the chill of the night. Jukes felt his soul swell as he held her close.

Oh, God, it feels good to be held.

Old Tom Rayburn was as good as his word. The porch light was on, and Jukes could see that the storm shutters had been pulled back.

Taking the flashlight out of his bag, he shone it around the weathered front door.

"It seems so much smaller and shabbier than I remember."

"That's only normal."

The old wood planks creaked under their feet as they stepped up to the door. It was unlocked. Rayburn knew that nobody would be around, and he didn't lock and batten down all the cabins until the first week of November. Leaving the door unlocked was something that people still did in these parts. How alien it seemed to Jukes, a native of New York City. His own apartment door back home had four locks on it.

He twisted the knob and swung the door open. Its rusty hinges creaked loudly, like they hadn't been opened or oiled in years.

He felt the wall next to him and found the light switch. It clicked on and the old room was bathed in weak yellow light. Rayburn had turned on the power, and Jukes was grateful for the illumination.

The furniture was unsophisticated, to say the least, and the dust was thick over most of the room. The shabby look of the place, with its hopelessly warped flooring and its cheap wall coverings, gave him a chill. It was something that he hadn't felt in decades.

The place gave him an unmistakable case of the creeps. The

smell was damp, the memories painful. He walked in very slowly, careful to avoid touching anything. It all seemed somehow tainted.

"Let me take a look around first, before we get settled. You never know what kind of animals might get in. Why don't you stay here?"

Fiona nodded. "Be careful."

Jukes systematically began to search the house. First the bedroom. The lightbulb in the hall was burned out. Likewise the bedroom light. He clicked on the flashlight again and inched along.

The bedroom was dreary, and as he splayed the light across the walls, a gloom seemed to settle over him. The peeling wallpaper cast uneven shadows, and the bed, devoid of sheets, looked as cold and unappealing as a coffin. The mattress sagged in the middle with the weight of an invisible body. The metal frame was rusted, and the whole room smelled of mildew.

He shone the light on the closet door. A new chill went through him as he pondered whether or not to open it. He knew he had to, just to be totally sure. The thought filled him with dread, and he had to force himself onward. He tiptoed up to it and listened.

His mind, already stretched to its limit, threatened to play tricks on him. He thought he heard shallow, raspy breathing coming from inside. He had to shake his shoulders to get rid of the gooseflesh there, but it didn't help.

What did he expect to find? The Banshee, her unearthly body coiled and ready to leap out at him as soon as he touched the door? Or Bobby Sudden, murder in his eyes, about to lunge at him with a butcher knife? Or maybe just more bitter memories?

His mind raced. Jukes knew he'd best get it under control or it could be a very long night. He took a deep breath, grasped the door handle, and yanked it open.

A rusted coat hanger fell from the upper shelf and startled him. He jumped back as if it were a poisonous snake. It rattled to the floor with a forlorn metallic clatter.

"Are you OK?" Fiona called from the living room.

"Yeah, I'm fine. It's just a little dark in here."

He peered into the empty closet. Jukes felt his heart pounding in his chest like a runaway pony.

He shone the light up and down inside the forlorn old closet and backed away. Satisfied that the bedroom was secure, he moved back out into the hallway.

Never an overly religious man, Jukes said a silent prayer, a true testament to his growing unease.

"OK in the bedroom. I'll check the basement next."

He approached the basement door stiffly. It stood before him like the entrance to a tomb. He gripped the flashlight in his hand tightly.

"Before I go down there, I want to check something."

Fiona didn't answer. She stood in the center of the room shivering, half with the cold and half with the anxiety of the old cabin. She wondered if she'd be able to sleep in here.

Jukes walked back into the front of the house, where the electric lights still burned reassuringly. There was a utility closet in the kitchen, a walk-in pantry. He opened it and shone the light inside. The empty shelves looked back at him. He stepped inside.

In the back of the pantry, above the top shelf, was a false panel. He removed the loose board that hid a long space from view and reached inside.

His hand touched something cold. He wrapped his fingers around the object and carefully pulled it out.

All right! It was still there after all this time.

Incredibly, his old .22-gauge hunting rifle hadn't changed a speck. Wrapped in a couple of garbage bags, it had stayed dry over the years, and it looked as good as the day he'd hidden it there. He felt around inside the wall for a box of shells. Bingo! He thanked God for one of life's little victories.

He checked the gun. It looked fine. He loaded it up and put a handful of shells into his pocket. The smell of gun oil still clung to it, and he wished he had time to clean it properly.

It had been at least thirty-five years since he had last fired the weapon, when he had killed a raccoon. His parents had been very upset with him for doing that. It was only with the agreement that he would never aim it at anything living that his father had let him have the lightweight .22. Jukes was looked upon as a perfect son, an angel who would never do anything wrong. When he'd abused that privilege, it shocked his parents in a way that he'd never been able to rectify.

Jukes still felt bad about that. He felt bad about the cute little raccoon he'd killed and worse about disappointing his father. What had he been thinking? It was too long ago to remember.

Memories washed over him as he held the rifle in his hands.

Would the gun still work? It had been stored in the secret place for thirty-five years. He'd always kept it clean and oiled.

Jukes Wahler knew deep down inside that it would work; otherwise he wouldn't have wasted his time pulling it out of the wall. Besides, he had no other weapon, except the Swiss army knife he had brought along with the flashlight.

He cursed the fact that he'd left New York without another weapon. He didn't want to confront Bobby unarmed. The knife wouldn't help him much in an open fight; Bobby was young and strong, and he . . . he wasn't.

Jukes knew he didn't have the killer instinct that allowed guys like Bobby to hurt other people. In a physical confrontation, the good doctor would no doubt be afraid of hurting the other person.

Still, he had this mental image of cutting Bobby down. After all, he was the avenger now; he was the stalker. He had the rage, the anger. He didn't need anything but his own righteous conviction to nail that squirmy toad, right? Wrong. He needed the rifle, and as it rolled on his hands he felt the fire and passion of his youth rising up within him.

Of course the rifle would work. Just because it had been sitting in a wall for thirty-five years didn't mean a thing. It was primed for duty then as now.

He checked the barrel and pulled back the bolt. Everything seemed all right. He wondered if he should go outside and fire off a shot to test it but decided not to. It would attract too much attention. Old Tom Rayburn would probably hear it and come over for a little look-see.

Jukes cradled the rifle in his arms. He felt brave and invincible with it, just as he had so many years ago.

Fiona's eyes were wide as he walked back into the room carrying the rifle.

"What's that?"

"It's my old rifle. It was right where I left it. I thought it might be a good idea in case there's any animals down there."

He knew what he had to do next, and he also knew that he'd been procrastinating. The cellar, he had to check the cellar.

CHAPTER
NINETEEN

O'Connor studied the door with the black dog painted on it. Like all the doors in the warehouse, it was metal-plated and built for security. He put his ear against it and listened.

A loud rock band was pounding away in the next studio, making it hard to hear anything.

Ska music.

But O'Connor did hear something else. Rising above the music was the sound of a motorcycle, coming from behind him.

O'Connor spun, and the sound got louder. Someone was driving a motorcycle down the hallway.

O'Connor dived for cover, crawling behind a trash container down the hall.

Bobby Sudden roared around the corner a split second later, gunning his motorcycle. He looked crazed, as if he been running and fighting.

Bobby frantically unlocked the door, cussing and fumbling with the keys.

He dashed inside, leaving the door ajar.

O'Connor slipped out of his hiding place and approached the motorcycle. He stealthily planted a magnetic homing device under the rear fender and crawled back behind the garbage container to watch.

A few minutes later, Bobby reemerged, dragging Cathy. O'Connor watched intently as Bobby threw her and a saddle-bag across the bike and started the engine. It roared loud and throaty in the enclosed hall. O'Connor could smell the acrid taste of carbon monoxide, and Bobby turned and pointed the bike back down the hall, back to the loading dock door.

He gunned the engine and drove the bike down the hall. O'Connor heard it rattle through the loading dock.

O'Connor stood up. He knew he had about fifteen minutes to follow Bobby, as the range on the homing device was limited, so he wasted no time getting back to his vehicle—the rented Jeep Cherokee. From his laptop computer O'Connor tracked Bobby over a grid of maps, out of the city and to the north.

The hunt had begun.

The door to the cellar had a stark and ominous look to it, like so many of the doors you see in horror movies. Jukes could almost hear the trailers: "Don't open that door! Don't go down the stairs! Don't go into the cellar!"

There was nothing really distinctive about it. It was just an old wooden door. Jukes had seen it before.

Yet he felt a great amount of trepidation about opening it. Holding the rifle in his hand, at the ready, he put his other hand on the doorknob.

He shook his shoulders, shrugging off the goose bumps. He kept the gun pointed at the center of the door.

He slowly turned the knob, heard the lock disengage, and felt the pressure on the door release. Then, in a smooth, quick motion, he pulled it open toward him.

There was only darkness, and the dank odor of mildew.

The steps went down into the blackness as if they descended into the bowels of the earth, into Hell itself. Cool, fetid air came up to greet him, to welcome him into the abyss.

Come on down, it seemed to say. *We've been waiting for you.*

A small puddle of light illuminated a portion of the dirt floor. The world was reduced to that size, and Jukes's concentration followed the same periphery. One inch beyond that limited circle of understanding, the darkness swam like a thousand black eels.

He looked around for a light switch and then remembered that there was no light in the cellar, never had been.

Jukes thought it odd that these cabins had cellars at all. But it was one of their distinctive selling features. Dirt floor cellars were considered very chic in the 1950s, especially around these parts. Maybe they intended to make them into bomb shelters, he thought cynically.

The steps were moist and unsafe. For a moment he considered forgetting about it, but a search was a search, and he would never feel safe enough to sleep unless he knew for sure. Bobby could be hiding anywhere. Jukes wanted to secure this area once and for all; that meant getting on with it. The rifle felt substantial and powerful in his hands as he descended into the unknown.

His first step brought forth such creaks and groans that he almost cried out in surprise. The steps actually seemed to bark like a living thing as soon as his weight was brought to bear.

He made his descent gingerly.

The basement was small, low-ceilinged, and not very hospitable. Nature had nearly reclaimed it. There were many huge spiderwebs, Jukes noted unhappily.

He shone his light around and saw nothing. Over in the corner was a wood box. It was taller and longer than a coffin but just as foreboding.

He reluctantly put his gun down and, with his flashlight in his left hand, opened the box with his right.

He pulled the lid up and looked inside. What he saw there made him jump.

Two feral eyes shone up at him from the dark. They glowed like fluorescent gems. He gasped, profoundly frightened, and stepped back.

There was a scuffle of claws and teeth; he dropped the lid and screamed a short burst. His shaking numbed him for a few seconds, debilitating him, costing him valuable gun re- trieval time. He reached for the rifle, knocked it away, rum- maged for it again, and cursed.

Inside the box, the scuffling continued. Then, it receded into the earth below.

Raccoons, he thought. *Jesus, that woke me up.*

Fiona called from the door, "Jukes! What's going on down there? Are you all right?"

"Yeah, I'm OK. It was just a raccoon. I surprised him."

"Well, come back up here. I don't like this. That cellar gives me the creeps."

"I'll be up in a second."

"Don't you think you're overdoing it? There's no one around here."

Jukes spoke loudly toward the stairs, trying to sound confi- dent. "I have to make sure. We're not going to spend the night in a cabin in the middle of the woods until I know that every square inch of it is safe."

He realized he was sweating uncontrollably, almost gasping for breath, and shivering like a wet dog. On unsteady legs he walked toward the stairs, surveying the room with his flash- light as he went. He looked back again, became still, and lis- tened. The industrial pounding of his pulse was all that came to his ears.

"OK, I'm coming up," he said so she could hear.

When he was satisfied that there were no people or ghosts or creatures down in that earthen pit, he made a quick retreat back upstairs.

"It's all right. The place is clear."

"Thank God for that. Does this cabin have a fireplace or something? Let's try to cheer it up a bit."

"Are you scared?"

Fiona smiled. "Not as long as I'm with you."

"You think I should erase the tire tracks from the car?"

"Why?"

"In case Bobby comes along."

"Now I'm scared. You really think he'd come here?"

"I don't know, but this is where the Banshee said I'd find Cathy."

"OK, erase the tire tracks if you like, but I think you're getting carried away."

"It'll only take a minute; I'll be right back. There's a wood-burning stove in the living room and some firewood on the porch."

He went back out into the night. The wind was soft and fragrant through the pines. Their limbs brushed and rattled, rubbing each other intimately, sending dust and pine needles off into the waiting world.

He used a branch to sweep away the tire marks, feeling a little silly doing it.

Maybe Fiona is right; maybe I am overdoing it.

Bobby Sudden piloted his motorcycle into the green possibilities of pastoral New York State, unaware that he was being followed.

Cathy, sluggish from drugs, clung to his back like an infant baboon. One or two times she leaned too far to the left or right and came into danger, for a split second, of falling off.

Bobby pushed her back with his free arm and shouted for her to hang on.

He wasn't quite sure what to do with Cathy, but at this point he knew he couldn't keep her. Cathy had become a liability, too strung out on drugs to be any good to him as a lover or a model and too docile to take out his pent-up hostilities on.

Once or twice he considered letting her fall off the bike and smash her stupid head on the roadway at seventy miles per hour. But the cops would find her and link her to him.

No, he couldn't do that.

But he had made a personal decision that, one way or another, up at the cabin by the lake, he would lose her.

He'd never considered murdering Cathy like he had the prostitutes. She was different. It seemed to Bobby she liked being abused, that she actually enjoyed his humiliating games of bondage and scenario.

That turned Bobby on. So few things, outside of murder, did. That meant Cathy was a good thing.

But she'd let herself go and now she looked like an anorexic coke whore, and he seriously doubted he could get a boner even if he beat her to within an inch of her life.

Besides, she was too hot right now. Jukes was no doubt looking for her and had probably pulled the cops into it. Her corpse showing up anywhere would most likely put Bobby squarely at the forefront of any murder investigation.

And Bobby couldn't afford that. He had too many skeletons in his closet, literally.

His mind stung from the revelation that somehow the cops had tracked him down to the theater. How was that possible? There were no physical clues to link that part of him with the murder investigation. It had to be a phenomenal, once-in-a-lifetime coincidence.

Bobby knew the way to the lake; he'd been there before with Cathy. He expertly guided his bike over the hills and past the boarded-up stores and onto the dirt road leading to the cabin.

Cathy hung drunkenly on, and he cursed her as a useless deadweight, intent on slowing him down.

George Jones followed Bobby's trail through the alleys. The dogs found the wig, then lost the trail. Twenty blocks later, somebody found a guy in a dumpster with a broken arm, and Bobby's gun. He'd tossed it into the dumpster behind a warehouse used for rehearsal studios.

They found Mohawk, barely conscious, his arm shattered. The paramedics were loading him onto a gurney when George arrived.

"Where did he go?" George asked.

Mohawk, thinking George meant O'Connor, the arm breaker, managed to speak. He said, "Bobby's studio, last door in the corner, dog painted on it."

George rushed to the door, shot the lock off, and opened it.

Inside, he found the computer with the pictures of Dolly Devane.

And Cathy.

"Holy shit," George said. "Looks like we found Dr. Wahler's sister."

CHAPTER
TWENTY

Fiona brightened the cabin considerably. She'd started a fire in the fireplace, done some basic house-cleaning, and made the bed. It wasn't perfect, but it was better. The cold, dusty cabin now hummed with warm life.

Jukes replaced the lightbulb in the barren bedroom, and they made love again. Afterward, Fiona drifted into sleep, secure and safe in the arms of her lover.

Jukes, however, was restless and consumed with the Ban-shee's prophecy. He believed that Cathy would be here, and Bobby, too. He believed a showdown was coming. He strengthened his resolve that this time, he would not back down. This time, he would save Cathy.

Jukes stared at the peeling paint of the ceiling and wondered about the complicated lines of fate that had brought him here.

"They will appear to be a series of unlikely coincidences," O'Malley had said.

Another thought occurred to Jukes—maybe Cathy didn't want to be saved. He'd considered that before, even though it hurt him deeply. Maybe it was her destiny to be the victim, just as it was his to endlessly try to rescue her.

He eased himself from the bed without waking Fiona and padded into the living room. He slipped on his coat, hefted the rifle in his hands, and went out onto the porch to wait. If Bobby came, Jukes would be ready.

The temperature was dropping and Jukes pulled his collar high, propped the rifle under his arm, and rubbed his hands together. He hunkered down against a pile of firewood and looked for a place where he could stay out of sight.

The porch area opened into a workshop/toolroom that had been built along one side of the cabin. There were tools hanging from the walls; Jukes recognized a power drill and a belt-sander.

Jukes decided it would be warmer and safer to wait in the workshop, so he propped up a piece of log to sit on. He positioned himself near the screen door where, in the dark, he could look out onto the porch and the front area beyond.

Jukes heard a curious sound coming from somewhere in the dark beyond the porch. At first he thought it was an owl—an upper-mid-octave mournful *whoo, whoo*, but the more he listened, the more it seemed to him that it was not an owl but a woman crying. He could hear a tremble in the tone, like a grievous angel sobbing over a lost soul.

Jukes listened carefully, thinking it might be Cathy, out there in the night, in need of help. Taking his flashlight, he went outside and scouted the area around the house, finding nothing. The sound faded and left Jukes perplexed.

He returned to his perch in the toolshed.

Twenty minutes later, against his will, he dozed off.

He awoke with a start, wondering how long he'd been asleep. An odd sound roused him. It was a gentle thumping above his head.

He looked up and saw the moth, one of those huge luna moths, pounding headlong into the lightbulb. Drawn by the light, it frantically flew toward it, trying to merge with it, only to eventually die of exhaustion.

Momentarily hypnotized by the sight, Jukes forgot where he was and what he was doing.

It all came back in a few seconds. He looked out across the porch and into the yard.

Something was different.

Jukes cursed himself for being so lax. In his stressed condition, his mind was losing track of the little things, all those little details that could be so important now. What the hell was different?

The porch light is on!

Of course! But had he left it on? Damn! He couldn't remember for sure. He remembered coming out to the porch and entering the workshop in the dark. Had he gotten up and turned it on? In his groggy state, Jukes tried to sort out the details.

After a careful mental review, he came to the hazy conclusion that he had not turned the light on.

OK, then who did?

Adrenaline pumped. He instantly went into a state of edginess that made his skin crawl.

Maybe Fiona got up and came out here looking for me, he thought. That was a good, plausible explanation. But some sixth sense tingled in Jukes's mind—everything was so strange, so alien, his life had been in such upheaval lately, that somehow the disorientation actually had begun to work in his favor. He found himself primitively come alive with the challenge.

Whatever the reality, he knew he could face it. Within the false security of that sense of well-being, he got his second shock.

There was movement in the darkness beyond the porch.

He sat up, the rifle cold and numb in his hands, and strained to see.

The Banshee was there.

She was standing just out of the pool of light thrown by the porch light.

He clearly saw her now through the shadows. She was unmistakable, her pale skin luminous against the darkness. The movement that caught his eye was the ghostly waving of her hair as she combed it, in a breeze that didn't exist in Jukes's universe.

My God, what's she doing here?

She stood deathly still, a specter in the dark, generating her own ghostly light.

Jukes's heart jumped up into his throat.

Was he in danger? Did the Banshee want to kill him? She'd been stalking him for days—maybe he, not Bobby, had become her target.

He remembered Fiona's words. *I must be an empath, a sympathizer.*

But Bobby, he's a different story. The bastard fits every criterion, he's asking for it.

The only thing that perplexed Jukes was the fact that Bobby didn't have prior knowledge of the Banshee, something that Loomis had insisted was important: "The Banshee only kills those who know her face, Doc."

But who's to say that Bobby didn't know her? Who's to say she hasn't been stalking him for days?

Bobby was in the network of those she'd already touched: Loomis, himself, Detective Jones, and Cathy.

Jukes smiled. *Wouldn't it be nice if she's out here waiting for good old Bobby-boy to arrive.*

Jukes enjoyed the thought. Revenge would be so sweet, he thought. Justice would be sweeter.

Of course, he couldn't be sure of anything. The Banshee, as far as he could see, didn't seem to follow any particular set of rules.

He watched her long red hair undulate as she combed. Jukes became mesmerized by the rhythm of the strokes.

The smooth, cool metal of the rifle felt reassuring. His hand slid over it.

He tried to stay focused. Jukes had Bobby to worry about now, no need to let his mind wander at this crucial point. *For-*

get about the Banshee, he told himself. Bobby was coming, and he was dangerous.

But it was impossible to take his eyes off her.

He was too busy staring at her to notice the hand that slipped over the fat part of the gun and began to gently remove it from his lap.

He looked up a split second too late.

Padraic O'Connor struggled to keep the signal from the homing device within range. He'd been following a dirt road for about ten minutes, along the edge of what appeared to be a large lake. He lost the signal from time to time as he passed through crests and valleys. He threaded through the trees slowly, not wanting to get too close. His headlights had been off for the last few miles as the signal faded in and out.

Damn, maybe the batteries are weak. I better keep movin', he thought. *I could lose him among the trees.*

The signal winked out. O'Connor cursed the delicate electronic equipment and kept the vehicle rolling through the pine needles.

Somewhere up ahead they'd be stopping, he thought. Otherwise they'd just circumvent the lake and come out where they started.

Bobby's fist hit Jukes on the jaw, in about the same spot it hit him the night Bobby took Cathy. At the same instant, Jukes felt the rifle jerk out of his hands. The next thing he knew, he was looking down the barrel of his own weapon, past the trigger, past the faded wooden stock, into the distorted face of Bobby Sudden.

"Well, well, Doc. Imagine running into you here."

"But how—"

"Hey, I'm not stupid, man! I mean, look what I found . . .

you sitting here with a fuckin' gun! What were you gonna do with that? Shoot me? Blow my brains out?"

Jukes's heart sank. Anger and defeat mixed in his gut like two unstable chemicals, causing strange and unpredictable reactions. He immediately thought of Fiona. Was she still sleeping in the bedroom? Had Bobby already discovered her and tied her up? Or worse?

Jukes was genuinely shocked and surprised that Bobby had sneaked up on him and couldn't take his eyes off Bobby to see if the Banshee was still there.

Jukes swallowed hard and grit his teeth.

"I parked down the road," Bobby continued, "about a mile back. I hiked up the rest of the way, just in case something funny was goin' on. Good thing I did. Beautiful, huh? You know what your problem is, Doc? You think everybody is some kind of fuckin' idiot like all your half-assed patients. You didn't realize that stupid old Bobby was as smart as you, did ya? Nah, your ego's a few sizes too big for your head, and that was your downfall."

Jukes bit his lip. The scumbag was right; he had grossly underestimated his enemy. That was the kiss of death in any battle. It looked like this one, the battle of Lake Pierce, was over without a shot being fired.

Bobby looked wild and dangerous in the half-light. He held the rifle almost up against Jukes's chest. Sweat was on both their faces, even though the night was cool. Jukes let Bobby talk, wondering what the desperate man was going to do next.

"So now it's down to this. I got a mind to pull this trigger right now. What do say about that?"

Jukes just stared back at him, his lips sealed.

"I said, what do you say about that? Answer me!" Bobby screamed. The sound of madness in his voice shook Jukes to the core.

Fiona must have heard that, he thought. *Is she OK? Did he already get to her?*

"I can't tell you what to do," he answered evenly.

"You're goddamn right you can't. Save the headshrinkin' for your patients."

Jukes was right about one thing: whatever he said wouldn't matter much now. He didn't intend to beg, however. A catharsis had taken place, and Jukes Wahler had changed in the past few days. He was stronger now, and he wasn't going to give Bobby one ounce of satisfaction. Instead, he took a different tack.

"Why did you do it, Bobby?"

"Do what?"

Jukes leveled his gaze at him. "Why'd you beat her?" he asked softly. "Why'd you beat Cathy?"

Bobby sneered. " 'Cause she wanted it. Shit, man, she loved it. It turned her on. Your sister's a real kink, a freak; didn't you know that? She's a sicko, Doc; all I did was answer the call of nature."

Jukes's eyes filled with hate. "You're a real asshole, Bobby."

"You've got a hell of a lot of nerve tellin' me that," Bobby spit. "I'm the one with the gun."

Jukes could feel Bobby taking the bait. He'd pulled him into this conversation against his will; now he hoped that it wouldn't backfire on him.

Jukes screwed up his newfound courage. "Fuck you! Go ahead, shoot me, if that'll solve all your problems; shoot me, you pathetic son of a bitch! You think you've got trouble now, shoot me and you can never go back. Think about that. The cops will be on your trail forever. You'll be on *America's Most Wanted* every week; you'll never get a night's rest again. Behind every door, every window, you'll think somebody's watching, and they will be, Bobby; they will be."

Jukes watched the storm clouds gather in Bobby's eyes. They were locked on his, the gun barrel inches from Jukes's chest.

Bobby said, "Cathy's the least of my problems. And blowin' you away don't mean a thing to me. You have no fuckin' idea what I'm involved in. I make the ultimate art."

There was a stillness in the air that seemed to numb them both.

Then, in a motion as fast as sudden death, Jukes's right hand flashed out and tried to knock the rifle away. At the same time he tried to snake his other hand around the barrel and jerk it out of Bobby's hands. Jukes put everything he had behind that move. It was, without a doubt, the boldest single thing he had ever done.

The gesture didn't work. Bobby was ready for it and smacked the rifle barrel against Jukes's hand. Pain flared across his knuckles. The hand was knocked away harmlessly.

A split second later, the rifle pointed into Jukes's face. He blinked and held his breath.

Bobby pulled the trigger.

Nothing happened.

They were both frozen in time, shock settling over them like radioactivity. Then all hell broke lose.

Jukes leaped at Bobby like a pit bull, biting, punching, kicking, scratching, knocking him down in a hail of blows. He wrestled the rifle from Bobby's hands manfully and rammed the stock back into his face. Surprised by his own success, Jukes fought harder and more viciously than he'd ever fought in his life.

The rage had been bottled up inside him for years, going all the way back to the incident with the boy at the boat dock. Now, ironically, within fifty yards of that very same pier, his moment of truth was at hand. Jukes struck out not only at Bobby, but at that kid on the pier, the kids in school, and all his other failures. He struck back at life, and it felt good. The dam had burst.

Yet even now, at the height of his passion, with the rifle butt in Bobby's face and the opportunity to smash his enemy senseless at hand, Jukes hesitated. Somewhere in his mind, he grappled with a fundamental moral question that had plagued him from childhood: *Can I really hurt this person?*

Jukes had already made the decision to ram the rifle into Bobby's nose and end the struggle, but in the time it took to reason it out Bobby countered. Ever the resourceful street fighter, Bobby kicked Jukes in the balls. Jukes doubled over, his eyes watering in pain, but bit back the numbing debilitation between his legs and fought on.

Both men battled as if there were nothing else in the world. They fought their way across the toolshed. Bobby, the younger, tougher man, fought to gain the upper hand. He fought a vicious and dirty fight, repeatedly going for Jukes's eyes.

Jukes did all he could to keep from being blinded, but the doctor was hurting in several crucial places.

They traded blows and Jukes tried to keep up. He felt his strength eroding as the stamina of the younger man became a factor.

Jukes gasped for breath.

Bobby kicked him hard in the chest and sent him flying into the corner, clutching his ribs.

Then something on the workbench caught Bobby's eye. He reached for it. When Jukes saw what it was, he froze. Time froze. Everything froze.

Bobby had gotten hold of a portable battery-powered hand drill with a three-sixteenth-inch drill-bit in it, snatching it from its recharging cradle like a pistol. He flicked it on and the Black & Decker variable-speed, reversible wood drill came to life.

The sound paralyzed Jukes, a hellish whine, as Bobby revved

the RPMs up. The drill bit twisted demonically. Jukes could see it was black carbon steel, as hard as industrial diamond.

Bobby held it out in front of him like a knife, letting it whir in Jukes's terrified face.

Jukes had nowhere to go. He put his hands up to protect his face, and Bobby drilled a neat three-sixteenth-inch hole through the center of Juke's palm. Jukes screamed.

Blood squirted out in both directions, spraying the faces of the two men simultaneously. Bobby pulled it out with a rev. The bit was wet and red, spinning a fine mist of Jukes's blood around the room.

It was hard for Jukes to fathom the sadistic cruelty behind Bobby's glazed eyes. He seemed to be in a deep, violent trance. Jukes tried to wedge himself ever deeper into the corner.

This is how it must have been for Cathy, he thought.

Bobby brought the drill to Jukes's temple and held it there, a mere quarter of an inch away from his brain. "Here's your lobotomy, Doc. Where do you want it? In the forehead?"

Jukes stared at the spinning drill bit, his eyes locked on the tip. His life began to flash before him.

He held his breath. The drill whined and spit blood. Bobby's hand moved closer.

The door banged open.

"What the hell!" It was old Tom Rayburn, his shotgun at the ready, a look of total surprise on his face.

Bobby saw the shotgun first and reacted by throwing the portable drill at Tom's weathered face.

An explosion rocked the cabin. Its percussive, air-shattering effect left all three of them temporarily deaf.

The gun had blown a hole in the ceiling; dust and wood chips rained down on them. Tom had not been careful with the safety. When he raised his arm to block the oncoming drill, the gun discharged.

At first, Bobby thought he was hit, but he soon realized he

wasn't. He jumped up and ran past Tom and into the night, knocking down the older man as he went by.

Tom struggled to his feet and saw the blood on Jukes's hand. "Holy shit! Looks like he drilled ya!"

Tom Rayburn helped Jukes into the cabin. They found Fiona tied up in the bedroom.

"Jukes!" she cried. "Oh, my God! Are you all right?"

"He's been drilled through the hand!" Tom shouted. "He's bleeding like a son of a bitch! Help me get him bandaged."

Fiona rubbed her hands together, trying to get the circulation going. The ropes had been too tight, and she'd suffered. But now, with Jukes hurt, she had to be able to help.

Tom got Jukes to the bed. A trail of blood followed him.

"See if there's a first-aid kit somewhere in the cabin! They usually have something for emergencies!"

Fiona ran through the house, opening drawers and cupboards. In the bathroom she found a blue-and-white plastic Johnson and Johnson box.

Jukes was on the bed, blood running down his arm, when Fiona came back.

"Do you know how to do it?" Tom asked.

"Yes! We have to wash the wound first, then treat it and get it bandaged. Get some towels; I'll do the rest."

Together they managed to get Jukes's hand bandaged.

"Wrap him in blankets!" Fiona said. "Hurry! He's probably going into shock!"

Tom brought blankets from all over the cabin, and they wrapped Jukes like a mummy.

"Is there a phone around? We have to get some help."

Tom nodded. "The closest one is at my place, on the other side of the lake."

Fiona looked at Tom. "You'll have to go for help. Call an ambulance, and the cops, too. How soon can you get there?"

"Takes a while, but I'll hurry."

"We've got to get Jukes to a hospital."

Jukes opened his eyes and spoke through clenched teeth. He said, "What if Bobby comes back?"

"I'll leave her my shotgun," said old Tom.

CHAPTER
TWENTY-ONE

O'Connor heard a gunshot.

He rounded a turn and saw the lights of a cabin up ahead.

He stopped the darkened Jeep Cherokee and turned on his flashlight. From the duffel bag in the seat next to him he pulled out the stainless-steel cylinder, the human skins, and the bones.

He tightened the skins across the top of the cylinder, using a bracket to fasten them snug against the rim. He twisted the screws until the skins were stretched taut across both ends.

He quickly attached a gun belt to the cylinder and slung it across his back. The bones dangled from a piece of rawhide around his neck. He took his night goggles, some rope, and his gun and left the vehicle.

O'Connor stepped into the woods and disappeared.

Bobby ran through the trees like a wounded bear.

The forest was dark and the moon shadows deep and deceptive. Branches slapped and scratched at him as he ran at a full gallop into the night.

He smashed his knee against a tree and yelped. As he bent over to rub the painful spot, he looked over his shoulder and saw nobody coming.

He hurried back to the clearing where he'd left his motorcycle and Cathy, handcuffed to the handlebars.

Bobby crashed into the clearing and cursed. "Come on! We gotta get outta here!" He came at Cathy with such animal aggression that she flinched as if preparing for a blow. "I'm not gonna hit you! Jesus Christ, Cathy! What do you take me for?"

"Don't touch me!" she screamed. "Why did you have to handcuff me? It hurt my hands."

Bobby looked exasperated. "You were whacked-out. I can't have you wandering around out here in the dark. It's for your own good."

Cathy shook the hair out of her eyes. "Oh, give me a break! There's nobody around here for miles. The place is all closed up for the winter."

"There's people up in the cabin."

"People? But who . . . Oh my God, is it Jukes?"

"Wait a second; I have to find the handcuff key."

Cathy stamped her foot. "Is my brother in the cabin?"

Bobby ignored her and fumbled for the key.

"Answer me!" Cathy demanded.

"Yeah. He's up there with some chick."

Cathy's tears erupted suddenly. A damn of pent-up emotions had burst inside her. Her voice trembled slightly. "I heard a gunshot. . . . What happened? Did you shoot him?"

"No. . . . He tried to shoot me."

"Jukes wouldn't hurt a fly, Bobby. And you know it."

He fitted the key into the lock and snapped the cuffs open. "Come on; let's get outta here right now."

Cathy rubbed her wrists. "If you hurt my brother, I'll—"

"You'll what? You can't do a thing, little girl. I own you, remember?"

Cathy's face hardened. "You'll never own me."

"Look, baby, I know it looks bad, but we can make it. We'll go out to California. I've got some friends there. We can start over."

"No." She shook her head.

"I've got a half-ounce of the good stuff; we can last for a long time. You know you're gonna need it. What's gonna happen when you start gettin' sick?"

Cathy wiped her tears and glared at him defiantly. "I'd rather die than do that stuff again. It's killing me, Bobby. *You're killing me.* Can't you see that?"

Bobby tried to smile, but it came out more of a grimace. "All I can see is the little girl I love."

"I'm not your little girl anymore, Bobby. It's over."

"You don't know what you're saying."

"I know exactly what I'm saying. I'm saying I don't want to go on like this anymore. You've been abusing me, and I'm not going to take it anymore. You've hurt me enough."

Bobby spit, his anger rising. "Do you have any idea what kind of stress I've been under lately? It's driving me insane. You're not making it any easier."

Cathy narrowed her gaze, focusing on Bobby's face in the moonlight. Suddenly angry, she wanted to say something that would hurt him. "I know all about you," she whispered.

Bobby made a strange face, a kind of half-smile that looked dangerous. Cathy's bravery withdrew; she realized that she could be signing her own death warrant by revealing what she knew about the pictures on the computer. She fell silent.

"Yeah?" Bobby said. "What do you know?"

Cathy shook her head. "Nothing. Forget it."

"What do you know?" he shouted. "Tell me or I'll—"

"You'll what? You'll what, Bobby? What will you do? Kill me?"

Bobby exploded at her and she jumped away. He lunged again but misjudged the distance between them in the half-light. He tripped and fell, cursing, into a blanket of pine needles.

Cathy snatched up a stick, a piece of deadwood. It seemed frail and puny in her hands, and she tried not to visualize it breaking like balsa wood over his head.

Bobby scrambled to his feet and faced her. He had a crazed look in his eye and another one of those deadly half-smiles on his face. He laughed. "You're gonna fight me with that? You gotta be kiddin'. I'll shove that thing down your throat!"

Cathy held the stick up and waved it in his direction. "Try it! I don't care what happens as long as I make a stand. I've got nothing to lose anymore."

Bobby charged her and she swung the stick.

It cracked over his head, breaking in half. Bobby grunted and dropped to one knee. But instead of staying down, he shook his head and stood. He had a trickle of blood on his forehead.

Cathy pointed what was left of the stick at him. "I saw the pictures! I know about the dead girls! At first I couldn't believe that my Bobby, my own boyfriend, was a murderer. I thought maybe somebody else took them, or maybe they were fakes, but now that I see what kind of person you really are . . . I know it was you."

Ignoring the stick, Bobby slapped her hard across the face. "You'll pay for that," he sneered. The blow knocked Cathy sideways to the ground, and she put her hand out to break the fall.

At the moment his slap made contact with her, a sharp cry rang out, loud and agonizing, from somewhere in the woods behind them. The sound was unnaturally shrill, as if whatever made it felt Cathy's pain at the exact moment of impact.

Bobby looked up in alarm, expecting to see some kind of wild beast sprint into the clearing. The cry hung in the air, echoing across the lake.

All the ambient sounds of nature, from the insects to the wind, ceased abruptly. In the supernatural vacuum that followed, Bobby's breathing seemed to thunder from his nostrils.

"What the hell was that?" Bobby said.

Cathy shivered. She'd never felt more fear than this. At that moment, facing the raging bull, alone in the night against

Bobby, and with that ungodly sound still echoing in her head, Cathy's mind stopped reasoning.

She'd reached the point of complete sensory overload. She stopped thinking about everything. All she could do now was react. Self-preservation willed her new strength.

She leaped to her feet, like a sprinter from the starting block, and ran. She pumped her legs with all her might, supplying surprising power to her first stride. It carried her clear of the lunging Bobby.

On the unstable carpet of pine needles he lost his footing momentarily. As Bobby faltered, Cathy escaped into the woods.

Bobby ran after her, the breeze picking up suddenly as he navigated between the trees. The wind swished through the boughs, creaking the branches, and made odd moaning sounds. But then another sound grew out of the wind—a ghostly wail that sent shivers down Cathy's back. It rose and fell, like a group of old women keening for the dead.

Cathy ran in the direction of the lake. It shimmered between the trees with the iridescent reflection of the moon, beckoning her.

Once she reached the lake, she could follow it to the cabin, and Jukes.

Jukes and Fiona looked up when they heard the unearthly sound.

"Oh, God! Jukes, what is it?"

Jukes lay shivering on the bed, huddled in blankets. His eyes snapped open when he heard it. They listened as a sound unlike anything they'd ever heard rose and fell in the sky somewhere outside their cabin. It started something like the sound of a cat in heat, then rose to a wolf howl, then continued to climb and change timbre until it reached a screaming crescendo of operatic proportions. It seemed, at its peak, to come from all directions, as if the very air molecules were resonating sympathetically.

"It's the Banshee . . . ," whispered Jukes. "She's here."

Fiona blanched and her eyes watered. Her mouth hung open to speak, but no words came.

Jukes Wahler took a deep breath. "Sit me up," he said.

"What? Sit you up? Is that what you said?"

Jukes nodded. "Come on; hurry."

Fiona's hands reached out and stopped. "I can't; you're in shock. You'll kill yourself."

"Oh, for Christ's sake, Fiona, help me up. Please."

Against her better judgment, she helped him into a sitting position.

"Something's happening out there," he said.

Fiona looked at him, on the verge of tears. "Jukes, I'm afraid. Please don't say you want to go outside. I don't want to hear that."

Jukes shook his head. "If Bobby's here at the lake, then Cathy probably is, too. We can't stay here."

"It's too dangerous, Jukes."

"You realize if Tom doesn't make it, or if there's a problem, we still have to get out of here and find a hospital on our own. You can drive. I'll navigate."

Fiona wrung her hands. The look of consternation on her face seemed almost beautiful to Jukes.

Bobby chased Cathy along the lake shore. With his long legs and demonic energy, he gained ground quickly in the open space. They sprinted past the dark cabins, past the boat docks, and across occasional stretches of imported beach sand.

Cathy panicked when she ventured a look over her shoulder. Bobby would catch up in a minute or two.

With bursting lungs and burning legs, Cathy ran through the limits of her pain. Knowing she would rather die than submit to Bobby again, she made a personal vow to fight to the end.

Bobby howled like an animal behind her, closing fast.

O'Connor used his night-vision goggles to thread a path to the lake. Through the infrared lenses he spotted two bodies running along the water's edge. They were coming toward him.

He quickly moved into position behind a tree next to a sagging wooden boat dock.

The sound was all around him now, louder than he'd ever heard. Realizing it would get louder, O'Connor inserted his earplugs.

He chambered a round in his .45 automatic, checked the ammo clip, and crouched behind a lone tree near the water's edge. He could see them clearly now in his goggles.

It was Cathy Wahler, running for her life.

On her heels was Bobby Sudden.

O'Connor slung the cylinder off his back and wedged it between his legs. He aimed his gun in the direction they were coming and waited.

Fiona started Jukes's car, then went back into the cabin to help him out.

The sound that had come and gone earlier now returned. An eerie wailing, longer notes this time, and louder.

Fiona spoke nervously, trying to keep Jukes's mind occupied. "Nothing like sound waves to scare the hell out of you. Some sound frequencies can go right to the neurocenter of the brain and trigger involuntary reactions. That's why your skin crawls at certain sounds, like fingernails on a chalkboard. But what we heard earlier was like a combination of everything that ever put me on edge. I swear, in that last crescendo, I thought I heard a baby crying."

"It's the song of the Banshee," Jukes said. "You're listening to the sound of death."

Fiona put Jukes's arm across her shoulders and walked him toward the door. He winced but gamely kept moving, concentrating on each step.

"I'm getting weak. Whatever you do, don't stop moving forward. Just get me into the car, please."

Fiona put up a brave front, even smiled. "Sure, honey. Nothing to it."

The wailing modulated to another crescendo, so loud this time it shook the windows. The cabin vibrated as if a tornado were circling it.

"Hurry!" Jukes shouted into the fury.

The song of the Banshee suddenly rose an octave. The swooping, impossible sound waves jarred them. A piercing high note shattered all the glass in the house. The windows exploded inward with the force of a cannon.

Fiona screamed.

Bobby Sudden caught Cathy at the end of a mad dash and tackled her from behind. She went down hard on her hands and knees.

The wailing swelled to a roar.

At first they both ignored it, but that became impossible. The sound swirled around them like a sonic hurricane. It was pure sound, without any discernible source, coming from all directions.

The pitch began to rise. The next series of notes hit every frequency the human brain reacts to—a baby crying, a lover's moan, a woman screaming in pain, a police siren, and, finally, an all-out shriek that shook the trees. It blocked out every other sound or thought.

Bobby struggled with Cathy, rolling along the ground near

the water's edge. She fought tenaciously, but Bobby soon had her on her back.

With the terrible sound bearing down on him, Bobby slammed Cathy's head against the ground. He grabbed a handful of hair and pounded it down again. Had they not been this close to the water, where the earth was soft, he would have fractured her skull. As it was, Cathy grunted and lost consciousness.

Bobby felt her go limp beneath him.

The sound roared like a jet engine.

As he stood and brushed himself off, Bobby noticed a woman standing on the dock. The sudden realization that she was there jolted him, as if he had entered a dark room and turned on the light, only to find someone standing there.

Bobby recoiled.

It was the woman he'd seen in the alley the night he killed Dolly, the one who had pointed to him from the movie screen.

"Oh, shit!" he shouted. All sound seemed to escape his mouth before the words were formed, swept up into the raging storm of noise.

She was illuminated clearly in the dark, her skin luminescent. She stood there silent and pale, while Bobby's breath came in ragged, inaudible gasps.

"Who are you?" he shouted at her. "What do you want?"

The woman combed her hair slowly, her mouth open as if she was singing. Bobby tried to pull himself away and run, but now, with the sound of her wailing penetrating his skin, he felt strangely drawn to her.

Bobby's memory began to dissolve. He tried to concentrate on escaping, but he could feel his mind draining away like sand through dirty fingers.

He visualized his motorcycle and pictured himself roaring down the dirt road to freedom, away from all this crazy shit. The more he thought about it, the more he couldn't remember, and the more blank spaces his memory held. In a few more seconds, he wouldn't be able to recall his own name. The data was being sucked out of him, leaving him an intellectual husk.

The repetitive motion of her hand slowly stroking down with the comb through her crimson locks hypnotized him.

Pinkish tears, large and compelling, formed in her eyes and rolled down her cheeks with exquisite slowness. She was painfully beautiful to Bobby, and suddenly he could think of nothing else but going to her.

He found himself taking step after step toward her. He reached out in her direction and stumbled over Cathy's body.

He fell, then got to his knees and looked up at the mystery goddess, tears blurring his vision.

Suddenly, the sound storm stopped. The frogs and crickets fell silent. The wind stilled. The trees, restless a few minutes ago, stood straight and stiff. The air seemed unnaturally heavy.

Bobby couldn't take his eyes off her; he felt her image burning into his mind like a radioactive memory, erasing all else. His pupils were sensitive to the light radiating from her skin; he had to shield his eyes.

She glowed brighter now, more ghostly.

A whiter shade of pale.

The light seemed to be coming from under her skin. She shimmered like a fluorescent tube.

Bobby began his rapture.

Jukes and Fiona looked down at the lake in awe. The Banshee glowed in the darkness by the water's edge like an archangel. Her ghostly light illuminated a circle that encompassed the entire dock area.

And there was Bobby Sudden, on his knees, reaching up to her.

The sound that had been a hurricane a few moments before

had stopped suddenly and given way to a preternatural silence that seemed deafening by contrast.

"Oh, my God," Jukes whispered. "That boat dock, the hill . . . It's the same place the bully challenged me when I was a kid. It hasn't changed. Bobby's kneeling at the exact spot."

Fiona pointed to the left. "Look! Isn't that Cathy?"

Before Jukes could say anything to stop her, Fiona ran down the hill to Cathy's side. Jukes watched as she knelt by Cathy's side.

"She's alive!" Fiona shouted.

In the stillness of the moment, the words reverberated Jukes's heart like a church bell.

The Banshee pointed at Bobby and began her final song. Her mouth opened, and the most ungodly, mournful sound that Jukes had ever heard came out. Different from the shrieking hurricane that had preceded it, which sounded like a choir of anguished voices, this was a solo. One single, mournful voice rising in the night, expressive in a way a group can never be.

The tone was something no human voice could ever hope to create: part wolf howl, part siren, part screaming baby, part Jimi Hendrix guitar squeal, it floated upward with hair-standing, alien dissonance.

"Banshee," whispered Jukes, though none could hear. "You came back."

The Banshee's head turned and she looked at Jukes. It didn't actually turn; it rotated unnaturally, swiveling on her neck like a doll's head. Her face vibrated, changing expressions faster than the eye could follow.

Jukes saw the look in her eyes and felt a stab in his heart. In that brief second when their eyes met, just like the first time he saw her through the window of the delicatessen, Jukes felt some understanding pass between them.

He realized instantly that she would destroy Bobby. He also understood she had a soul full of torment so vast she could

never express it to any living creature. Jukes felt the weight of
her burden in his heart and sensed the undying passion for revenge she'd held inside for centuries.

He looked inside her.

It was there, in the dark ocean of the Banshee's soul, that he
saw himself.

Himself!

Jukes shuddered against the night. His damaged hand was
swollen and screamed with pain, but somehow, in the Banshee's presence, it didn't matter anymore. Nothing mattered.

Numbed, he stood there gaping at the grievous angel, with a
mind anesthetized by what it had witnessed.

Jukes struggled to concentrate, but the great and shocking
revelation lingered. He had seen himself in her.

The sound of her solo wailing penetrated the woods like a
beacon. A song of terrible, destructive beauty began.

The Banshee turned her attention back to Bobby.

Her mouth opened wider. The notes of the song she sang became impossibly high and dissonant. It broke the threshold of
pain, vibrating his eardrums violently. Bobby Sudden put his
hands to his head and screamed, but no one heard.

Jukes also brought his own hands up. He wondered how long
the sound would continue and how high it would modulate before it damaged his brain. Surely it would make them deaf. Or
kill them.

Jukes wondered if anyone had ever heard the song of the
Banshee and lived.

Then, he saw something that made his heart stop beating. It
disturbed him in a way that nothing ever had.

The Banshee changed.

It happened quickly, in the space of a heartbeat. But to Jukes
it seemed much longer, now that time had become distorted.
He watched as she mutated before his eyes and all the while the
ungodly sound increased.

Her young, pale face stretched, aging incredibly in a matter of seconds, like rubber—a latex contortion of pain and sorrow. Her skin became wrinkled and her eyes seemed to protrude from her eye sockets.

Her head swelled, the space between the eyes increased, and the entire grotesque visage appeared to pulse as it expanded. She seemed to be changing not only on the outside but on the inside as well. Jukes sensed the storm clouds gathering across her soul.

The song had become pure vibration, a powerful, immobilizing ringing in their ears.

They were all locked in a moment that couldn't be. Impossible, yet it was happening.

A vortex of energy swirled around them, emanating from the Banshee. It sucked them in, pulling at their bodies and souls.

The Banshee was now a monstrous hag, like Medusa of mythology, something so hideous, to look upon it meant death.

Her head tilted back; her mouth opened wider than human skin and jawbone could stretch. Her song jumped another octave.

Her shriek filled the valley like a jet engine.

The trees shook and bowed to the sound. Animals fled for miles around. All around the lake the eerie siren soared and peaked. The Banshee, her transformation complete, stood before Bobby a heinous, wailing specter, calling out for justice from beyond the grave.

Her mournful cry intermingled with a new sound, far off in the distance, the sound of approaching police sirens. The combination of the two created a skin-crawling dissonance that echoed across the still water like some nightmare electronic effect.

The avenging angel focused on Bobby. His eyes rolled back

into his head until only the conjunctiva showed. He slapped his hands to his ears in a futile effort to block out the sound.

Blood ran from his nose, his eyes, and his gaping mouth. His tongue bulged, the soft tissue there splitting open. The vibrations shook him to the bone, rattling his flesh, vibrating his very atoms to the point of combustion.

The otherworldly nature of the sound penetrated everything, distorting the laws of nature. Jukes and Fiona, now trying to protect their ears, were miraculously not affected by the higher frequencies that threatened to destroy Bobby.

It was like standing next to a tornado intent on destroying the house next door yet leaving your home untouched.

The Banshee directed her song in a concentrated beam at Bobby Sudden.

The hands on Bobby's ears began to move. They inched across his face like fleshy spiders, working their way into his mouth.

Bobby's expression changed. His eyes showed utter terror and disbelief; rapture was replaced by panic.

His hands, working against the desperate will of his body, dug into the sides of his mouth until blood appeared.

Then, as if in a dream, they began to pull back the skin.

With the Banshee's wail reaching new heights, Bobby's hands began the dance of death. Completely against his will, he began to destroy himself.

While Jukes and Fiona watched in horror, Bobby ripped his mouth open, unhinged his jaw, and began peeling his skin back up over his head. His hands worked with unnatural strength, like metal pliers against his soft flesh.

He was turning himself inside out, the bloody inner skin reversing itself like an old, bloody overcoat.

Blood flowed freely off him, muscles glistened, and a peek of white bone showed here and there. He hadn't quite gotten the skin flap over his head when he stopped being alive.

He crumbled to the ground in a bloody heap, lifeless and horrible as mutilated carrion.

The corpse belched open and spilled its contents onto the ground. All that was Bobby emptied out.

CHAPTER
TWENTY-TWO

The song of the Banshee stopped.

It faded gently from the air, gone like a cool breeze. The effect was like a change in air pressure. The wind returned; the insects began. Things eased.

The Banshee did not change back into a young girl again. Her face remained the same terrible mask of sorrow that had destroyed Killian, Loomis, and now Bobby. Yet her tears flowed on as if she were sorry for it.

The grievous angel stood before them. She raised her arms into the nighttime sky and began to dissipate like a cloud.

O'Connor had watched the Banshee closely. He wore protective goggles and earplugs, but he heard it nevertheless. It penetrated and chilled his Irish blood as cold as a Belfast New Year.

He had waited until the Banshee destroyed Bobby, for he knew that was Bobby's destiny and he could not interrupt it. He hunkered down, in the shadow of the tree, with the leg bones in his hands and the cylinder between his legs. He put his gun on the wet turf next to him, where he could snatch it up quickly if needed.

He held the femurs up, uttered a string of ancient Gaelic incantations, and beat the drum with all his might.

The sound resonated though the night, along with O'Connor's incantation, which he shouted at the sky. The Gaelic mixed with Latin. The two languages stumbled over each other in an awkward chant, casting a conjuration.

The Banshee stopped disappearing. She looked in the direction of the drumbeat and wailed again, but this time the sound seemed arrested by the drumbeat and O'Connor's baleful chant.

The drum hummed and resonated as the human bones stimulated the skin covering it.

Ta Toooommmmb. Ta Toooommmmb. Ta Toooommmmb.

The skins vibrated, pounding a rhythmic tattoo into the sky, and the Banshee began to descend.

Her hair moved with the invisible suction the drum created. Her head shrank, the eyes retracted, and the skin cleared. In a twinkling, the rose of her icy beauty bloomed again, and she became young.

The Banshee wavered, her image distorting as if being viewed through shimmering heat waves.

Then she was in front of O'Connor. He didn't see her move. She just winked across the space between them. She didn't glide or walk to get there; she just materialized at the new location. Then she was closer still; another wink, and her hands were reaching toward the drum.

"Oh, my God!" Fiona cried. She suddenly realized what O'Connor was doing.

He's capturing the Banshee.

Fiona remembered that in some cultures there existed old folkloric techniques for capturing a wayward spirit in an iron drum. Ghost catchers in the sixteenth century allegedly had employed this method. Somehow the soul found the vibrating metal drum irresistible and could be tricked into entering, and there it became stuck.

While Fiona watched, the Banshee wavered again, becoming even less distinct as she moved toward the drum. The compelling rhythm resonated like faraway cannon fire.

The air itself began to get thick, as if the supernatural forces on display were overloading. The pressure increased with the passage of each heartbeat/drumbeat.

The atmosphere became oppressive; the air molecules felt heavy and full of electricity. They crackled with energy. Fiona found it hard to breathe; the air seemed too thick to pass into her lungs. She sucked it in, but there didn't seem to be enough oxygen in it to sustain her. She felt as if she were drowning. Her ears popped.

O'Connor began to chant higher, his voice modulating up like that of a crazed Benedictine monk, singing out the guttural phrases of two dead languages in time to the infernal drum. His voice distorted in the strange air. It sounded as if he were miles underwater, with thousands of tons of pressure per square inch closing around him.

The incantation ended. O'Connor shouted at the Banshee in English but kept on pounding the drum.

"We come! We come! We catch you in the iron drum!"

The Banshee began to elongate; she was being sucked into the stainless-steel cylinder.

"No!" Fiona screamed. "No! Don't do it! Let her go!"

The cadence of the bones striking the human skin had a mesmeric quality. The Banshee's face distorted and she wailed a heartrending cry.

Fiona saw that the Banshee was being pulled into the spirit catcher. The woman's fear turned to pity for the Banshee, that her magical existence should stop here, at the hands of this horrible man.

"We come! We come! We catch you in the iron drum!" O'Connor repeated, singsong.

He shouted with his head thrown back, the veins on his neck bulging, talking in tongues, babbling his simple rhyme.

Fiona's fear reached a climax. Her heart pounded furiously, threatening to leap out of her chest and run away. She screamed, but the sound was instantly stifled in the turgid air.

The Banshee continued to dissolve; her image now streamed
into the drum, melting like watercolor paints down the drain.
Fiona sensed a titanic unseen struggle.

She wanted to move but couldn't.

O'Connor's eyes were locked on the rapidly disintegrating
form of the Banshee. His voice still clung to the drumbeats
like water clinging to a windshield. He kept up the nonsense
chant.

"We come! We come! We catch you in the iron drum!"

In a few more seconds he would have the Banshee. She
would be trapped inside the drum until he let her out. It would
be O'Connor's ultimate moment of triumph. He had done
what no other could.

He had caught the Banshee!

The bloody bitch is mine, at last, he thought.

Just a few more seconds, that's all it would take. Then she'd
be on her way back to Ireland, where she belonged. Just a few
more seconds and the deaths of his father and brother would
be avenged. Just a few more seconds and the Black Rain would
live again. Suppose he turned her loose on the oppressors back
home? God knew they had the blood of women and children
on their hands.

Oh, the terrible possibilities!

Revenge was at hand.

The Banshee's image became indistinct; it drifted into the
drum like smoke being sucked through a fan.

Jukes stared at the same place the local boy had stood so many
years earlier, hitting Cathy and daring Jukes to do something
about it. That was the scenario, repeated over and over again in
their lives: Jukes does nothing while Cathy gets hurt. The bully
challenges, Jukes backs down, ad infinitum.

But no more.

Except now, when he looked down at the dock he saw not the boy, but O'Connor.

It looked to Jukes like the drum was somehow pulling the Banshee in, inhaling her, and it didn't seem right.

For the first time in his life Jukes felt absolutely no fear. He didn't think but, rather, acted instinctively. Jukes bounded down the hill and launched himself at the man with the drum.

From the corner of his eye, O'Connor saw Jukes Wahler flying through the air at him. It all happened in the space between drumbeats.

Jukes tackled O'Connor from the side while his arm was up, poised to strike the drum, hitting the big man in such a way that the bone was jarred loose from O'Connor's left hand and went spinning across the ground to where it landed in front of Fiona.

The drum rolled away, making a hollow thumping sound as it bounced downhill. It splashed into the lake, sending crazy ripples radiating over the surface. The moonlight reflected off the hundreds of shimmering little humps of water, all moving outward in formation.

The Banshee, still attached to the drum, twisted and writhed as it rolled, struggling to free herself.

She stopped fading. The air pressure changed.

Jukes's hand had been numb until the collision with O'Connor. But the impact sent a shock wave of pain through his body that threatened to render him unconscious.

With superhuman determination, Jukes soldiered on—kept moving and stayed focused. He drove O'Connor downhill to the water's edge.

The painful hole Bobby had bored into Jukes's hand seemed to radiate energy now. He transcended the pain.

Jukes Wahler fought like a man with nothing to lose and the world to gain. He rammed his good fist into O'Connor's face,

putting the full weight of his body behind it. O'Connor turned
and deflected a portion of the blow, and Jukes couldn't swing
his other hand.

Jukes's heart sank when he realized that his initial attack had
done little but jar the drum loose. He hadn't hurt O'Connor
at all.

Padraic recovered from the surprise quickly. He was, after
all, a trained killer, a guerrilla commando with years of life-and-
death experience, and Jukes, the good doctor, was no match.

O'Connor kicked Jukes in the stomach and, when he doubled over, chopped down hard on the back of his neck.

"You bastard!" O'Connor screamed. "Do you have any idea
what you've done? I nearly had her! You fucking ruined everything!"

Jukes fell and rolled into the water. O'Connor was on him instantly, raining blows.

"I'll kill you for this!"

In water up to their waists, O'Connor held Jukes down.

Stars swirled before his eyes like tiny tropical fish and he
couldn't breathe. Jukes faced death. Somewhere in his mind,
the Banshee sang.

Fiona ran toward Jukes and O'Connor. It all happened too
fast—Jukes came out of nowhere; then he and the Irishman
were in the water struggling. Jukes was hurt.

Fiona charged toward them.

Her rage was channeled by a single thought; it focused on
saving Jukes.

She watched as O'Connor held Jukes's head under. She
reached the water's edge and splashed toward them desperately.

She was distantly aware of the Banshee, rising above them
with her hair streaming, watching O'Connor. Her mouth came
open to sing.

O'Connor heard the first notes of the Banshee's death song

and cringed. His earplugs had been knocked out in the struggle, the goggles were gone, and the drum now rolled in the lapping waves twenty feet away.

Fiona punched O'Connor's face. Then again, and again. She tore at him with her fingernails, but O'Connor held Jukes down like a machine. He endured Fiona's blows, single-minded in his pursuit of drowning Jukes.

Fiona used every pound of courage in her body and hit O'Connor as hard as she could in the nose. She thought she felt something break.

Jukes had been under now for almost a minute. Fiona panicked and tried to pry O'Connor's hands loose, but they were like iron.

The Banshee sang high and clear, like an operatic declaration of vengeance. Her voice became excruciatingly loud in a matter of seconds.

In one soaring, unreal glissando, she peaked.

O'Connor's heart exploded. His chest blew open in a red eruption that rocked the water. Fiona, sprayed with blood, frantically dived for Jukes, who'd gone under and stayed there.

She found him immediately, bobbing just below the surface. Where O'Connor had been standing a moment ago now there were only parts of him, floating in the black water streaked with red.

The Banshee was gone.

George Jones and the local sheriff arrived just ahead of the ambulance. As they rounded the lake they saw a blinding light in the sky, hovering just above the lake. An unbelievable sound came from it, like a woman wailing as loud as a jet engine. As they drove closer it drowned out the sound of their own sirens.

Now George could see the image of a luminous woman, hovering above the water, casting a blinding light. Two figures were plainly visible: a woman struggling with a man.

"What the hell is that?" George said.

The sheriff shrugged. "I don't know, but it sure is loud."

They stopped their vehicles and ran toward the lake, despite the sound and light.

George looked up just in time to see the man's chest explode as if it had been hit with a hollow-point .57 Magnum slug. The man's upper body disintegrated as the woman dived under the water.

By the time George was close enough, he could recognize Jukes Wahler, bobbing to the surface in the woman's arms.

Fiona pulled Jukes toward the shore and looked up to see George Jones coming toward her.

"Help me!" she cried. "He's not breathing!"

The paramedics from the ambulance were right behind George, and they carried Jukes to safety. Fiona followed them in a willful frenzy; George had to hold her back while the paramedics administered critical aid. Time stood still for her while Jukes struggled for life.

After several anxious moments they revived him. The sound of his coughing brought tears of joy to her face.

"Oh, God! Oh, my God," she sobbed and fell into George's arms. He comforted her.

"Did you see Cathy?" she asked.

George nodded. "They found her back up the hill. They're taking care of her now. I don't think she's hurt too bad."

"The Banshee saved Jukes's life. She killed Bobby Sudden . . . and him." Fiona pointed at the human debris floating in the water.

"What was that thing in the sky? Did I really see that?"

Fiona looked at George, her eyes glistening with tears. Her lower lip trembled, and she began to sob.

The sheriff's men gathered around Bobby Sudden; his steamy ruins had already begun attracting insects.

Flashing red and blue lights filled the night.

Jukes Wahler opened his eyes and looked down at himself surrounded by paramedics. He watched and wondered if he'd
died. He was floating above the scene, out of his body, as light
as air.

He saw Fiona crying.

I must be dead, he thought.

The Banshee appeared next to him, a beautiful young girl
again, the eternal tear glistening in her eye. She looked at Jukes
and shook her head.

Jukes realized that he was alone with the Banshee in her own
universe. He'd left his body behind and entered the spirit
world.

She gazed into his eyes, past his heart, and into his soul.
Jukes returned her gaze and saw himself clearly in the reflection, pitiful and helpless, and profoundly longing to be alive.

That's what she sees, he thought. *She sees the real me, all of me.
She sees the dark side. The hypocrite, the coward, the liar, the fool,
everything.*

He panicked for a moment, realizing that everything about
him was suddenly laid bare. His own fears and doubts were revealed to her as if they were nothing but an inconsequential
passing cloud. To her, with the weight of centuries on her
shoulders, that had to be what they seemed, as formless as
clouds, drifting through one small corner of time. Insignifi-
cant. One microscopic frozen moment held against the infinity
of her domain.

But she also sees the good. That's the saving grace.

Jukes thought, *Why do you walk the earth? Why can't you be
free?*

The mighty Banshee, the eternal avenger of womankind, si-
lenced him with her soundless command.

Self-realization flooded Jukes.

The time had come, he realized, and he'd faced his own failures and fears. For so long he had tried to help others; now he was finally able to help himself.

Physician, heal thyself.

He realized the monstrous thing O'Connor had almost done. Destroying the Banshee would be destroying nature. She was the uncomplicated truth, unspoiled by logic; simple as fate.

She pointed down at his body, and he understood it was not time for him to die yet. He had to return.

Then she disappeared, a shadow exposed to light.

Come back!

But she was gone on a wisp of smoke, and there was nothing left but the hushed sigh of the wind across the water.

Come back!

Someone shouted, "He's comin' around! Looks like he's gonna make it!"

Jukes opened his eyes and saw Fiona elbowing her way through the paramedics.

"Is Cathy OK?" he asked.

Three people answered in unison, yes, she was.

Fiona threw her arms around Jukes and said, "I love you."

Jukes managed a smile. "I love you, too. Can we go home now?"

EPILOGUE

After hours of surgery to repair his hand and an eternity in the recovery room, Jukes now had his chance to talk to Fiona and George.

Fiona stood next to his hospital bed and explained to George and Jukes what she could. "Cathy's already in detox," she said.

"Detox?"

"Yeah. Bobby had addicted her to heroin. The medics found out when they treated her for her other injuries."

Jukes said, "Jesus. No wonder he could control her so easily."

"Well, it's over now. Thank God she's OK, and thank God you're still alive."

"It must be our luck," Jukes said.

Fiona shook her head. "Luck had nothing to do with it. It was fate. Fate and the Banshee."

George raised an eyebrow. "You're losin' me. What does fate have to do with it?"

Fiona held Jukes's good hand. Her voice was warm and soothing.

"The Banshee is a creature of destiny; she follows the lines of fate. You've heard that old saying that a butterfly flapping its wings in China affects the weather in New York. Well, that's actually true in certain respects.

"Human beings live lives of interlocking destinies. One person touches another, who touches another, who affects the fate of still another. We're all wrapped up in it, the tangled web of fate, and none can escape.

"The Banshee isn't so much a master of fate, because I don't think she can change destiny, but she can manipulate it and place herself at crucial junctures, like waters flowing in a stream that forks, carrying some one way and some the other. She knows what will happen, and she appears at the precise moment that will affect destiny the most."

Fiona pointed at George. "What were the odds of you stumbling onto the one clue to Bobby's whereabouts? Then equally improbable was the fact that Bobby would be in the theater when you went to look."

"A series of unlikely coincidences," Jukes said. "That's what O'Malley said."

Fiona shook her head. "It was more than coincidence; it was fate—fate carefully manipulated by the Banshee, don't you see? Bobby would be in that theater at some point, and George would have gone in at some point, and at some point Panelli would have been shot, but only the Banshee knew when and how. She simply tipped the first domino over and caused events to fire off at intervals that best suited her plan.

"You could say the series of unlikely coincidences was nothing more than the Banshee's carefully choreographed dance of destinies."

George smiled. "I think you guys are cracked."

"But you saw it with your own eyes."

George shrugged. "My eyes ain't that great."

"George will never admit that anything supernatural exists; it's not his nature," Jukes said.

"Damn right it's not. Everybody thinks I'm a psychic now; it's terrible. I do good police work, that's all. Nothing spooky about that. You'd think the newspapers never heard of a successful investigation. If I get hunches, I play 'em. Sometimes it pans out; sometimes it doesn't. You never hear from those jokers then."

"Was Bobby the strangler?" Jukes asked.

George nodded. "We had some experts go over his computer, and they turned up some very grisly evidence. Bobby had an extensive business going on the Web, selling digital photos of murder victims. The FBI's got it now. The trail leads all over the world. There's no shortage of sickos these days.

"And the guy you thought was Charlie O'Malley was really a terrorist with an outlaw group called the Black Rain. His real name was Padraic O'Connor.

"I got this thing pretty much nailed down, except for everybody thinkin' I'm a damn soothsayer."

Jukes said, "Well, George, that's your fate."

George nodded. "Yeah, I guess so, but all this supernatural crap is outta my league. Speaking of fate, what does the future hold for you?"

Jukes looked at Fiona. "Fiona and I are getting married. Cathy's going to be in therapy for a long time. When she's finished, we'll take care of her until she's back on her feet."

Jukes paused and smiled as if enjoying some private joke. "And then, I'm gonna take some time off and learn to play the drums."

"The drums?"

"Well, George, you never know."